MW01114452

PRAISE FOR

CITY OF HERETICS

BY HEATH LOWRANCE

"***City Of Heretics*** is one of those books that don't come around very often, a novel that brings joy and pleasure because of the way it's written. Brooding, fresh, dark, eventful, full of suspense and tension and nigh on perfect. A must."

—**Nigel Bird**, author of ***Ain't That a Kick in the Head***

"***City of Heretics*** is a modern noir evoking the classics of the 50s & 60s. It's the story of an undeviating, relentless, compulsion. Crowe is just out of jail and only has one desire – to take down the people responsible for setting him up. The only consequences Crowe considers are whether or not his actions will move him any closer to payback time. And he doesn't walk away from any of this lightly."

—**Seth Lynch**, author of ***A Dead American in Paris***

HEATH LOWRANCE

CITY *of* HERETICS

A NEO-NOIR NOVEL

2021

THE CITY OF HERETICS

Published by Shotgun Honey Books

Shotgun Honey
215 Loma Road
Charleston, WV 25314
www.ShotgunHoney.com

Cover Design by Bad Fido.

First Printing 2021.

ISBN-10: 1-956957-01-4
ISBN-13: 978-1-956957-01-3

10 9 8 7 6 5 4 3 2

ALSO BY HEATH LOWRANCE

The Bastard Hand

Dig Ten Graves

I Was Born a Lost Cause

Hawthorne: Tales of a Weirder West

CITY OF HERETICS

1

He saw the Ghost Cat twice. The first time: a cold and icy morning in the middle of nowhere, and him sprawled out on a desolate two-lane road, blood freezing to his face, spent cartridges scattered. January Third. From the corner of his eye he saw it moving amongst the dead, searching...

He remembered thinking death. *The Ghost Cat means* death.

Some weeks later, he would see it again for the second and last time, and again it would follow at the heels of violence, rubbing against its ankles and purring. If he'd had any doubts then about what it meant, those doubts were laid to rest.

That long and brutal January, all sorts of things were laid to rest.

The room was dark when Crowe came in. He stopped in the doorway, key in hand, and tensed up. He'd turned on the floor lamp before he left, he was certain, but now the light was off and the room was pitch-black.

Pitch-black, which meant that the curtains had been drawn as well. And he knew he'd left them open.

So he stood there in the doorway, silhouetted against the dim light from the landing and making a wonderful target for whoever was in the room. He waited for a long minute, expecting any second to see a tire iron swoop out of the darkness or feel a bullet plow into his guts. But then a familiar voice said from the darkness, "Well? You gonna stand there all day or you gonna come in?"

Crowe said, "Turn on the light."

"What, you afraid of the dark?"

"Turn on the goddamn light."

A hoarse chuckle, a creak of imitation leather, and the light snapped on.

The little room, illuminated by the weak yellow light, looked only slightly less seedy than it did during the day. Small kitchenette in one corner, rumpled bed in the other, and between them a small sitting area, just a love seat and a cushioned chair with a scarred coffee table between them.

Chester Paine sat in the chair by the window, a nasty grin spread out across his long face. After seven years, he looked exactly the same—slick black hair, a pencil-thin mustache under a thin nose, small, expressive eyes gleaming blue in the pale light. He was about Crowe's age, late '40s, but there wasn't a single new line on his face or gray hair on his head. The only thing new was the suit; it was well-pressed and expensive. A sharp Burberry overcoat was draped over his knees.

Buds were in his ears, attached to an MP3 player he held in his hand. He plucked the buds out and Crowe could vaguely hear the strains of a Tom Waits song— "Misery is the River of the World" —before he shut it off.

He spoke in his raw Mississippi drawl, "Howdy, Crowe. Happy New Year."

Crowe shut the door behind him. While Chester smiled, he strolled over to the small stove in the corner and put some water on for coffee.

Chester said, "No beer in the fridge. And no bottles in the cabinet. You on the wagon or something?"

"What's with turning out the light, Chester? Seems a little dramatic, unless you were thinking of plugging me or something."

"I wouldn't shoot you in cold blood," he said. "I reckon I just like having the element of surprise."

He'd just pulled out a pack of cigarettes, so Crowe grabbed the little tin ashtray out of the cupboard and took the two steps that brought him back into the sitting area. He eased onto the battered love seat across from Chester. "Hope you don't mind if I light up, Crowe," Chester said. "You want one?"

"No thanks."

"I'm on these French smokes now, American cigs don't have any taste anymore."

He lit one of his French cigarettes and a plume of gray-black smoke wafted away from his head. It smelled awful.

Outside, the wind howled against the single window and ice rattled the panes.

Memphis, New Year's Eve, near midnight, the wind sweeping across the waves of the Mississippi River and pasting the streets with clinging wet ice. The ice wouldn't stick, and tomorrow the only signs of it might be a felled power line or two, but the cold was vicious.

It was a long goddamn walk from the bar on Madison to this hovel, a rented third-floor room near Front Street in an old converted cotton warehouse. There were a few of them downtown, harkening back to the Gilded Age when cotton was Christ. Most of them were pretty pricy. Crowe's wasn't.

And now here was old Chester. From far away, bells tolled, goodbye, goodbye to the old, and welcome the new, a year of promise and goodness and hope. Crowe heard people cheering somewhere far away, and fireworks. He said, "Well. Whatever's on your agenda, it's gotta be pretty goddamn important. Hell of a night for a social call."

Chester nodded. "How's things, Crowe?"

"Passing fair. You?"

"Same shit, different day. You know how it is."

"Yeah. What brings you around here?"

"Well," Chester said. "I was in the neighborhood. And seeing as how you haven't bothered to come around since you got out of stir, I thought I'd check in with you."

"That's mighty neighborly of you, Chester."

"I'm a neighborly sort of fella, you know that."

They let that one hang out there for a long minute. Chester puffed on his cigarette, stinking the place up good and proper. Crowe heard the water start to boil and got up to make the coffee. He brought Chester a cup. Chester sipped it, made a face, set it on the coffee table between them. "Instant coffee," he said. "Things are never that bad, are they?"

Crowe sat down again and cupped his between his hands. He didn't look at Chester.

Finally, Chester said, "Got some work for you."

Crowe shook his head. "No. Thanks anyway."

"Oh, I see," Chester said. "You're gonna take one of those other hundred jobs people are trying to throw at you, right?"

"Chester—"

"I hear that bank manager job pays real well. And the executive president gig has a real good benefits package. Which one you thinking of taking on?"

"I'm weighing options presently."

"Yeah, sure. But in the meantime you need money. Even a dump like this costs something. And the economy being what it is and all, I've managed to get a good thing lined up for you. I put in a good word for you, and—"

"No."

Chester scowled, took a last drag on his smelly cigarette and crushed it out in the tin ashtray. "Lemme guess," he said. "Going straight, right? Giving up the old life. Prison changed you, you've paid your debt to society and turned over a new leaf. Realized the error of your ways. Yeah?"

Crowe didn't answer him.

Chester shook his head. "Well now, that's pretty noble, I gotta say. Too bad it's a load of shit, though. Right?"

Again, he didn't require a response. Chester never did, really.

"A load of shit, Crowe. Going straight ain't in you. You can pretend all you want. And just because you ain't got no booze in the place, that don't convince me. You think not taking a drink is gonna make you a better person?"

Crowe said, "You want to hang around and talk about old times, fine. But I'm not interested in what you're bringing me."

Chester nodded, something like disgust twisting his narrow face. "Old times. Yeah. Let's talk about old times. I don't know, maybe you have changed. There is something different about you, I gotta admit. You got that hang-dog expression, the kind you see on the faces of losers. Seven years in stir, hey, it can break a man, sure. But I reckoned you for tougher than that."

"Did you?"

Chester stood up, looked down at Crowe. His impeccable coat fell to the floor, but if he noticed, he pretended not to. "So what happened, exactly? What happened to old Crowe? The biggest bastard I ever knew. The cat who'd knock a man's teeth down his throat for smiling at him wrong. The cat who'd break someone's arm 'cuz he didn't like his choice of whiskey. What happened to old Crowe?"

"What makes you think something happened to him?"

"Because the old Crowe wouldn't even bother saying that. The old Crowe would just sock me one, right on the jaw."

"Is that what you want me to do?"

He chuckled. "No, not really. I've seen what happens when you sock someone. They don't usually get up on their own."

"You're just gonna have to get used to it. Find some other thug to hang around with. There's plenty of them out there, you know."

Chester eyed him warily, taking inventory. "Okay," he said. "Okay, Crowe. But the facts still remain. You need work, and I have work for you. You remember Vitower? Marco Vitower?"

"Yeah."

"He's running the show now, since the Old Man died, about two years ago."

"Not interested."

"Oh, for fuck sake, at least hear me out! It's about Murke. Peter Murke, you know? That fucking psycho. You heard about him while you were in the joint, yeah?"

Crowe stood up, picked Chester's coat up off the floor, and with his other hand grabbed Chester by the collar of his expensive suit and hefted him around the love seat. "Hey!" Chester said. "Listen to me, man! Vitower wants to take Murke out!" Crowe opened the door and shoved him out onto the landing. He bounced against the far wall, looking too stunned to be angry. He'd dropped his MP3 player. Crowe stooped to pick it up and flung it at him. Chester fumbled but managed to catch it.

"I don't give a damn about what Marco Vitower wants," Crowe said. "Happy Fucking New Year." He slammed the door before Chester could say anything.

Crowe waited for a minute at the door, listening. He heard Chester mumble under his breath, straighten out his clothes, and then his footsteps walking away, tapping down the wooden steps. Crowe had expected a *this ain't over* or a *you just wait, I'll be back*, but he'd apparently decided to bide his time.

Crowe went to the window and opened the curtains. Ice gathered at the corners of the glass. Just over the rooftops to the west, he could see the slow muddy waters of the Mississippi roiling and tumbling under the Bluff, and the lights of a moored barge near the marshy Arkansas bank. There was no moon and no stars, and the barge lights looked like glittering lost planets, reflecting dimly against the rushing universe of the river.

Crowe gazed past his own reflection and thought his thoughts.

2

Mid-morning, the first day of the New Year, Crowe forced himself out of bed, stumbled into the bathroom, and took a long shower. He didn't get out until the hot water crapped out on him.

He was less than three days away from seeing the Ghost Cat for the first time.

He shaved carefully, straightened his tie, and took a cold, hard look at himself in the mirror.

He saw a man with a 50th birthday coming up in a couple of weeks, but with a slightly somber look that made him seem much, much older.

Crows feet had formed around his eyes and mouth during his years away from the world, and more than a sprinkling of gray had somehow appeared at his temples when he wasn't paying attention. His face looked long and lean and hungry. They'd given him back his old suit when he got out—and admittedly it was a fine suit—but it hung on him now as loose as an elephant skin. He looked seedy and run-down. He looked like a criminal. It was a little hard on him. He'd always been a bit vain about his appearance.

Almost 50 years old, he thought. *Fuck. Didn't I just turn forty?*

He had a suit and a few bucks and an apology that they

couldn't line up any work for him presently because of the shit economy, but at least he didn't have to endure parole, and so the world was his oyster.

"Happy New Year, Crowe," the landlord said when he passed his door. He leaned against his doorjamb, smoking a cigarette. His wife hated tobacco smoke in their apartment. He was a stringy, bony man in his mid-fifties who always smelled like a dusty book. The oversized, threadbare sweater he wore made him look even flimsier.

"Morning, Harriston."

"Say, you ain't goin' out like that, are you?" He waved his cigarette at Crowe's jacket. Crowe nodded, and Harriston said, "Damn, it's colder'n a witch's titty out there. Ain't you got a winter coat?"

"I'll be fine."

"Gonna catch yourself the pneumonia is what you're gonna do."

"Take care, Harriston."

Crowe started down the stairs and Harriston said, "Oh, say, I almost forgot, hold up a minute there, Crowe."

He took a last long drag of his cigarette, holding up his other hand in a 'wait-a-minute' gesture, stubbed the butt out in the standing ashtray by his door, and scurried off inside his apartment. Crowe heard him calling, "Hey, Luella, where the hell's that envelope?" A mumbled response from a deeper room. "What do you mean, *what* envelope? The goddamn envelope for Mr. Crowe, woman! Can't you get off that goddamn computer for two goddamn minutes?"

He came back out carrying the envelope in thin, nicotine-stained fingers. "This was in the vestibule door this morning." He handed it to over. It was addressed in a fine, feminine scrawl.

Crowe shoved it in his pants pocket without opening it. He knew who it was from. "Thanks. And tell the missus I said Happy New Year."

"Will do," he said. "And if you come back here hacking

and coughing with the pneumonia don't come crying to me about it."

In the vestibule downstairs Crowe pulled the envelope out of his pocket and crumpled it up. He tossed it in the trash can by the door.

3

Outside the building, the wind snapped down out of a slate sky, so bitter it stung his freshly-shaven cheeks. Traffic was light on the street and even the pedestrians had apparently taken a powder. He had a brief moment of disorientation, wondering where the hell all the people went, before he remembered it was a holiday. New Year's Day. And ungodly weather to boot.

He had some eggs and bacon and a bowl of fresh fruit for breakfast at a diner just off Front. The local news was on the little flat screen television over the counter and the stiffly-smiling blonde broadcaster was talking about Peter Murke. Murke had been all over the news since Crowe had gotten back. He had a hearing coming up tomorrow to determine if he was of fit mind to stand trial for murder, and after the hearing he'd spend the night in a holding cell at Memphis P.D. before being shipped off to Jackson for evaluation.

Crowe watched with interest, thinking about what Paine had said the night before. Vitower wanted to hit Murke. No surprise, considering what had happened to Vitower's wife. He'd need to find out more about Murke.

After breakfast, he hailed a taxi and started to look for Robert Radnovian.

The last couple days, Crowe had been digging around for

him, checking some old haunts, looking for a possible lead on a safe place he could talk to him. In a pinch, he could've just called Radnovian's office at the Sheriff's Department, but that would've meant embarrassing questions. Not that Crowe was concerned about his comfort—but if Radnovian was squeezed, he wouldn't be any good to Crowe.

Radnovian was a bad guy's wet dream. He was a cop, very well-connected, who'd worked his way up from Vice to Internal Affairs over the course of twelve years, so he knew scores of people and had dirt on just about every single one of them. He was also that rarest of things—a functional heroin addict.

His addiction to smack made him very easy to work with.

Crowe had his old home address, and the address of a girl he saw on and off, depending on how available the drugs were. He also had the latest address for Jimmy the Hink's place, where Rad spent a lot of time. It was sort of a private club for lowlifes and hopheads. That was where Crowe finally found him.

The house was on the north side, in the shadow of the freeway that wrapped itself around Memphis like a boa constrictor. A shabby place, even by that neighborhood's questionable standards. Ice clung to the dead remnants of lawn, nudged around broken glass and rusty auto parts. Crowe told the driver to wait, gave him a twenty to hold his nerves at bay, and trotted up the rickety front porch.

The front door was wide open, letting in the cold. Crowe walked in.

Three men and two women lounged around the front room. One of the women had nodded off with a needle stuck in her arm, the back of her head slumped against a threadbare sofa. The others were in various states of oblivion, working with the tiny dose of heroin on the table in front of them. Also on the table were a couple of syringes, a spoon with a burnt-out middle, and two or three back issues of *People* magazine.

One of the men had a lighter and another spoon, doing it the old school way, and the others watched him, rapt. None of them paid any attention to Crowe.

When he was halfway into the room, one of the guys finally looked up and said, "Oh. Hey, brother. Can you close that door? It's fuckin' freezing, man."

Crowe went back and closed the door and the guy said, "Cool, thanks, brother. You up?"

He indicated the heroin the other guy was cooking up, and Crowe shook his head. He passed through the room.

There was a filthy kitchen beyond that, stinking of the rank garbage overflowing from a little trash can, and two men who clearly weren't junkies were lounging, one at the table and the other against the cabinets.

They both came to attention when Crowe strolled in. They were dressed in classic street thug attire—wife-beater tees, baggy pants with the boxers showing over the top, ball caps and gold chains and all that. They had training weight muscles and tattoos. No marks for originality.

The one who'd been leaning against the counter took a step toward Crowe, saying, "You lost, old man?"

"I'm looking for someone."

"Yeah?" he said. He looked as if he expected his day to get really interesting, out of nowhere. "Who you looking for?"

"A guy named Radnovian."

The other one didn't get up from his chair. He said, "We don't do names here. What's your boy look like?"

Crowe said, "He looks a little like you. Except better dressed, and not so fucking ugly. You seen him?"

Both of them went all wide-eyed, and the one sitting down shot up and into Crowe's face. He said, "I know you didn't just say that. Tell me you didn't just say what I thought you said."

The other one pulled a gun out of the back of his waistband but kept it low, just so Crowe could see it.

The one in his face said again, "I know you didn't say that."

Crowe was long past the stage in his life where these sort of kids amused him. He said, "Where's Jimmy the Hink?"

The one with the gun said, "You a pig?"

Crowe shook his head.

"What you want with the Hink?"

Crowe grinned at him. "Tell you what," he said. "Why don't you *make* me tell you?"

The gun-boy scowled, but the other one was starting to look a little uncertain. He said, "You got some guts, old man. Maybe we should see what they look like all over the fucking floor."

Crowe had already decided on the fastest way to drop the two jokers—a fist in the throat would take down the closest one, and a heel just below the kneecap would cripple the other, followed up with a fist directly behind his left ear. Piece of cake.

But he didn't have to do a thing. From the other side of the kitchen, a familiar voice said, "You ass-wipes better back off. Dat Crowe you fucking wit."

Jimmy the Hink filled up the doorway pretty thoroughly. He was a fat ugly man in an ugly orange blazer, his pale head patchy with psoriasis. He sucked on a peppermint. Crowe could smell it from across the room, even over the stink of the garbage.

"Heya, Crowe," he said.

"Heya, Jimmy."

The two thugs backed off. The one with the gun looked unsatisfied.

"I take it you here to see ole' Rad." He still spoke in that weird, pseudo-Cajun cadence of his, although as far as Crowe knew he'd never been anywhere near Louisiana.

Crowe nodded. Jimmy brushed dandruff off his shoulder, said, "C'mon, I take you up dere."

The thug with the gun was standing in the way. Crowe looked at him, and, without breaking eye contact, the thug stepped back. Crowe walked by him.

He followed the Hink down a short hall to a staircase in back. They passed a couple of rooms with an assortment of junkie-types lounging around; old and young hippies, street bums, prostitutes, pretty much the whole catalogue. You had to sort of give it to the junkies, Crowe thought—these were people who'd given up on ambition. And who could blame them?

Ambition is a bitch. It makes people do horrible things. People without ambition are the happiest people on earth.

The Hink spoke to him over his shoulder as he waddled up the steps. "You been gone a long time, ole' Crowe. They got you all locked up in da big house, yeah?"

"Yeah."

"Yeah. That change a man. I been dere too, you know."

The Hink had been the Old Man's operator for as long as Crowe could remember, and now he was working for Vitower, doing the same job—selling heroin, operating little fly-by-night 'safe houses' for addicts to crash in, as long as they had the cash. Not that he ever had the pleasure of meeting his employers face-to-face. The Old Man would never have allowed himself to be seen with someone as crass as the Hink, and Crowe could only imagine Vitower felt the same way.

At the first door at the top of the stairs, the Hink stopped. He jerked his head at the door, and dead skin sloughed off and floated away. "In dere," he said. And then, "Listen. After you bidness done, come down and talk wif me? I gotta thing, could use you."

"Some trouble?"

He frowned. "Some trouble, yeah."

He trudged off, back down the stairs.

Crowe watched him go, thinking about how quickly old patterns re-emerge in this life. Back in the day, he used to do odd, unpleasant jobs for the Hink, out of nothing but pure altruism—and, of course, the fact that he always enjoyed a good bit of ugliness. He opened the door without knocking and went in.

4

Rad was sprawled out lazily on an overstuffed sofa in the middle of a nearly bare room. There was a widescreen TV in front of him showing cartoons, and between that and the sofa a long, low coffee table. All his gear was spread out there. A candle was burning and the room smelled like synthetic apple pie.

He looked up at blandly. Crowe hardly recognized him.

He'd lost a good thirty pounds, and his off-the-rack suit hung on him comically. He'd lost a lot of hair, too. What was left clung haphazardly just above his ears and at the moment was ridiculously unkempt.

He was well-shaven, though. He always carried a portable electric razor with him, and used it four or five times a day.

He said, "Is that… is that Crowe?"

Crowe nodded, and Rad said, "No shit. Well I'll be damned. Crowe is back." And then, "That can't be good."

He didn't stand up. From the way his gear was spread out, Crowe could tell he'd only just that moment shot up and was waiting for the bliss. Seeing Crowe walk in probably wasn't what he had in mind.

He'd been on the Old Man's hook back in the day, had managed to secure a steady line of smack in exchange for… well, whatever the Old Man needed. He'd picked up the habit back in the late '90's, when he was still with Vice, working undercover. Posing as a heroin addict.

Eventually, we become what we pretend to be in this world.

There were a few officers with the Shelby County Sheriff's Department who suspected the truth about Radnovian, but the fact that he was with Internal Affairs now and could destroy them completely with one phone call kept them quiet.

Crowe said, "Catch you at a bad time, Rad?"

"Naw, man, not at all. Why don't you, like, siddown or something, though. It hurts my neck to look up at you."

Crowe sat down next to him. Rad looked at him with hooded eyes, and Crowe could see the drug starting to take effect. His facial muscles were slack and he sort of smiled weakly. "I heard you were out," he said. "Good for you. Fresh start. Debt to society paid, and like that."

"I'm a reformed man."

Rad laughed, not so stoned that he would believe something like that. "I take it you're here for something shapasic. Shpacific, I mean. Shit." He shook his head sharply. "*Specific*. You're here for something *specific*."

"I need to know about Peter Murke."

His mouth opened and closed a couple of times. He said, "Peter… Peter Murke. Ah, no, man. No, no, no, no, no."

"Last I heard, he was about to face a competency hearing."

"No, man, come on. Christ."

"Rad," Crowe said. "For the last few days, I haven't done much. But as of today, I'm a very busy man. Stop wasting my time."

Rad grumbled and slouched lower on the sofa. "Vitower sent you, right? Whassa crazy bastard gonna do?"

"I haven't seen or talked to Vitower since I've been back."

"No, man. No way."

Crowe hit him in the teeth. Rad grunted once, clutching his mouth, said, "Shit! Ah, fuck, man!"

"Things are a little different this season, Rad. We ain't buddies, you and me. And I'm not *asking* you to talk to me. You understand?"

Rad looked at him resentfully. Crowe gave him a minute to gather himself. Finally, he pulled his electric razor out of his coat pocket, flipped it on, and ran it over his face. It seemed to relax him. He said, "Yeah, okay. I reckon things are different, huh? Not that I ever thought we were buddies."

"You're trying my patience, Rad."

"Okay, okay." He seemed entirely straight now; the fist in his face had sort of dispelled the heroin rush a bit. He flipped off the razor and put it away. "Fine. You wanna know about Murke, fine. He got some good slimy attorneys, tryin' to pass him off as crazy, sayin' he's not responsible for what he did. They're trying to get an appeal on his conviction."

Murke had been apprehended about two years before and charged with the murder of a thirteen-year-old girl named Patricia Welling. But he was the prime suspect in many more murders, possibly as many as sixteen in all. Every last victim a woman, but that was all they had in common. The D.A. went over every scrap of evidence they had, but, despite that they knew Murke was their man, they had nothing solid, nothing that would stick. Nothing except for Patricia Welling. There they had him with strong DNA evidence and a witness who'd seen him with the victim.

He'd been convicted on a single charge of first degree murder, given a hefty life sentence without parole.

That much, everybody knew. It had been all over the papers, had even scored national headlines for a couple of months. But like any ugly media story, there was much more to Murke's saga than that.

Crowe said, "An insanity plea? That hasn't worked in the state of Tennessee in, what? Decades."

"Whatever, that's what they're gonna try. They're gonna transport him to the psychiatric hospital in Jackson. He's gonna undergo a complete psych eval. It's not gonna do them any good. Any shrink they can get to say Murke is too crazy to be convicted, the prosecution'll come up with three more to say he's sane as rain. But they're going through with it anyway."

"When are they transporting him?"

Rad sighed. "Jesus, Crowe."

"When, Rad?"

"The third. Tuesday. Tuesday morning. What the hell are you gonna do about it? Ambush the goddamn transport van?"

Crowe smiled. "Not a bad idea."

Rad shook his head. "You're goddamn nuts. Maybe they should take *you* there. Honestly, man, don't even tell me what you have in mind, I don't wanna know."

"Did you think I was gonna share with you, Rad?"

Crowe found it all very interesting. Interesting, because one of Murke's victims—his last, in fact—was Jezzie Vitower. Wife of Marco Vitower.

Opportunity wasn't just knocking on the door. It was walking right in, flopping down on the sofa, and opening a beer.

He stood up. "I'll be in touch."

Rad frowned and pulled out his razor again. "Well, you know, that's something to look forward to, I reckon."

5

"Dese boys," the Hink said. "They been in the neighborhood, see. They been around, and they got no bidness here."

"Outsiders?"

"Yeah. Dis new gang popped up in the last few years, while you was away. Bad Luck, Inc, dey called. Dese fellas wit' dem."

The Hink's office was in the far back of the house, down a long crumbling hallway hidden by a ratty curtain. It was barely big enough for his desk and two wooden chairs, and there were no windows. He had a poster hanging on the wood-paneled wall of a Hispanic girl holding her large breasts up, as if waiting for an inspection. Several large stacks of money were on the desk; must've been close to fifty grand just sitting there.

"Lotsa new faces dese days, you know," he said, and Crowe nodded. It had been happening since long before he got sent up, the slow infiltration of major gangs into Memphis from Chicago and L.A. The scenery was changing all the time. "But so far," the Hink said, "we been okay. We do what we do, and they do what they do. Respectin' borders, right?"

"But now they're getting bolder."

The Hink nodded. "Since Vitower been runnin' the show, things got a little more stable. The new gangs listened to him, respected him, cuz he black, not like the Old Man. Dey made deals, shook hands. But dese new boys, Bad Luck, dey don't care 'bout none a' dat. Dey come in, dey do what dey want. Down the South side, dey already runnin' everything, and now dey movin' north and east and you can't hardly scratch your balls wid-out hittin' one wid your elbow."

"I'll do what I can. But I don't know what good you think it'll do. It's not like running them out of the neighborhood is gonna do much for you, long term."

He shook his head, and a little flurry of dandruff floated to the desk top. He brushed it away from the stacks of bills. "I don't care 'bout no long term. I'll be outta this block in another three weeks or so anyway, it'll be time to move somewhere's else. But for now, I need dem outta my hair."

"You clear this with Vitower?"

"I don't need to clear nuthin' wit Vitower," he said, frowning.

Crowe leaned back in the rickety wooden chair, mulled it over for a second. The Hink drummed his thick fingers on the desk.

"Okay," Crowe said. "I'll see what I can do."

The Hink grinned, an expression that looked painful for him. One big hand grabbed a stack of bills and handed them across the desk.

"Dat's two grand dere, for your trouble," he said. "Get yo-self a coat, why don't you? You too old to be runnin' around wid-out a coat."

Crowe took it, slid it in the inside pocket of his jacket.

6

From half a block away, Crowe could see her in front of the building. Even from the distance, he knew it was her. She wore a long gray wool coat with a white fur collar. Probably fake fur, but who could tell? Her hair was the color of oxblood, wavy but not quite curly, long and flickering in the wind like the flame of a huge candle. He paid the cabbie off half a block away and walked the rest. She saw him coming but only stood there, hands thrust into her pockets, shivering.

Closer, and they made eye contact. He went over in his mind if he should just walk right past her or actually stop. Her pale cheeks were flushed with cold. Her nose, slightly too long, burned pink and her green-gray eyes, which he'd always thought were too big, were cradled by thick black eyeliner. She looked like a gothic raccoon.

Without really making the decision to, he stopped in front of her.

She said, very softly, "Welcome home." Her voice was just like he remembered, just like he'd remembered all those black, black nights in prison. Deep and dark, with that soft lazy accent that absolutely refused to commit to a vowel. Like many in Memphis, she was really more of a North Mississippi girl.

He nodded. "Well, you know, it's good to be back."

She nodded back at him. And they didn't say anything for a long moment.

Then, "You wanna invite me in?"

He shrugged and opened the door for her. She went in, past him, and he smelled *her* smell. That smell did something to him. He had a lot of memories tied up with it.

She paused in the vestibule and he didn't look at her. He went up the stairs slowly and she followed.

Inside, she took off her coat, looked around for a coat rack, and finding none, tossed it on the loveseat. She wore a simple green tee-shirt, tight around the breasts, short enough to show just a peak of her midriff. Hip-hugger jeans. She was in her mid-'30's, had put on a few pounds since he'd seen her last, but the extra weight looked good on her. She'd always been too skinny.

She put her fists on her hips and looked at him.

The old thing came back, horribly. Take her. Throw her on the floor and take her. He'd thought about it often enough in prison. Pretty much every lonely fantasy he'd had involved her.

He said, "Okay. You want coffee?"

"I hate coffee."

"I don't have anything else."

"Tea, maybe?"

"I don't have anything else, Dallas."

She walked past him, gazing around the room. Her eyes flicked over the narrow little bed and the beat up loveseat and the scarred coffee table. She sat in the easy chair by the window, just like her husband had the night before, and crossed her legs like she owned the goddamn place and said, "My letter. Did you get it?"

"Yeah."

"Well?"

"I didn't read it."

"What?"

"I threw it away," he said. "You shouldn't be here, Dallas."

She said, "If you'd read the letter, you'd know that this is exactly where I should be."

"Well, I didn't read it. I think you should go."

He couldn't read her face. But he never could. He remembered looking down at her, he remembered her body under his, and blue light coming from somewhere, her gazing up at him with those green-gray eyes half-closed and mouth part-open, sharp little teeth clenched, sweet breath against his cheek. And the smell of her. A flower, after the rain. Even then, he couldn't read her.

They'd been sleeping together for almost two years before Crowe went to prison. They never talked about her leaving Chester or anything like that. They weren't children, with stupid and unrealistic ideas about each other. What they had was nothing.

She sat there in his easy chair with her oxblood hair all crazy and wind-blown. Most women probably would have been touching it, trying to fix it up, but not Dallas. She didn't care. She knew it looked good that way.

She said, "They released you on Christmas Eve, gave you a bus ticket back to Memphis and a hearty slap on the back. You stayed at a motel on Union your first night. And then you paid the first and last month's rent on this place the next day. Are you out of money yet?"

He thought about the two large in his pocket, but said, "Just about. Why, you need a loan?"

She laughed without amusement. "I wouldn't call it a loan, exactly, Crowe. I wish you'd read the letter. It would make all this easier."

He stood by the loveseat, arms crossed.

She said, "A lot's happened in the last seven years."

"Yeah."

Again, they went silent. After a few seconds, she said, "Maybe I will have some coffee after all. Do you mind?"

"You know what? I just remembered. Chester was here last

night and he drank up the last of it. You remember Chester, right? Your husband?"

Her eyes narrowed. "Oh, Crowe. What's that all about? Was that supposed to make me feel all ashamed? All morally inferior to you?"

"No. It's supposed to make you realize I'm all out of coffee."

She laughed again, the same humorless version. Crowe sighed and plopped down on the loveseat next to her coat. Two visitors in two days. The place was turning into a veritable social Mecca.

"Okay," he said. "What's the story, Dallas? Why are you here?"

She frowned and pushed her hair out of her face. She looked away from him. "You really are… unhappy to see me. Aren't you?"

He didn't answer her.

"Seven years," she drawled. "That's an awful long time, huh?"

"It's a long time."

"And things have changed an awful lot. I mean… my life is… different than it was before. And you, well. I can hardly imagine."

She was doing the *sincere* thing now. He'd seen her do it before, but never to him. That had been, probably, the best thing about what they had; no deceit had been required. She'd never said anything like *I love my husband, I really do, but…* or *Chester doesn't understand me* or *you make me feel things…* All of those things would have been lies, or at least pointless justifications. Neither of them was interested in any of that.

But now here she was, trying to use emotion against him, the way she probably did to Chester all the time.

She said, "Do you remember, Crowe… do you remember that time we drove down to Oxford? You wanted to go visit William Faulkner's house."

"Yeah, I remember."

She smiled and shook her head. "And I said, what are you, kidding me? Faulkner's house? Like you ever read a book by

William Faulkner in your whole damn life. And then you… started telling me about that one book… what was it?"

He said, "*Sanctuary*."

"Right. *Sanctuary*. About that Temple Drake woman, right? And she was supposed to represent, what was it, Southern womanhood?" She laughed. "But poor old Temple wasn't really such a sweetheart, was she?"

"I remember all this, Dallas."

"Yeah. And then that brute, Popeye, rapes her."

"I don't remember going into that much detail about it."

She shook her head. "No, you didn't. But, after you told me about it, I went and checked it out of the library. It was a horrible book. I really hated it. What it said about us. About humans. The lawyer in that, what was he called?"

"Benbow, I think."

"Right. Something like that. A decent fellow, yeah? But so completely… ineffectual. Everybody in that book, all these horrible, nasty characters, were able to cause change, were able to make things happen. Everyone except him. The one decent person in the whole awful book. Jesus, did I hate that book."

He said, "The Ladies Book Club isn't until next week. You'll have to come back."

She grinned ruefully. "Sorry. It's just that, well. I can't think of you anymore without thinking about that book. And our drive to Oxford. It was such a nice drive. And Faulkner's house, well… remember?"

"I remember. I was bored."

"Yeah. And I was the one who actually got something out of it. I went and read that book, after you went away, and you know what? It sort of helped me get over you."

"Get over me, Dallas? There wasn't any goddamn thing to get over. Why are you feeding me a line?"

The whole time, she hadn't really been looking at him, only casting her eyes here and there, fixing her gaze on his tie, on his hand, on the refrigerator. Now she looked at him and the playfulness evaporated. She said, "If it was just you and me, Crowe, you'd be right. If it was just you and me, I'd have nothing to get over at all. You were a good fuck. You were fun to be around. You didn't talk a lot so that I'd have to pretend to be interested in what you said. It was pretty ideal. The only time you yapped too much was that one time, when you told me about William Faulkner and that god-awful book. And look what that got me. But it's not just about the two of us."

"If you think Chester—"

"And it sure as hell isn't about Chester."

Crowe was getting irritated. "Okay. Who else is it about?"

She said, "I wish you'd read the damn letter."

"Who else?"

Her mouth went all hard and she took a deep breath through her long, narrow nose. She said, "I have a son now. His name is Tom."

"What?"

"He'll be seven years old at the end of this month."

It got quiet then. He looked at her. Her gaze strayed away, focused on the refrigerator again, the stove, the sink. The muscles in her jaw clenched and unclenched.

She cleared her throat and said, "It was that night, when we went to Oxford. We spent the night at that cozy little motel in Holly Springs?"

He nodded, remembering it pretty well. The condom broke, and they had a few moments of tension before shrugging it off. He remembered her laughing uneasily, saying, *well... if I get knocked up, don't expect me to name the kid after you. I don't think Chester would dig that so much...*

Two stupid, ruthless, amoral people, him a strong-arm thug for the Old Man, supposedly Chester Paine's best buddy, and her a fashion-obsessed party girl, too young for him, married to a very dangerous little man who was also too old for her and living it up for all she was worth.

Jesus Fucking Christ.

Crowe said, "Chester didn't mention a kid."

"He wouldn't."

"Yeah, I reckon he wouldn't. Okay. Tom, eh?"

She nodded. "Thomas Paine. Like… the guy, you know."

"Thomas Paine, yeah. *Age of Reason*."

She nodded again. "I'll tell you the truth, though. That was a complete accident. I didn't know who the hell Thomas Paine was until later. Don't tell anyone that."

Crowe laughed shortly. She knew perfectly well who Thomas Paine was. Women can be strange sometimes, he thought; why pretend you don't know something when you do? Do some women still cling to the idea that men like a stupid broad? But what did he know, maybe some men do. Dallas Paine was a lot of things, but she wasn't stupid.

The thought that she was playing him crossed his mind, but only for a moment. If he'd wanted to, he could demand DNA tests, solid evidence, all that. But no. She wasn't playing him---well, she *was* playing him, but she wasn't lying.

He said again, "Okay. What can I do?"

She said, "You don't owe me anything, Crowe. I know that you don't. I… I came here to see you, not because I think you have some responsibility to me. You don't. I came because I need your help. I do. And I thought, if you knew about Tom, it might… persuade you a little. It might give you a good reason to help me."

"What sort of help?"

She leaned forward in the easy chair. The green tee-shirt tightened against her breasts, and now that he knew she was a mother, he thought he could see it a little—she was a little thicker around the middle, maybe. The breasts were fuller or something. It could have been his imagination. She said, "I want to leave. I want to take Tom and leave Chester and just… get out of Memphis. I want to get far away."

"Well, why don't you, then?"

"Money. I need money."

"So withdraw a few thou from the old joint account and split."

She shook her head. "It's not that easy. Chester is… well, he's different than he used to be. Like I said, a lot of things have changed these seven years. Things you couldn't imagine. You know that Marco Vitower is Chester's new boss?"

"I remember hearing something about it."

"Well… Vitower's wife was murdered, just a couple of years ago. You know that, yeah? And after that, Chester started… well, he started keeping me on a short leash. He… he fixed it at the bank so that I couldn't withdraw any money without his permission. He took Tom out of public school and hired a private tutor. He just went… well, he went kinda weird."

"And you think it has something to do with Vitower's wife getting killed?"

"Yes. Well, maybe. I don't know and it doesn't matter to me. But that's not even the real reason, Crowe."

"What is?"

She looked at the floor. "The real reason is… please, please don't laugh at me."

"Just spit it out."

"I need to get away from this life, Crowe, because I found God."

That one stunned him a bit. He couldn't tell if she was pulling his leg. He said, "You found God."

"Yes."

"I didn't know he was missing."

"I know you're cynical about things like that, but don't make fun of me. I took Jesus as my personal savior, and I just want out. I want to scoop up Tom and go somewhere far away."

Crowe leaned back in his chair and looked at her. Found God? *I go away for seven years*, he thought, *and everyone gets all delusional on me*. He tried to look thoughtful and said, "You need money, then."

She nodded, and the green-gray eyes glistened a bit. Helpless little animal. Helpless little Goth raccoon, with her black eyeliner and crazy oxblood hair and wistful scent. She said, "But you don't have any money. I don't know what made me think you might. If you had money, you wouldn't be staying here, would you?"

She grinned at the lack of hope promised by the flat.

He said, "Tell you what. You stop bullshitting me, maybe I can get some cash."

"Bullshitting you?"

"About this 'God' thing. You're no Jesus freak, so stop lying to me. What did you think, I'd cave if I thought you'd lost your goddamn mind?"

She stared at him for a long moment, and then a guilty smile crept over her face. "Okay. The truth is, I did try it out while you were gone. I did join a religious group for a while. It didn't take."

"So."

"So... it didn't take, but some of the things it made me realize stayed with me."

"Like the need to get away from Memphis."

"Yes."

He nodded. "Fine. So maybe I can lay my hands on some money."

She swallowed hard and licked her lips. "How?"

"Don't worry about how. Just go home now. Give me a call in a few days."

"You have a phone?"

"Oh. No, I don't. Right. Well, swing by then."

She stood up, and for a moment she was entirely too close, close enough that he could feel her body heat radiating. He stepped away from her.

She said, "But how?"

"You probably don't remember, Dallas, but I really hate answering questions. Just do what I say, okay?"

She frowned. "I'll come by in a few days, then. And Crowe..."

"What?"

"Thanks. Thank you."

"Shut up, Dallas. And leave the Christians alone, what did they ever do to you?"

She said, "Do you... well, this is sort of an awkward question, but do you want to meet him? Do you want to meet Tom?"

He said, "No."

She nodded, grabbed her coat off the loveseat and started toward the door. He watched her, and when she had her hand on the knob he said, "Hey. I have a confession to make."

She turned to face him. "What do I look like?" she said. "A priest?"

"I never read *Sanctuary*. I never read a goddamn Faulkner book in my life. I got all that info from the Cliff's Notes."

She threw her head back and something like an actual real laugh came out of her. She said, "I should've known. I can't believe a word you say, Crowe."

And that was something they had in common.

7

He trotted down to the package store for a six-pack after Dallas left and then went immediately back home. He spent the rest of the day drinking beer, sitting at the window and staring at the sliver of the Mississippi that he could see over the rooftops. Tugs drifted up and down, black smoke pluming out of their stacks and into the gray sky. By four o'clock, the gray had deepened and a cold rain started, sluicing away whatever traces of icy snow had been left from the night before. A smattering of half-ass fireworks went off somewhere close to the bridge, a muted green and red; a last pathetic left-over from the New Year celebrations.

By five, he'd downed three bottles of Amstel Light and felt pleasantly light-headed. His tolerance for alcohol wasn't what it used to be; another side-effect of seven years as a guest of the state. He burped luxuriously and stood up.

He hadn't foreseen the complication with Dallas and the kid, but after thinking it over decided it didn't matter. He kept sort of examining it, though, thinking it *should* make things more difficult, thinking he *should* feel something about having a son he knew nothing about.

He was a father.

No, that was bullshit. He was no father. Having a kid doesn't automatically make you a father, does it? Not in the strictest sense. He didn't know the kid, didn't want to know the kid, would never know the kid.

But he wished she hadn't told him about it. He couldn't afford that sort of distraction.

It didn't change anything, though. He would have a great deal of money before this was all done and he could afford to throw some Dallas's way.

In the bathroom, he took a piss that seemed to last ten minutes, and then wobbled to the kitchen and found a box of saltines he'd bought his first day back. He sat in the easy chair and ate them, indulging his inner gourmet.

He fell asleep in the chair for a while, which kept him from fretting about what to do for a few hours. He had fitful dreams about Dallas. He woke up about eight, had the usual moment of disorientation, wondering why his cell looked different, but shook it off, ate some more crackers and brushed his teeth.

Then he set about putting together a make-shift sap. With a kitchen knife, he sawed a big chunk out of the back of the imitation leather chair, about two feet by two feet. He had a jar of change on the kitchen counter-- He dumped about three dollars' worth of dimes onto the chunk of material, bundled it up, and secured it with a heavy piece of twine. The lump it made was about the size of his fist, and a good solid weight that he could swing easily. He shrugged on his suit jacket, shoved the sap in his outside pocket. He headed out the door.

8

Memphis had always been attractive to organized crime for the same reason Fed-Ex loved the place: location. If nothing else, Memphis is well-situated as a hub, a place to launch off from to someplace with better prospects.

The Old Man had been a relic, even before Crowe got sent up. He was a hold-over from the days of the Irish mob that saw its hey-day in the fifties and early sixties. They'd never really got a great toehold in Memphis to begin with—while other cities had been easy pickings for crime families, Memphis was more or less protected by Boss Crump, an officially-elected criminal. But they managed at least to get by, under the radar.

But by the seventies the L.A. gangs like the Crips had started setting up and it wasn't long before others from Chicago followed. The meager old white guys had gotten lax and lazy, sitting around in diners or strip clubs counting money, while the young Turks took it to the street and got their hands dirty. The new breed had a sense of unity and purpose that the old guys had forgotten.

The Old Man saw all these changes happening, but by the time he decided to do something about it, it was too late. He started courting the black gangs, making deals, treating them the way he would've treated any powerful rival—with respect.

He started employing blacks and Hispanics into his ranks, even letting some of them into the inner circle.

No one would ever have guessed the remnants of the Irish mob would ever make nice with the black gangs. There was too much animosity, stretching all the way back to right after the Civil War, when newly-freed blacks managed to snag the jobs in Memphis that used to belong to the poor Irish. Crazy that something like that would dictate the tone of relations for almost one hundred and fifty years, but that's the way things worked.

But the Old Man saw the writing on the wall and did what he had to do, and that was how Vitower eventually came to power. The white mob went down without a shot fired; it just transformed itself into a black mob. Easy as that.

The Old Man was shell-shocked, out of his element, in those long years of transition before Crowe went to prison. He didn't seem like the Iron Man he'd been before. He hesitated. He hem-hawed on important decisions. He knew he'd become a dinosaur, and that meant that Crowe was one too, Crowe and all the other white guys in the ranks. Extinction couldn't be far off.

It didn't trouble Crowe. In those days, he actually believed that eventually he would be out of the life. He'd go to the country somewhere, or maybe the ocean, and live out his peaceful old age in a shack or something. He didn't care what would happen to the mob after that. It would have nothing to do with him.

That was before prison, though, before he understood. He was already in his old age. Forty-nine wasn't particularly old for most people, but for men in his position it was downright ancient. He was already extinct.

The cab driver was an old black guy with strangely reddish hair. Driving south on Danny Thomas, he kept sucking his teeth and saying things like, "Back in my day, it didn't look nuthin' like this. It's a damn shame is what it is, the way it's all fell apart. This city used to be something. And now look at it. You know, I been robbed three times in the last two months. I don't even know why I keep comin' out. I don't even know anymore."

Crowe ignored him, spoke only enough to give him directions off Danny Thomas and back into Jimmy the Hink's neighborhood. The driver looked at him in the rear-view, wondering what a middle-aged white guy wanted around these parts, but he didn't ask, just said again, "I don't even know anymore."

About a block from the Hink's place, Crowe spotted them—three young black guys, huddled at a corner in front of an abandoned house. They were under the yellow acid glare of a streetlight. It was cold but they wore only hoodies with the hoods up to protect themselves from the wind.

He told the driver to stop, then snapped a fifty dollar bill at him. "Drive around for five minutes, then come back to this spot," he said. "There'll be another one of these for you."

The driver took the bill, said, "It's your funeral, I reckon," and then took off before Crowe even had the door closed behind him.

The three youngsters noticed him getting out of the cab, but didn't respond. They only watched from within the shadows of their hoods. He walked over to them.

When he was only a few feet away, one of them said in a quiet, deadpan voice, "You want somethin'?"

Crowe stopped, close enough to reach out and touch his chest if he wanted to. "What you got?" he said.

They eyed him up and down, checking out the suit and tie, and the one doing the talking pushed his hoodie back and cocked his head. He was a good-looking kid with a strong jaw and eyes that glittered in the pale streetlight. He had about two inches on Crowe.

He said, "You a little over-dressed for the occasion, old man. Maybe you lookin' for a dinner party, huh?"

"I found what I'm looking for."

"You lookin' for trouble, then. Blow, old man."

Crowe said, "You're in the wrong neighborhood, kid. What you wanna do is find someplace else."

They all smiled at that one. They always did. Crowe didn't know why he even bothered with it anyway. He watched as all three of them switched to swagger-mode, bumping against each other and laughing and imitating his bravado.

The talker took a step closer, leaving himself open to show his sheer confidence, and said, "I like your suit, old man, so I'm gonna give you one chance to walk the fuck away, or—"

Crowe hit him with a right in his kidney and before he could fall he head-butted him in the nose. The kid lurched backward, stiff-legged, his eyes dazed. The other two took almost three seconds to process before they moved.

The sap was in Crowe's left hand. As soon as the closest one was within distance, he snapped it backhanded at his face, like swinging a tennis racket. It cracked against his jaw and Crowe could see a couple of teeth surf out on a narrow wave of blood before the kid fell to the sidewalk.

The third one was expending a lot of energy with words—*motherfucker, I'm gonna fuckin' kill you*, that kind of thing. Crowe let him get close enough to take a wild swing that he sidestepped, and then Crowe was behind him, bashing the sap down on the back of his head, right at the base of the spine, the magic spot.

He went down without another sound.

Crowe stood over them for a moment, getting his breath back. It had been a few years and it took a little more out of him than he would've guessed.

The first kid, the one who'd done the talking, was still conscious. He curled up on the sidewalk, groaning. Blood streamed from his nose, but he was clutching his torso. A rabbit punch to the kidney. There aren't too many things much more painful than that.

Crowe was still getting his breath, trying to push down the adrenalin rush. Fifteen years ago—hell, even seven years—all of this would've been a walk in the park, but he wasn't a kid anymore, not like these guys. And maybe prison had made him a little soft after all.

Before the kid could pull himself together too much, Crowe got down on his haunches next to him and said, "What's your name, kid?"

Between clenched teeth, he said, "Mother… motherfucker…"

Crowe slapped him hard across the bridge of his broken nose and to his credit the kid didn't scream. Crowe said again, "What's your name?"

"Garay…" he said. "Garay. Ah, you motherfucker…"

"Listen, Garay," Crowe said, like a benevolent dad. "If I see you around here again, I won't have a sap with me. I'll have a knife. And I'll gut you like a fucking pig. You understand?"

He didn't answer, so Crowe hit him again. This time, the grunt of pain was louder, and he said, "Yeah, fuck, yeah, I get it… Jesus fuck, man…"

"Good boy," Crowe said, and stood up.

The cab was just pulling around the corner. It stopped at the spot where Crowe got out and waited. He walked over and climbed in.

"That was no five minutes," Crowe said.

The driver was looking at the three guys sprawled out on the corner. He didn't look at Crowe or say anything. Crowe handed him another bill, which he took and shoved in his pocket.

"Take me to the Cuba Libre. You know where that is?"

The driver nodded, and off they went.

9

The Libre was a nightclub just off Sam Cooper, glittering in the gray-black evening with pink and green neon, smack in the center of a small industrial area. The front was done up in a sort of Miami-deco style, with a rounded archway leading in and a curvy overhang with lights that were in constant motion. It was cheerful and decadent and made you want to have a tall, exotic drink.

The cab driver let him off, took a twenty dollar bill, and drove away. Ice had begun to fall again, and the wind swept bitter across the nearly empty parking lot, so cold it made his gums ache.

Back in the day, there was always a doorman at the entrance, but not now. He went in through the heavy leather-padded door and paused just inside for a moment to shake off the chill.

It was pretty much just as he remembered it. There were pictures of palm trees and famous Cuban guerillas. A short hall opened up into the club, a large, high-ceilinged place with more neon in funny shapes, dim track lighting in more pink and green and the occasional ocean blue. The Libre usually didn't get going full swing until after midnight, but he could smell the lingering richness of cigar smoke, marijuana, and earthy perfumes from the New Year's celebrations the night before.

To the left, wrought iron tables and chairs and a multi-colored dance floor and a stage for the rare live act that would show up. To the right, the long oak bar, lined with soft green plastic to rest your elbows on.

He remembered nights when the Libre was so jammed with sweating, drunk, desperate people that you could barely move three inches, but at the moment it was all but dead. A couple of businessmen-types, in good suits with ties loosened, sat at the far end of the bar, heads together in some sort of half-sloshed negotiations. At a table near the quiet dance floor, a young hipster couple slouched, each nursing lime green drinks in tall glasses.

A full-throated female voice said, "Well, fuck me seven ways to Sunday!" and Crowe saw Faith behind the bar, gripping a bar rag in one hand and grinning at him with her fine white teeth. "If it ain't goddamn Crowe, as I live and breathe."

She'd had a full-on Afro last time he'd seen her, big and well-coiffed, but now her hair was cut tight to the scalp and it made her look sort of like an action figure. She wore a tank top, revealing lithely-muscled light chocolate arms and a decent amount of cleavage.

He smiled and said, "Faith. Happy New Year."

"Happy New Year, the man says! Motherfucker, I haven't seen you in, what, five years? And now you just stroll in here like nothing and say 'Happy New Year'. Goddamn Crowe!"

It had been over seven years since he'd seen her, but he didn't bother with a correction. She came around the bar, snapping her bar rag in the air, and barreled toward him as if she was going to pop him one. She threw her arms around his shoulders and hugged him with fierce strength. She was taller than he remembered, the top of her head at eye level, and she smelled sort of intoxicating, like peppermint and rum. Up close he could see the dark cradles under her eyes, and the first traces of broken capillaries along the bridge of her nose.

She'd always been a drinker, Faith.

They'd gotten the attention of the two businessmen-types.

They looked up from their important deal-making and stared for a moment, but very quickly their gazes drifted to Faith's ass, and then back to their own concerns.

She held him out at arm's length, looked him up and down. "Jesus, boy, you done got skinny! Where the hell have you been?"

He shrugged. "Traveling the world. This and that. You know."

"Traveling the world, right. And all your travels led you right back to where you started, huh?"

He said, "What makes you think this is where I started?"

That Faith didn't know he'd been in prison told him a great deal. Chester had never mentioned it? Or Vitower, or anybody? So much for the irreplaceable hard-ass Crowe. She went back behind the bar, saying, "Well, if this don't call for a drink, I don't know what the hell does. Have one on me."

The three beers he'd had earlier were just about all the booze he needed for one day, but he pulled up a stool and said, "Thanks. Make it a—"

"Wait," she said, "Vodka gimlet, right?"

One of the businessmen tapped his glass on the bar, and Faith slid over to refill it with scotch— always the up-and-coming young executive's brand of poison. Smiling, she made her way back over to Crowe.

She said, "You in town permanent?"

He shook his head, and she nodded hers, and then the other businessman needed attention.

Crowe sat and nursed his drink.

This place, the Libre, was where he had his first introduction to the Old Man and his people. The Old Man didn't own the joint, but he carried on a great deal of private business here—Sunday nights always found him in one of the Libre's backrooms, going over weekly receipts or setting up new deals or plotting out how to screw with people in the coming week. It was also the place where Chester and Crowe hung around when they weren't busy with other work. Home away from home.

And Marco Vitower bought the place about a year ago. He

wasn't the sort to go changing things that didn't need to be changed, and what better way to cement the permanency of the Libre than to own it?

It was a Sunday night, which meant that, New Year's Day or not, Vitower would be here. Unless he wasn't.

A burst of customers showed up over the next few minutes and the next time Crowe turned around to look, the place had filled up, keeping Faith busy. When she finally made her way back over, Crowe said, "You still see Chester and the old crew around?"

"All the time," she said. "Chester usually swings by two, three nights a week. He'll probably swagger in here in pretty soon. I take it you didn't keep in contact with any of them after you left?"

"No, we kinda lost touch."

She mixed a Cosmo for a woman a couple stools down and said, "I asked about you a couple times after you left, but pretty much just got the cold shoulder. No one wanted to talk about it. It was like they were pissed at you or something."

He shrugged. "Maybe they were. But maybe if I smile and apologize real sweetly they'll forgive me."

She laughed. "Oh, I just gotta see that. Crowe says he's sorry. That's a riot."

The P.A. system crackled energetically and then a staggeringly loud bass drum started throbbing like a thermonuclear pulse. The dance floor was mobbed almost instantly, and like clockwork, as soon as the music kicked in around the bass line everybody was moving, the lights were flaring and pulsing, the floors were shaking.

Before prison, loud noise and mobs of people didn't bother him much; things were different now. He'd spent too long in relative silence, had grown comfortable there. The sudden assault of noise sent his nerves crawling and his head pounding almost immediately.

That's when Chester decided to spring on him. There was a hand on his shoulder, and Crowe spun around on his stool, his fingers automatically going to grab the hand and break it off the arm it belonged to. "Whoa, whoa!" Chester said, barely audible above the techno music. "Easy, man, it's just me!"

It took a lot of effort to rein it in, but Crowe managed to relax. From the corner of his eye he saw Faith take note of his reaction, a brief flicker of uneasiness stiffening her body. But then he smiled and said, "Hello, Chester. Maybe you can tell me. What exactly was it we enjoyed about this place?"

Chester nodded, said, "Yeah, right. I'm kinda surprised to see you here, Crowe."

"No, you're not."

"What?"

Crowe raised his voice a notch or two. "You're not surprised!"

"Right," Chester said, smiling and nodding. "Hey, come on with me. Vitower's in back, he'll be happy to see you."

Crowe took a last sip of his drink and left it half-finished on the bar and stood up. They started to walk away when Faith called, "Hey, Crowe!"

He stopped, and she said, "How you getting home tonight?"

"A taxi, most likely."

"No," she said. "I'll take you home."

"Thanks, but you don't have to do that. It's kind of a hike."

She grinned. "Not *your* home, dumb-ass. *My* home. I'm off at one tonight."

He shrugged and nodded, and he and Chester threaded their way through the crowds to the backroom where Marco Vitower waited for them.

10

He knew that Marco Vitower was running the show these days. That sort of info gets around, even in prison. He was surprised, though, when he first heard it. The Old Man was pretty firmly in charge when Crowe got sent up. When he died—congestive heart failure and who knew the old bastard even had a heart?—Crowe had assumed, as much as he'd even thought about it, that one of his closer advisors would take over.

But Vitower? Well, that had been a whallop, especially considering that he was—according to Crowe's sources—still enraged over the murder of his wife.

Marco Vitower, like a lot of the guys, had started strictly small-time. Everyone knew his legend. He was one of the first black guys to make a real mark, back in the days before the operations were almost entirely black, and lily-whites like Crowe and Chester Paine became the exceptions. Hired muscle before his eighteenth birthday, then bookmaking, and finally getting into the Old Man's good graces by killing a district attorney's assistant that had been snooping around. Whacked him, as they say in the gangster movies, *gratis*.

In those last days before Crowe's extended leave of absence, Vitower was pretty highly-placed, that was true. And by that time a good ninety percent of the Old Man's people were black—nobody could say he wasn't an equal opportunity sort of guy. But the top men, the men running the show, were white, still carrying on that questionable tradition of making wads of cash off the labors of black men.

And Vitower had the reins now. Pretty goddamn funny.

"Chester tells me you weren't interested in coming back into the fold," Vitower said. "Tell me that's not true."

"Back into the fold? What are you running these days, Marco, a church?"

He laughed good-naturedly. "Sure, why not? A church. And the city is our flock, right? I mean, I could think of worse analogies."

"Yeah, so could I."

"So, what's the story? Not interested in salvation?"

Crowe already grown tired of the church analogy, but Vitower probably could have kept it going all night.

He looked dramatically different from the last time Crowe had seen him. Seven years ago, he was a thug—a tattooed, gold-chain-adorned gangsta-type with personal gym muscles, the type you see all the time on cop shows. But even then, you could tell, the guy was just way too smart to go around looking like that. He was smarter than any of the gang, really. All that posturing and street-slang never seemed genuine.

He seemed to realize it now. The muscles and tattoos were hidden under the sleeves of a pretty tasteful pearl gray suit that he wore very well. His hair was cropped close to his head, and his strong jaw was clean-shaven. He looked respectable and trustworthy, and had that aura of casual authority that most leader-types have learned to cultivate from various books and seminars. The guy was a good ten years Crowe's junior, but he perched on the edge of his desk like a benevolent old master. His fingers, decorated with rings that glittered with gold and diamonds, drummed against his thigh.

Chester had slouched on a leather sofa across the room, smoking one of his smelly French cigarettes and watching with casual interest. There were two other men in the room, black guys who looked like proto-Vitowers, wearing good suits but without the panache of their boss. One of them stood by the door, the other hovered near Vitower's left elbow.

Crowe was placed in the seat of honor, a comfy high-backed suede chair right in front of the desk, with a pretty good view of the room. Vitower was saying, "I was a little offended, if you want to know the truth, Crowe. I mean, I sent Chester out to see you, as an emissary, really, and you just toss him out? Bad form."

"I was tired, what can I tell you? Chester picked a bad time."

Chester smirked, shook his head, and smoked his cigarette.

Vitower said, "I suppose I can understand that. Speaking frankly, you stopping by tonight sort of... lessens my annoyance."

"I thought it over, Marco. I figure I owe you that much."

It was a clean, spacious office, not the sort you'd expect to see in the back of a nightclub and nothing like the makeshift space the Old Man had utilized. A picturesque seascape in pleasing blues and greens occupied the wall behind Vitower's enormous oak desk. The carpet was a plush wine-red. An impressive bookcase filled almost one whole wall on the right, and the unread volumes that lined it were nice editions of various classics. A well-stocked wet bar sat next to the bookshelf. It looked more used than its neighbor.

The office smelled strongly of incense. The incense smell came from a small altar in the far corner. Sticks were burning, candles were fluttering, and a large photograph of Jezzie Vitower gazed out at the room with an innocence that only the dead are capable of.

Vitower caught him eying the little altar, and his mouth went tight. He said, "You don't owe me anything, Crowe. I mean, you and me, we hardly knew each other back in the day, did we? All the same, I'm glad you feel that way. I'd like to take you on. The Old Man always had good things to say about you."

"That didn't stop him from dropping me like a bad habit

when I got busted," Crowe said. He didn't mention the guy the Old Man had sent to kill him in prison.

Vitower nodded thoughtfully. "Yeah. Well, let's be honest, Crowe, you screwed up. I mean, you really blame him? You got yourself in a position where the Old Man couldn't do anything for you, not without getting himself involved. Right?"

Crowe smiled. "Would you have done the same thing, Marco?"

Vitower said, "Heard you swung by Jimmy the Hink's today."

"Word travels fast."

"What made you do that, I wonder?"

"I missed Jimmy's conversation and sparkling wit."

Vitower said, "Ha. Okay, fine. You don't have to answer. Are you still averse to signing on with me?"

Crowe glanced at Chester, who quickly looked away.

"My qualms about it," he said, "are not as pronounced as they were."

Chester sucked on his cigarette and, not looking at Crowe, said, "I'm glad you came to your senses, Crowe. I was kinda worried you were gonna flop around for a while, looking like an ass."

Vitower glanced over his shoulder at Chester. "Little passive-aggressive there, Paine?"

Chester shrugged, grinning. "I can't help myself. If you could've seen what he was like, back in the good old days… I mean, it's kinda funny. You'd never guess now, looking at him." He turned to Crowe. "No offense, there, old pal."

Crowe smiled pleasantly. "None taken, Chester. I'm just glad you were able to survive seven years without me covering your ass."

Vitower laughed. "Right. Take it easy, boys. You worked together well. I do remember it, Paine. And the two of you, working together again, is just what I need right now. Big things are about to go down. You probably already know some of it."

Crowe nodded at the altar to his dead wife and said, "Murke is being transported to Jackson on Tuesday."

Just the mention of Murke's name caused a massive change in Vitower's demeanor. The easy-going good humor vanished and the face went hard again, and he made a point of not looking at the altar. His voice was flat when he said, "Yeah. Tuesday."

Nobody said anything for a long moment.

Crowe knew a great deal more about the murder of Vitower's wife than Vitower could ever have guessed. In prison, he'd made the acquaintance of a guy named Pernis, who happened to be the lover of one of Vitower's old buddies from before he quit high school, a slight but menacing-looking man named Marvis Hicks. Sometimes Crowe had to pay Pernis in cash or cigarettes or even the occasional dime bag, but mostly Pernis was a more than willing transmitter of information. He liked to talk.

So this was what Crowe knew: Two years earlier, Jezzie Vitower was visiting her mother on Memphis's north side. By that time, the Vitowers were living on Mud Island, in an expansive stone house with five bedrooms, six baths, and a staff of four to run the place. Jezzie was four months pregnant. She'd been trying to talk her husband into buying a home for her mother in a nicer part of town, and it was something Marco Vitower had every intention of doing, eventually. As far as Crowe knew, afterward, he never did get around to it.

Jezzie left her mother's house at close to ten pm. She'd been there about four hours. Her car, a sporty dark green MG she'd had for less than a week, was parked half a block up the street, because when she'd arrived all the other spots to park along the curb were taken. The folks three doors down from her mother had been having a family get-together. It was kind of a miracle that the MG wasn't lifted.

Later, witnesses claimed to see a man wandering around the neighborhood, a white man, with longish sandy hair and a strangely wide mouth. Peter Murke. The descriptions couldn't have been more accurate.

But such is the world that three or four people spotting someone who looks like you in a neighborhood doesn't convince a jury that you murdered someone. When Murke was arrested, some two months later, the DA's office went over their evidence pertaining to every murder they were sure Murke had committed, and came up with only one they felt would stick. Thirteen-year-old Patricia Welling.

But the cops and the DA, privately and in conference with Vitower, were convinced that Jezzie was actually Peter Murke's last victim.

Pieced together, it looked something like this: She'd still been on the sidewalk, three steps away from her car. Between two houses, a walkway of broken and buckling concrete cut through to the next block; the walkway was walled on either side by some scrubby but tall bushes. The killer had been waiting there, crouched. When Jezzie passed, he swooped down on her, slapping one hand over her mouth, dragging her back into the shelter of the walkway. At the same time, he plunged a knife into her spine—a gutting knife, most likely, the kind hunters use to gut deer—and effectively severed the bundle of nerves there that controlled her motor impulses.

With his victim completely helpless, the killer dragged her halfway down the covered walk, straddled her, and went to work. He slit her throat first, a quick and clean stroke, designed more to silence her than anything else. And then he did what Peter Murke always did. He sliced her sternum to pelvis, like a surgeon, and proceeded to pull things *out* of her.

The whole thing must've taken about ten minutes. Fairly risky behavior on Murke's part. Some kids on the way to school the next morning found her, her heart, her liver, her intestines and lungs all laid out beside her and above her head. The killer didn't take anything with him.

A goddamn horrific murder, no two ways about it.

But the night Jezzie Vitower was slaughtered, Tennessee State smoked Jackson State, 20-14, in the Southern Heritage Classic. The story of Jezzie's murder got pushed to the back pages to make room for this obviously historical victory.

That, more than anything, stuck in Vitower's craw.

He said, "Tuesday, Crowe. They're going to take him up to

Jackson, set him down in front of some shrinks, and decide that he just can't be held responsible for what he's done. They'll decide he's crazy and needs help." His smooth hands clenched tight and his jaw twitched. "Needs help," he said again. "Poor old Peter Murke."

Chester said, "It don't seem right."

Vitower glared at him. "No. No, it doesn't, does it? First, the prosecutor's office insults me, right to my face, telling me that they aren't even going to mention Jezzie's murder when they present their case. They aren't even going to *mention* it. Only one victim mattered to them, a little white girl from goddamn Bartlett, a little white teenage whore wandering around in Midtown all by herself, looking for drugs. Because you know, even in Memphis, where the population is eighty-goddamn-percent black, the only murders that matter are the murders of white people."

Chester squashed out his cigarette in the standing ashtray by the sofa.

Vitower swallowed hard. "No offense meant, gentlemen." Crowe shrugged, and Vitower said, "As if that wasn't bad enough, right? Now, they're going to declare him a raving nutjob and set him up as cozy as can be at the state loony bin."

He slammed his fist against the desk. His rings thunked into the wood, leaving little round indentations.

Crowe said, "You want to make sure he never gets to Jackson. Right?"

"Yes," he said. "That's about the size of it, Crowe."

One of his proto-Vitowers went to the little bar, mixed a short gin and soda, garnished it with a lime, and handed it to the boss. Vitower took it without looking at the man. He threw it down his throat and handed the glass back. He was having a hard time holding it together, but the drink seemed to help.

Crowe said, "Why me, Marco? I mean, I understand why *now*, with him being transported, but why have me do it, and not one of your people?"

He grinned darkly. "For one thing, I'm looking forward to

being able to say you *are* one of my people. For another, there's a little bit of heat on at the moment."

Chester said, "Wills."

Vitower said, "Right. Eddie goddamn Wills. Sheriff's Department detective. Been giving me grief ever since the Old Man kicked."

Crowe said, "A cop, Marco? Since when has a cop been able to give you any trouble worth talking about?"

"Since Eddie Wills. He's trouble. One of the cops other cops don't like. Hard-ass, follows the rules as loosely as possible without losing his job. And he's got a hard-on for me."

Crowe grinned at him. "What did you do to the poor fella?"

Vitower smirked. "Damn if I know. But the fucker keeps picking up my people on any minor charge he can—he even busted Maurice here for littering once. Threw a cigarette wrapper on the street, fucking Wills shook him down."

One of the proto-Vitowers, Maurice, Crowe guessed, nodded, and that was about all he had on the subject.

"Whatever his damage is, he's been snooping around, making himself a nuisance. Thanksgiving, the sonofabitch was even parked outside my house. On Thanksgiving!"

Chester said, "Maybe he's just thankful for you."

"Right. Whatever, I wish the bastard would just go away. In the meantime…"

Crowe said, "Murke's being transported by the Sheriff's Department in an armored vehicle. What do you think we can possibly do about that? He'd be pretty damn near untouchable."

Vitower straightened his collar, which didn't really need straightening, took a deep breath, and smiled. "Pretty damn near," he said. "But not entirely. You find a way, Crowe. You find a way to kill that motherfucker before he makes it to Jackson."

Crowe said, "The odds, Marco, aren't good."

"I know. That's why I want you to do it. Here's the thing. This is a shit job, and I don't want to risk any of my long-time people on it. I don't really believe that you'll be able to pull this off, not without getting killed or caught."

Crowe said, "You need someone expendable."

"No, that's not it. I'm giving you Chester, and as many of my boys as you need, and none of them are expendable as far as I'm concerned. What I need is someone to take the heat if it all goes south. That would be you."

He smiled, and it wasn't the easy-going, leadership seminar smile this time. It was the predatory smile of a reptile. He said, "All my resources will be at your disposal. Like I said, you'll have Chester here as your right hand. You do this, Crowe, and you can consider yourself back in my good graces. That is what you want, yes?"

Crowe nodded. What he really wanted, Vitower couldn't afford.

But he said, "Fine, Marco. Consider Peter Murke dealt with."

11

That night he dreamed about the Ghost Cat, although he didn't know at the time that's what it was.

It had all the surreal logic of any nightmare: alone, in a tangle of forest tainted an unnaturally dark green. Rain pattered on the canopy of leaves overhead and drizzled down in misty silence. But it wasn't him, exactly. He was small, and had the physical sensation of being a young boy.

A cat—*the* cat—came out of the dark green undergrowth and nuzzled against his ankles, purring. He reached down to touch it and it lifted itself up on hind legs for a moment to meet his palm with a narrow head before rubbing against his ankles some more. The cat was sleek and jet black, with a blue-ish sheen, well-cared for. A white spot on its forehead formed an almost perfect cross.

But something felt wrong. They were too alone, him and the cat. It shouldn't have been here, in this dark place. He felt a shameful rage welling in him when he realized this. He felt a strange betrayal. The cat had trespassed in his world, the one place he was safe from… from whom? From *them*.

The cat was looking at him from the base of a huge maple tree, about five feet away. Dark gray eyes glittered. It was sitting and looking at him and then for a split-second he saw what it was *going* to look like, with its jaw ripped wide and one arm torn away, blood seeping into the undergrowth and insides scattered, and he tried to say, Go away cat, don't let it happen, go away, but no words would come. It only gazed at him in that curious cat way, and the horrible vision of its end flashed before him again, and he knew he was some sort of Holy Man right then, some sort of Sacrificial Priest. Choking back a sob, he took a step toward it.

And woke up, feeling an unsettling sort of *holiness*, of dark and ugly *divinity*.

The nightmare shook him up. Crowe had killed men. He'd put many more in the hospital. He had every intention of carrying on in that manner.

But he liked animals. He didn't like to see them suffer, particularly cats. He'd sooner kill a man than a cat.

He dozed off again pretty quickly. Faith woke him some six hours later, close to eleven in the morning. She'd just gotten out of the shower, and smelled clean and raw as she worked her lithe brown body over his under the blankets.

"Time to get up," she said, nipping at his jaw and neck with her sharp little teeth. "I'm not quite done with you yet." He could smell rum on her breath already.

The night before, they'd stopped and bought two bottles on the way, and within an hour they'd finished the first one. He had one drink. In bed, she kept her drink on the nightstand and went often to the kitchen to refresh it. She eventually passed out on top of him.

They had rough, awkward sex after she woke him, and an hour later he was finally out of her bed and in the shower. Her place was in Midtown, near Overton Square, and driving there from the Libre in her Honda Civic they passed about a hundred bars. He wondered why she worked at the Libre, when there were so many other bars to choose from, but he didn't ask. People just do what they do.

She was in the small and homey kitchen, just setting out plates for eggs and bacon and biscuits out of a tin when he strolled in, tucking in his shirt. The second bottle of rum was on the counter, opened and about a third empty. He ignored it.

"You made breakfast," he said, more than a little surprised.

She cocked her head at him, grinning. "Uh, yeah? Breakfast, it's something people do, you might've heard something about it?"

She was wearing nothing but lacy panties and an undersized man's tee-shirt, and he realized it was the first time he'd ever seen her in the daytime, in natural light. She looked smaller somehow, more vulnerable. From her stance, a little defensive, he could tell she was afraid he was going to be a bastard—the old 'get-laid-get-out' routine.

"You have fresh fruit?"

She smirked. "Fresh fruit, he says. You'll eat eggs and bacon, and like it."

The breakfast looked great, and she looked great, and he sort of didn't mind being there so much. He sat down at the breakfast table and ate.

He had six thousand dollars in his pocket, rolled in large bills. Vitower called it a 'retainer', and suggested that he use a big chunk of that to buy some good clothes. Between that and the two thou from Jimmy the Hink he was doing okay. Finishing the last of his bacon, he said, "Hey. Get dressed. We're going shopping."

Standing at the kitchen counter and drinking orange juice, she said, "You're pulling my leg, yeah? You don't strike me as the type who spends much time at the mall."

"That's true. And that's why I need you along. I'm buying some fresh threads today, and you're going to pick out three or four dresses you like or jeans you want or whatever. I'm buying."

She said, "My mama always told me, never say no to a man offering to buy you clothes."

While Faith was in the bathroom getting ready, he used her phone to make a call. Radnovian picked up on the fourth ring. "Make it important. I'm trying to sleep."

"You can sleep when you're dead."

"Who the goddamn hell is this?"

Crowe identified himself, and Radnovian said, "Ah, Christ. Didn't I just fucking talk to you? Like, yesterday? I swear, you do this shit to me on purpose."

"I don't do anything on purpose, Rad," Crowe said. "Things just sort of happen."

He snorted into the phone. "Innocent bystander to life, as usual, right? And I'm going to assume this ain't a call just to see how shit's going."

"At the moment I have some pressing business. I need to know more about Peter Murke."

"Jesus. What about him? I already told you everything I know about it."

"They're transporting him tomorrow, yeah? I need to know what route they have in mind."

Rad said, "What route? Christ, Crowe. From Memphis to Jackson, you can't get much simpler than that. You throw the prisoner in the back of the armored van, you start the engine, you drive away. Simple."

"For a prisoner as high profile as Murke? They're gonna be cagey."

Rad said, "Sounds to me like you're anxious to get back to prison. That's not the sort of info someone on parole usually has a hankering for."

"I'm not on parole, Rad. When all this is done, I promise that if I have to get arrested I'll let you collar me first."

"Lucky me. Tell me one thing, Crowe. Why do you need to know this stuff?"

"Some questions are better left unasked. Especially for guys with certain illegal habits."

There was a brief flare of silence on the line, before Rad puffed air through the headset and said, "There *is* some concern about Murke's safety on the trip. We had a tip-off a few days ago that some fringe group yahoos might be planning an ambush on the transport van. I mean, it's a long shot, right, but the D.A. really wants to see this come to trial, and he's not willing to risk it." He paused, and Crowe could hear him swallowing hard, weighing things in his head. He said, "You, uh... you wouldn't happen to know anything about said fringe group, would you?"

"I'm a moderate. What route are they taking, Radnovian?"

He huffed and puffed, but in the end he spilled.

Crowe said, "One other thing. There's this Sheriff's dick named Wills. Eddie Wills. You know him?"

"Ah, Christ, don't tell me you're gonna involve yourself with Wills, man." Crowe could hear him shifting around; his bedsprings creaking. "Crowe, I won't lie to you, man, you really stress me out."

"I don't have any immediate plans involving Wills. But what's his story?"

"His story is one that's seriously screwed up. You probably already know he's targeted Marco Vitower. Wants him to go down in a big way. His job, basically, is to keep tabs on Vitower's org, you know, watchful eye and all that. The D.A.'s been trying to build a case against Vitower for a couple years now. They don't wanna take any chances until they know they've got him on something big."

"But this Wills guy isn't the patient sort, I take it."

Rad said, "Wills thinks Vitower killed the Old Man."

"Why should he care?"

"That, Crowe, is a source of never-ending speculation. Maybe Wills had some kind of arrangement with the Old Man. Maybe they were old drinking buddies, who knows? The point is, Wills has been dangerously close to losing his badge over this. At this point, there's no telling what the crazy bastard will do. I'd advise you to steer clear of him."

"Noted," Crowe said.

He was standing by the window while talking to Rad, and

happened to glance out just then. A kid was standing in the parking lot, not far from Faith's car. He looked somewhere in his mid-twenties, wore a hoodie that Crowe recognized.

Rad was saying, "Hey. Assuming you survive whatever crazy shit you're about to pull, you should swing by and have a few beers. Catch up, yeah?"

His brief flare-up of anger at being compromised yet again had dissipated. Even what Crowe had told him the day before about their new status quo didn't seem to sink in. That's the way of the heroin user, Crowe thought. After a while, they lose their sense of outrage.

The kid in the parking lot glanced up at the window, and Crowe saw the strong jaw and glittering eyes in a smooth brown face. It was the kid from Jimmy the Hink's neighborhood, the one he'd kidney-punched and head-butted yesterday. Garay, his name was Garay.

Rad was still talking. Crowe hung up.

12

He was leaning against Faith's Honda but stood up straight when he saw Crowe coming across the parking lot. He looked confused for a half-second, but gathered his wits quickly.

"You," he said. "I thought it was you. Sonofabitch."

"What are you doing here?"

"I was gonna ask you the same question. Motherfucker, you are just about the last fucker I expected to see today."

Both his eyes were puffy and he had a bandage across the bridge of his nose. Anger simmered in his eyes and he jammed his hands into the pockets of his hoodie and did an agitated little shuffle. He shook his head, kept shaking his head, as if he couldn't think of quite what to say and could only marvel at it. "Motherfucker," he kept saying.

Crowe said, "Remember, Garay, how I told you yesterday. If I saw you again, I'd slice you open."

"Naw, man. You said if you saw me in *that* neighborhood. You didn't say nothin' 'bout no place else."

He looked happy with that, like he'd gotten Crowe on a technicality. Crowe almost had to laugh. "Okay," he said. "I'll ask you one more time. What the fuck are you doing here?"

"I was gonna ask you the same—"

"I'm asking *you*, Garay."

He looked sullen, took a deep breath and spat out, "What the fuck you doin' with my sister?"

"What?"

"My sister. You were up in her apartment. What the fuck are you doing up there?"

"Your sister. Faith is your sister?"

"Ever since I was born, motherfucker. What are you doing with her?"

That time Crowe did laugh, and Garay said, "Ain't no laughing matter. That's my big sissy you fuckin' around with."

"Okay," Crowe said. "Well, you answered your own question. You *know* what I'm doing here."

"You using her to get to me?"

"Don't flatter yourself, kid. As far as I'm concerned, any business you and I had was finished with yesterday."

He sneered, huffed air out through his bandaged nose, and then winced. Crowe gave him a moment to get used to things. Finally, Garay said, "You telling me that, just by coincidence, you hooked up with my sissy?"

"We've known each other a long time."

"She didn't mention no old white dude."

"She didn't mention a thug younger brother, either."

"Shit, motherfucker, you know you're old enough to be her daddy."

He was right about that—Crowe was more than twenty years older than her—but he said, "Jesus, kid, how old do you think I am?"

He smiled unpleasantly. "Old enough," he said. "Old enough to know better."

He couldn't argue with that one either, so he let it go. Instead, he said, "You don't have to like it, kid, but that's the way it is. Did you have something you wanted to say to Faith?"

"Whatever I have to say to her I can say without you around."

"Suit yourself."

He shook his head again and reached into his pants pocket for car keys. He started toward a pimped-out silver Grand Prix parked a couple slots away from the Honda, said, "This ain't over, man. This ain't fuckin' over."

He got in his car, pulled out and drove away. Crowe watched him until he turned off onto the street.

He didn't mention anything to Faith about her brother. He wanted to mull it over for a while first. And besides, he had things to do.

He bought four suits, English cut, all in muted conservative colors, one a pearl gray number similar to the one Vitower had on the previous night. He liked that suit. He waited while they were being tailored, and in the meantime bought four shirts and some silver cufflinks. Underwear, tee's, the whole nine. Faith picked out five neckties for him, three of which he put back because they had patterns on them. He only ever wore solid colors, especially in neckties. Finally, he spent a wad on a warm Burberry overcoat in gray wool, and two pairs of comfortable black Italian shoes.

They found so many dresses and blouses and sexy underwear for her that it actually required a clerk to take it all to the car. They split up for about an hour and when they met up again she smelled like booze. He was spending money like a fiend.

And the whole time, he was working it out in the back of his head; not a fool-proof plan, exactly, but a plan anyway. What would he need? Guns. A heavy, durable vehicle. Two men with him, Chester and one other, someone who could double as a driver/gunman. Two other men as back-up, in a separate vehicle, driving about ten minutes behind them. What could they expect? The driver and four Sheriff's Deputies, all armed, according to Rad.

What else? No killing the deputies. That would bring down entirely too much heat. Not that the rest of it would be forgiven with a wink and a nod, but shooting down cops, well. No thanks.

So the guns would be just for show—and just for Murke—

and they'd need some non-lethal gear. Tasers? Too unreliable. Tranq guns. Vitower could probably get his hands on two or three of those. Duct tape, the all-purpose crime product. Rope, or handcuffs or something. Yeah, that would do the trick pretty well.

The situation with Faith and her gangster brother took up some space at the periphery of his thoughts, but only a little. He knew he'd have to deal with it more directly before too long, but for the moment he had bigger things.

He was a regular four-star general. Had it all worked out, no worries. He'd pull this job for Vitower, collect a massive amount of money, and then, well... then he would pay himself. Chester and Vitower, and then whoever the hell got in the way.

They had dinner at a Japanese place in Germantown. It was dark when they got back to her flat, both of them pleasantly exhausted. He lay on the sofa and she modeled her new wardrobe for him until he couldn't take it anymore and threw her on the floor, ignoring the sweet tang of rum sweat that came off her body, peeling off all her new things one by one.

They had some fun. He never even bothered to find out her last name. She'd be dead before the month was over.

13

The front steps of the courthouse swarmed with reporters, people carrying signs of protest, and curious onlookers, just waiting for Peter Murke to be escorted out and into the waiting transport vehicle. At exactly 10:30, they burst through the doors, ten armed men with the prisoner buried in their midst. Flashes went off. Reporters started yelling questions, shoving microphones and TV cameras in various faces, trying to bulldoze their way closer to Murke. On the periphery, the protestors shouted things like, "*Die, Murke!*" and "*Remember Patricia!*" and "*Give 'em the chair!*" As far as Crowe could recall, there wasn't even a death penalty in Tennessee, but that didn't stop them from wishing.

It was a circus, but only a one or two ringer. Peter Murke's days of inspiring a full-on three ring act were two years gone. There were bigger stories these days. The guards shoved their way through, stone-faced and stoic. The prisoner was shackled with chains on his legs and arms. His head was hidden in the hood of a heavy ski coat. He kept his face down.

From up the block, they watched the circus. Crowe had the back seat of the Hummer to himself, and had to peek between Chester and D-Lux to get a good view.

When the procession was a few steps from the transport

van, Crowe said, "Okay then. Head around to the back of the building. That's not Murke."

"How you know that?" D-Lux said. He was a big, wicked-looking guy with a shaved head and a neck as thick as Crowe's torso. His heavy fingers drummed impatiently on the steering wheel.

"Head around the back," Crowe said again.

Grumbling, he put the Hummer in gear, flipped on the radio, and in the best tradition of the sort of people who drive Hummers, did an illegal U on Main Street. Hip-hop came blaring out of the car's rear speakers, thumping too hard and rattling the windows and seats.

Chester irritably stabbed the off button with his finger. "Turn that shit off, man. We got work."

D said, "Motherfucker, you don't touch a black man's radio. If I turn the fucking thing on—"

"D, shut the fuck up," Chester said.

D shut up, but he didn't look happy about it.

They turned left onto the next street, just in time to see the real transport van nosing out of the alley behind the courthouse and hooking left, toward the river. Tricky boys, those Sheriff's Department cops.

"There it is," Chester said. "The fuck, man, don't you see the goddamn thing? Stay on it."

D scowled. "You wanna watch yourself, Paine. I ain't having it. I ain't having you disrespecting me."

Crowe said, "Both of you, shut up."

D timed the traffic flow nicely, swung the Hummer into the next lane without getting them killed. One guy in a VW van had to slow down two or three miles per hour because of them. He honked his horn uselessly, and D flipped him off.

They were about four vehicles behind the transport van. Crowe said, "Good. Don't get any closer, we aren't exactly unobtrusive in this monstrosity. Concentrate on the road. Chester, call the other guys. And keep your eyes on the van, you're navigating."

Chester said, “No shit. In the meantime, why don’t you just chill back there, huh?”

Crowe said, “Good idea,” leaned back in his seat, and bit into the apple he’d brought with him. He didn’t get fresh fruit in prison, and in the few days he’d been free he’d developed a real taste for it.

Chester snapped open his cell phone and barked at the person on the other end. There were two of them, a couple of Vitower’s lower-ranking goons, ordered to follow them and do exactly what Chester told them to do.

The weight of a revolver pulled the pocket of Crowe’s new overcoat out of shape. It was a Colt .38, with a three inch barrel. In his other pocket were a handful of speed re-loaders. A good reliable caliber, nothing fancy. If he had to shoot it he knew it wouldn’t let him down.

The transport van got on 51 from Riverside, by the DeSoto Bridge, headed east. The monstrous glass Pyramid reflected the churning Mississippi to their left. D did a good job staying a few car lengths behind.

There wasn’t much traffic on the freeway, so Crowe said, “Fall back a little, D,” and miracle of miracles D did what he was told without complaint. The weather had warmed up a little that morning, and all the clinging ice was gone, but the sky looked washed-out and tired, as if it had had quite enough.

The transport van took 14 up to the 40 connection, passing the exits for North Parkway, Jackson, Chelsea. Where 40 headed east, the freeway opened up and very quickly they left the city behind them.

For a long time, they rode in silence. The deputies had chosen 10:30 in the morning to avoid any remnants of rush hour, and it had paid off, especially heading away from the city. They kept a steady clip, about seventy miles per, not having to do too much weaving or changing lanes. Crowe, Chester and D followed in their giant gas waster/status symbol.

The tension had been rising steadily in their vehicle. Chester kept fingering the revolver he carried in a shoulder rig, tapping his foot rhythmically on the floorboard and grimacing. D-Lux drove stiffly, huffing and sighing every few seconds. Finally, D-Lux said, "Sure would make this drive a little nicer if a man could listen to his rhymes."

Chester glared at him. "You want a rhyme, D? Try this one: Roses are red, violets are blue, shut the fuck up. You like that one?"

D gritted his teeth. "Once more. Talk to me like that just once more."

Chester said, "Your job, D, is to keep your mouth shut and do what you're told."

"Aw, hell no. My job, motherfucker, is to drive you two lily-white asses and look good doing it."

Chester said, "Well, you're halfway there."

D huffed again. "Just my goddamn luck," he said. "Stuck in a goddamn moving vehicle with two goddamn crackers."

Chester said, "Crackers? Did you just say crackers?"

D said, "Yeah. You got a problem with that?"

"No, but it just reminded me I haven't had breakfast. Some crackers sound pretty good right now."

They eyed each other for a moment and then Chester grinned and D grinned and they started cooling off. D shook his head and said, "I changed my mind. Our man Crowe back there is the cracker. You, Paine, are the cheese."

That got both of them laughing. Crowe leaned back again and gazed out the window. They were giving him a headache.

Twenty minutes later, well and truly out in the boonies, the transport van left the freeway.

"There," Crowe said. "They're taking the scenic route."

As the deputies got further into the rural areas between Memphis and Jackson, the possibility of ambush became greater, so they had chosen this particular exit onto a state road that didn't see much traffic. It was one of about ten choices as a route to Jackson, and not a very direct one, either—it wound and twisted through heavily forested areas, simple two-lane blacktop that would add another hour, at least, to the trip.

Not a bad plan, unless the ambushers happened to know in advance which road the deputies had chosen.

They followed them off the exit. Crowe said, "Fall back a little more, D. We know where they're going, we're not gonna lose them. Chester, call the boys in the other car and make sure they know which exit to take."

"They know which exit."

"Remind them."

Grumbling, he pulled out his cell phone again and punched them in. He spat the exit number at them and snapped the phone shut again. "Happy?" he said.

Crowe wasn't, not really, but he didn't say anything. The closer they got to doing this, the less secure he felt about it. He wasn't scared, exactly—if getting killed is the worst thing that can happen to you, well, big deal, right?—but he didn't want the plan to fall apart. He didn't want to get taken out before he'd finished what he'd come back to Memphis to do.

They slowed down, deliberately losing sight of the transport van. The road was a lonely stretch of black, weaving through dense icy woods. They weren't far from the state park, deemed a wildlife sanctuary, but Crowe didn't see any wildlife other than the small mammal variety littered along the sides of the road. There's not much sanctuary against a ton of speeding metal on wheels.

No one in the Hummer said anything for a long time. They drove on through the woods, always just out of sight of the transport van. Crowe kept checking his watch.

When they'd been on the state road for exactly ten minutes, he said, "Okay. It's time. Chester—"

"Yeah," he said. "Calling." He dialed again, said, "Move it," and tossed the cell phone on the seat next to him.

"D," Crowe said, "Give this ugly thing some speed."

D slammed his foot down hard on the gas and they rocketed forward hard enough to push Crowe back in his seat. He handed a tranq gun to Chester, who took it with a sneer. They loaded them up.

Crowe could see the speedometer over D's massive shoulder. They hit ninety miles an hour, just coming around a wide curve, and the transport van was suddenly in front of them, doing about forty.

"Do it," Crowe said to D. "Just like you see on the cop shows."

"Oh yeah," D said. "I always wanted to do this. Brace yourselves."

About five car lengths behind the van, he swung out to the left, ready to slam their left rear with the right nose of the Hummer. Crowe held tight to his seat.

Right about then, their plans took an unexpected turn.

From the corner of his eye, Crowe saw a flash of steel through the trees off to the right, heard the deafening roar of a horn, and an enormous eighteen-wheeler carrying a full rig roared out of a hidden road and crashed full-speed into the side of the transport van.

D slammed on the brakes, slid out of control off the road.

Chester's head smashed against his window and he dropped behind the seat, out of Crowe's line of sight.

They were spinning, but Crowe was peripherally aware of the terrible screech of shattered glass and metal and wood as the eighteen-wheeler squashed the transport van against the line of trees like a bug.

And then they were hitting the trees themselves, only feet away. The airbags deployed, burying D and Chester, but the only cushioning for Crowe was the headrest in front of him. His head slammed against it and he dropped his tranq gun and everything went fuzzy and red.

For what seemed like a long time, nothing happened. He could only hear a kind of dim ringing in his ears, and couldn't get his head around what had just happened. *An accident? Were we in an accident?* And then, *A semi... a fucking semi-truck just came out of nowhere...*

Chester was saying, "What the fuck? What the fuck?" over and over again, weakly, but he sounded far away. D-Lux groaned, his huge fingers groping at the air in front of him.

Crowe wiped blood away from his eyes with the back of his hand and pulled himself up from where he'd fallen on the floorboards. "Chester," he said. "You good?"

"What the fuck?" he answered. He was good.

"D?"

D turned his head to look at him, and his eyes were glazed. Crowe said again, "D? You good, man?"

He nodded, and Crowe became aware then of noise outside the Hummer, voices raised, people yelling, and a flurry of activity.

At the same time he heard the crack of a powerful rifle shot, the front window of their vehicle shattered, and D's head exploded all over him.

Crowe dropped behind the seat, his hand instinctively going to the .38 in his pocket. Chester screamed something unintelligible and war-like, and before Crowe knew it Chester had bolted out of the Hummer and was firing like mad at someone. Crowe heard a volley of gunfire matching him.

Chester was providing cover. Crowe was sure that wasn't his intention, but that's what the jack-ass was doing. Crowe peeked over the headrest.

He counted seven of them.

One, a guy wearing a dirty yellow parka and snow boots, was firing a sawed-off shotgun at Chester, who was busy diving behind the tail end of the semi-truck.

There was a younger man dressed all in black, with a long trench coat and long, unkempt black hair. He too, was shooting at Chester, with a long-barreled revolver.

There was a muscular guy wearing a white tee-shirt and jeans a la James Dean. There was another, older guy with a red cowboy hat propped on his head. Another in a rusty metal mask. And two more in very ugly business suits right out of the mid-70's.

And Crowe found himself mimicking Chester, at least in his head.

What the fuck?

Five of them had guns, and were firing at Chester. From his angle, Crowe could see him crouched behind the semi, frantically reloading. He looked pretty panicked.

The two businessmen didn't have guns. One had a long wicked-looking knife, and the other a machete that was already stained with blood. They were using them on the Sheriff's deputies. Three of them were already dead, sprawled out along the side of the road like dolls that had been ripped apart by mad dogs.

Crowe looked just in time to see the rear door of the transport van pop open and the last of the deputies come rushing out, screaming and firing a shotgun. The businessman with the machete was right on top of him. With a face as placid as a spring day, he sliced off half the cop's hand, and the shotgun went spinning away with most of his fingers. The other businessman—his partner, Crowe assumed—flicked his blade and instantly the lower half of the cop's face was gone in a wash of blood.

Crowe saw movement inside the transport van. Peter Murke.

Chester had reloaded and was firing around the corner of the semi. "Crowe!" he screamed. "Mother of fuck, Crowe, help me!"

Crowe kicked open the door facing away from the road and tumbled out of the Hummer. Instantly, some of the shooting focused on him. Bullets pounded into the vehicle and the trees above his head, showering him with wood chips. He fired blind over the hood of the Hummer, hoping to get lucky. No one screamed out any death throes.

The rear of the transport vehicle was visible from where he crouched. The downside: they could see him as well as he could see them. The two businessmen were looking at him curiously, and between them the rough-looking fish-faced Murke was stepping down out of the van.

Crowe raised his gun and fired three times before he had a good bead and his closest shot ricocheted off the bumper of the van. Murke and the machete businessman flinched, but the one with the long knife only smiled and very casually flipped his blade at him.

It thunked into a tree, less than two inches from Crowe's head.

"Fuck!" Crowe scrambled out of the guy's line of sight, fumbling in his pocket for one of the speed re-loaders.

From the other side of the Hummer, bullets pounded into metal, and Chester was still screaming for help. Crowe reloaded his revolver as quickly as he could, but he knew he'd never be able to do it before the freaks had moved in on him.

A sudden intense pain in his left shoulder made him nearly drop the gun, and he looked to see a throwing knife sticking out of him. He gazed up in mild shock at the businessman. He'd crept up while Crowe was preoccupied, and was now smiling down at him from less than six feet away. Already, he had another knife in his hand and was getting ready to throw it.

Crowe lurched to his feet and bullets whined around him. The knife-wielding businessman threw his blade, and it caught Crowe in the right shoulder blade as he was turning to get away.

He stumbled forward, right into the other businessman, the one with the machete.

He pushed Crowe back with one hand, swung his machete at him with the other. Crowe felt the blade slice across his face and everything went like a kaleidoscope, different colors, spinning crazily.

Crowe was in the middle of the road, about to fall, firing at something he couldn't see. He could hear bullets pounding the blacktop, and then he could hear his own revolver clicking empty. In his peripheral vision, he saw Chester, laying face-up but not moving.

A bullet in Crowe's right arm then, like a hot lance, and he fell, fell far, far down, to the icy blacktop.

And there had been no time, no time at all, to even wonder, except in the vaguest way, who these people were or what the hell was going on. It all happened too fast. Seven killers, a semi-truck, four dead Sheriff's Deputies.

And three hapless crooks, down before they knew what hit them.

After that, the sound of another car arriving, and of Murke and the freaks escaping.

His new overcoat wasn't doing such a good job keeping out the chill from the blacktop. He sprawled face-down, tasting the copper tang of blood, but didn't feel much pain because the cold was seeping into his bones and everything was numb. Particularly, he couldn't feel his right arm. He didn't want to turn his head and look. What if the damn arm was gone completely? That would've been too goddamn depressing to even think about.

He gave his best effort toward lifting his head, but didn't have any luck. The road scraped his jaw and fresh warmth trickled down his temple. But by casting his eyes up as far as they would go, he could see the tail end of the Sheriff's Department transport van. The rear doors were thrown open, and one of the cops half-hung out of it. His hand dangled over the road. Three of his fingers were gone, from when he'd raised his hand to ward off the machete blow.

Crowe couldn't hear anything except his own heart pounding against the blacktop.

That was when the Ghost Cat came out of nowhere. It materialized before him, flickering like an ancient piece of film, black and white and ravaged by time.

Black and sleek, with the white cross on its forehead, like a Pentecostal. It meowed, but the sound of it seemed far away. It wandered around amidst the spent bullet casings and blood, sniffing, searching.

"Cat," Crowe said, for no good reason.

It looked at him with curious gray eyes, meowed again. He couldn't hear it now. It sat on the cold road, licked irritably at its hind-quarters, and looked at him one more time.

Then it disappeared. It just evaporated, like steam off the blacktop.

"No," Crowe said. "Come back."

He rolled his eyes back to a more comfortable position and saw Chester, about six or seven feet away. He was on his back, near the side of the road. He didn't look so good, but as Crowe watched him he saw his chest moving up and down—very slowly, almost imperceptibly, but moving.

The sonofabitch was alive.

Not far from his head, metal glinted. Crowe focused on it. It was a gun, a revolver. Not his, he had no idea where his was, and not Chester's or D-Lux's. One of the cops, maybe. He grasped at it with his left hand. His fingers barely reached the barrel, but he managed to snag it and painstakingly drag it toward him.

When it was close enough, he grabbed the grip. It was cold in his palm.

"Hah," he said to himself.

He extended his arm in Chester's direction, aimed the gun at the back of Chester's head, pulled the trigger.

The hammer slammed on an empty chamber.

"Sonofabitch…" he said. "Sonofabitch gun…"

He tried two or three more times, just for the hell of it, but no-go. He put the goddamn useless gun down next and closed his eyes. *Death. Ghost Cat means death. I dreamed about it. I dreamed about the Ghost Cat.*

That's when the ice started coming down.

He heard tires squealing as their back-up arrived, someone saying, "*Jesus Christ, what the fuck!*" and he thought about the lesson he should've known by now, the adage he'd had to learn the hard way, seven years ago: *That's what you get, fella, for going into something not* knowing.

That was all.

14

Our defining tragedy, Crowe once heard a melodramatic news anchor call it, the terrorist attacks of September 11, 2001. What the assassination of JFK was to a previous generation, or the bombing of Pearl Harbor, or any number of horrible things you can think of. Crowe remembered it very well, because at the time he was beating a man to death in a seedy hotel room off Elvis Presley Boulevard, in Whitehaven.

The little 13-inch TV was on the whole time, but he didn't notice it because he was preoccupied. He was pulling Leon Berry up off the floor for the third time, getting annoyed because Leon kept laughing, even with a mouth full of broken teeth. "Not the time for chuckles," Crowe said, and slapped him backhand across his jaw.

Leon grunted, blood spilling down his chin onto his bare chest, and laughed again and mumbled, "You gotta… you gotta do better than that…"

It took a great deal to get Crowe truly angry, but little Leon Berry was pulling it off. Crowe had come there to beat a little sense into him. He was into the Old Man for almost five grand, betting more than he could afford on a series of bare knuckle brawls over the summer, down near the state line. He'd ignored the Old Man's calls, and eventually dropped out of sight, and

Crowe had been the one tagged to track him down and make him see the error of his ways.

Finding him had been easy. Crowe knocked on his hotel room door, heard him fumbling around in there in sudden panic, and Crowe kicked open the flimsy lock with the heel of his shoe. Leon had been standing by the bathroom door, reaching with one long-fingered hand for a razor blade on the sink. When he saw Crowe, he went still.

Crowe grinned. "Leon. You don't call. You don't write. We worry."

Leon said, "There ain't nothing you can do to me."

"Well," Crowe said, closing the door behind him. "Why don't we just put that theory to the test."

Leon was wrong. Crowe did plenty to him. Only it didn't do any good.

This was the sort of thing that should've been par for the course. Just another day in the life. But instead, it turned out to be the day that changed everything. Leon Berry was no ordinary squelcher. And this was no ordinary morning.

The TV was on, and from the corner of his eye, Crowe saw a shot of the Twin Towers in New York, saw a newscaster looking grim, his mouth moving. Leon had turned the volume down.

Crowe didn't think anything about it. He had work to do.

He didn't know that Leon was one of those rare fellas who are practically impervious to pain. He didn't know the cops wanted Leon on a felony charge. He didn't know they were staking him out, in the very next room. He didn't know terrorists were throwing airplanes at the World Trade Center.

Didn't know, didn't know, didn't know. That's what you get for going into something *not knowing*.

He wound up doing a lot more damage to Leon than he'd intended, because Leon wouldn't stop laughing and carrying on. Holding him up by the collar of his dirty tee-shirt, Crowe smashed his fist into his nose, and Leon only grunted and kept laughing. Crowe said, "Leon. I'm getting bored with this. I don't wanna keep hitting you. Do us both a favor, and stop laughing."

"I can't... I can't help it," he choked. "It's not... it's not my fault..."

And went into another bout of hysterical cackling.

Later, he would read about people like Leon, people who have some faulty wiring upstairs, messing with their pain receptors. It wasn't a mental illness. It was a neurological thing.

Frustrating.

So he kept pounding Leon and Leon kept laughing and Crowe kept getting more and more angry. His knuckles were raw by then, Leon was missing several teeth, and his eyes shined out of the blood-red mask his face had become. Finally, Crowe saw his eyes shift over to the TV, and something like horror finally came into them.

That tore it. Crowe couldn't get the reaction he needed, but something on the goddamn television had affected him. Furious, Crowe hit him one last time, square in the left temple, and Leon went limp, like a hippie being arrested at a protest. Crowe let him drop, and he slumped lifeless to the floor.

He'd killed him. He could tell that much without checking his pulse. You do this sort of work as long as he had, you just know.

"Sonofabitch," he said. "Leon, you stupid little bastard."

He glanced at the TV to see what exactly had inspired the dread he'd failed to create, just in time to see what must have been the fourth or fifth replay of the footage they would wind up playing all week. The World Trade Center was smoking, and the second airliner was just crashing into one of the towers. And the whole goddamn thing collapsed.

"Sonofabitch," Crowe said again.

The cops burst through the door then, guns waving, screaming, "On the floor, now! Get the fuck down on the goddamn floor!" and they were all over him, throwing him to the dirty carpet, yanking his arms behind his back, cuffing him. They didn't pass up the opportunity to kick him in the head a couple of times, being the pragmatic fellas they were.

"Sonofabitch," Crowe said again, craning his neck to see the television. "Are you boys seeing this?"

"Shut up!" one of them said, and punctuated the sentiment with another kick to his skull.

They'd heard the whole thing between him and Leon, listening from the next room with the device they'd planted under Leon's bed. How long they must have agonized, surprised by the unexpected arrival of one of the Old Man's strong-arms, trying to decide if they should risk their operation by busting in and saving the day. By the time they finally decided, it was too late to save their suspect. Crowe's only consolation was they didn't know any more about the World Trade Center than he did.

He was charged with second-degree murder, given a ten-year sentence, and was in the State Penitentiary by late December.

The Old Man didn't do a goddamn thing.

Crowe tried to reach him, naturally. His obligatory phone call was directly to his office. The Old Man didn't take the call. He didn't send a lawyer. The bastard had washed his hands of Crowe completely. And later on, of course, he'd send the stupid punk to try to kill him.

They gave him a state-appointed attorney who went through the motions and shrugged philosophically when they sentenced him. "Good luck," he said when they escorted Crowe in cuffs out of the courtroom. "Be good. You'll never do the whole ten, so don't worry."

He was right, Crowe didn't do the whole ten. He would've done five, except for the killing in prison, which got him an extra two, and he was out after seven years without even a parole hearing.

Seven years, ten years, a hundred years. It didn't matter. It didn't take near that long for him to know what he would do when he got out.

Dr. Maggie lost her medical license fifteen years earlier for selling prescriptions to junkies. So Crowe had to laugh when she said, "In my professional opinion, Crowe, you should stay in bed for at least another three days."

His laugh didn't endear him to her. She glared from behind her John Lennon frames and tapped a pen against her large but firm thigh.

"Three days," he said. "Right. Doctor's orders."

"It's not as if you have anywhere to be, is it?"

Now she was just getting nasty. He grinned and let her push him back down against the pillows.

From what everyone had been telling him, they were in a large, frame farmhouse north of Memphis. He didn't really know, as he hadn't been out of bed in two days. He had a window he could peer out if he sat up, but the view was limited; the branches of a heavy magnolia tree, glimpses of gray sky beyond it. They could have been anywhere, so he had to take their word for it.

They were Dr. Maggie, Marco Vitower, and Marvis Hicks.

Crowe come to late yesterday afternoon, after being out for almost twenty-four hours straight, and the first face he'd seen hovering over him was Marvis. He'd said, "Well, I'll be damned, he's waking up," and then he veered out of sight and Crowe heard him calling, "Dr. Maggie, Crowe's waking up," and Crowe sort of groaned and tried to move an arm to touch his face—everything hurt—and Dr. Maggie loomed into view, pushing his arm back down, and saying, "Try not to move, Crowe. You're okay now."

He wasn't convinced, but he let her push his arm down. Marvis said, "Long time no see, Crowe. Sure hate that we meet again with you in such sorry-ass shape."

Crowe said, "Where?"

Dr. Maggie told him about the farmhouse then, and how their so-called back-up had come upon them sprawled around on the blacktop.

Marvis said, "They put you boys in the Hummer, managed to get it separated from the tree it was attached to, and they all got the hell out. They said it was a crazy scene. What the hell happened?"

And Dr. Maggie said, "Not now. Let him rest." She looked down at Crowe and said, "I have to call Mr. Vitower now that you're awake. He'll want to talk to you."

Crowe said, "Chester?"

She nodded. "He's here. Worse shape than you. I pulled a bullet out of his stomach, and another had gone through his leg and hit the femoral artery. He's in and out of consciousness."

Crowe didn't like the way the room smelled, sort of antiseptic and musty at the same time, and he didn't like the glaring yellow of the walls and he didn't like the way his pillows were bunched up under his head. It was hard to talk; something was on the left side of his face that made moving his mouth difficult. He managed, "He gonna make it?"

"The worst is over, he's fine. The man you all refer to as D-Lux… was dead long before he got here."

He didn't need her to tell him that; he'd seen the man's head explode. But he was relieved about Chester. Couldn't have him dying, not yet.

She perched her considerable hips on the side of his bed and went on to tell him all the juicy details about his own condition, making sure to use laymen's terms. He'd been shot in the right arm, but it was the least of his wounds—the bullet had torn through the outer layer of muscle. He'd have a small scar, but after a few weeks normal mobility would return, she said. He'd lost a lot of blood from the two knife wounds—one in his left shoulder, another in the back, low and between the shoulder blades—and muscle had been seriously damaged on both of them. They could affect his mobility pretty seriously, and could potentially be painful for years to come.

"The thing that's most distressing, though," she'd said, looking very serious, "is the gash across your face." He reached up again to touch the area she was talking about, but again she pushed his hand down. "I'm… I'm pretty certain I was able to save the vision in your left eye, but, well. I'm not an eye surgeon, am I?"

"My vision?"

"The blade was apparently slashing in a *downward* motion," —she illustrated, slowly karate-chopping the air in front of her as if he wasn't sure what she meant— "and it got you from right above your left brow and down to your cheekbone. I'm afraid you're going to have a very noticeable scar, Crowe."

So that was what was all over his face, bandages. The whole thing started coming back to him then, the squad of killers, the eighteen-wheeler, the slaughter. And the Ghost Cat.

He said, "Food."

Dr. Maggie nodded. "Of course. I'll have the man fix you up something. Marvis will bring it up for you. I'm off to call Mr. Vitower, I'm sure he'll want to see you."

Crowe mumbled, "Bet he's worried sick about me."

She cocked one formidable eyebrow behind her wire frames. "Most men take at least an hour after waking from a near-death experience to regain their bad attitudes."

He didn't answer her, and she sighed resignedly and left the room, Marvis trailing her.

Later, Marvis brought up a bologna sandwich and a bowl of cream of mushroom soup. Crowe ate left-handed since his right arm ached too much for use, finished it in no time flat, and drained three glasses of water, which he knew he would regret later when Dr. Maggie brought the bedpan up. Marvis, a stout little man in his early '30's, with a receding hairline and skin the color of used-up coal, showed him that morning's newspaper.

BOLD AMBUSH, ESCAPE OF KILLER PETER MURKE, the headline read. The lead story said that Peter Murke was at large, and that the transport vehicle had been ambushed in route, smashed by an eighteen-wheeler, which led the very clever authorities to wisely conclude that Murke had been aided in his escape. Four Sheriff's Deputies were dead, one had been rushed to Baptist East, where he was currently listed in critical condition.

The story didn't say anything about signs of another vehicle, or the possibility of a third party. But then, it probably wouldn't have.

Crowe started nodding off after that, but when Vitower showed up Marvis shook him awake to talk to him. Vitower looked drawn and tense, anger simmering behind his cool façade. Crowe had to run over the whole crazy story three times before Vitower was satisfied, although *satisfied* wasn't quite the right word.

He sat on the edge of Crowe's bed, where Dr. Maggie had sat earlier, and nodded grimly and gritted his teeth and black clouds played in his eyes. He smelled like gin. He said, "This… this is completely fucked. All over the motherfuckin news, and nothing to show for it. I need you to still be in this, Crowe."

Crowe shrugged. "As Dr. Maggie pointed out, it's not like I have somewhere better to be."

Vitower said, "What kind of fucked-up plan were you running? Ambush the fucking truck? Sonofafuckingbitch."

He stood up and paced around the room for a long minute, furious. Crowe watched him until he calmed down and came back and sat at the edge of the bed again.

Vitower said, "But on the other hand, what plan could have foreseen a goddamn eighteen-wheeler smashing into the van out of nowhere? Or a bunch of weirdos slaughtering everyone?"

"I'll admit, I didn't see it coming."

That drew a slim, reluctant smile. He said, "Rest up while you can. You promised me something and you're gonna deliver, motherfucker. As soon as Dr. Maggie says you're okay to get up and around, we start over."

Crowe went to sleep after that. It was the next morning when Dr. Maggie started pulling up her dubious medical credentials and telling him that, in her "professional opinion", he had to stay in bed for three more days.

He kicked the blankets off and sat up, feeling woozy. His

blood by then was about half-composed of pain meds, but he managed to make it to his feet and took a moment to make sure he wasn't about to drop. Dr. Maggie folded her arms and glared. She shook her head, turned on her heel and walked out of the room.

He braced himself on the side of the bed, waiting for his head to catch up with the rest of him. They'd stripped off his clothes, so he was shivering in nothing but boxer briefs, and his body looked unhealthily thin and pale.

After a few minutes, he felt okay enough to pull on the khakis and tee-shirt Marvis had left out for him. It wasn't easy, pulling the tee-shirt on—his right shoulder ached fiercely, and the wound in his back felt as if it would bust open whenever he moved his arms higher than mid-level. The neck of the tee pulled against the bandages on his face when he slipped it over his head, and he tried not to think about that particular wound. A scar on his face, well, that would be pretty goddamn inconvenient. In this line of work, any distinguishing marks, as they say, were a hindrance. But losing the vision in his left eye would be considerably *more* than inconvenient.

He left the room, walking fairly straight, out into the hall. The walls were bare and the pine wood floor was cold on his bare feet. Chester was bedded up in the room almost directly across.

Crowe opened the door and went in. There was more light than in his room. Two windows instead of the one, facing east and the mid-morning sun streaming in. Chester was sleeping in a metal frame bed, looking very small, with the blankets pulled up to his sharp chin and a heavy growth of beard on his face.

Dallas half-dozed in a fat easy chair by the windows. She looked up when Crowe came in but didn't say anything.

She looked tired. Her hair was pulled back and half-covered by a kerchief. A threadbare blanket was thrown over her legs. Crowe said, "The distressed wife, keeping vigil over her ailing husband."

She said, "Marvis didn't call me until Chester first woke up, early this morning. So I haven't been here long enough to qualify as being on a vigil."

He almost asked her who was looking after her kid, but didn't. Instead, he said "Has he been awake since you've been here?"

"Yes. He didn't say much, though. Just 'oh, hello' when he saw me. He nodded when I told him Tommy was at home with the sitter. And he kinda chuckled when I told him you were in the other room."

"It's good that we can laugh about it now."

She stood up and stretched cat-like, the slim muscles in her arms and legs taut and her smooth white stomach showing between jeans and sweater. She had a new tattoo there, just above her belly button, in red and black, but it was too small to be able to tell what it was—some sort of cross or something. He looked away from her.

She said, "Lucky I was able to get the day off from work."

"Work?" Crowe said. "What, you have a job now?"

"Yeah. Some people do work for a living, you know."

"Don't give me that. You don't have to work."

"Has it ever occurred to you that maybe some people want to work?"

"No, not really."

She huffed. "Funny. Chester said the same thing. I got a job at the Mall of Memphis about four months ago. Working the evening shift at the shoe store."

Crowe said, "Well, you always were obsessed with shoes."

Chester snored peacefully. Crowe gently lowered his blankets a bit and saw the bandages around his torso. Dallas joined him next to the bed, standing entirely too close, and said, "What exactly happened out there?"

"That's what I've been trying to figure out."

She laughed softly. "Another daring adventure with Crowe and Paine comes to its inevitable conclusion. You two will be hard-pressed to top this one."

"I suppose so."

Her smell, again, that flowery scent that always went right to his head. He moved away and went to the windows. Another bleak winter morning out there, an expanse of dead brown grass trailing away from the house, into some sparse woods beyond an unpainted wood fence. In the distance, he could see a road, winding away toward what he could only imagine was civilization. A farmhouse in the middle of nowhere. The Dr. Maggie Memorial Hospital for the Criminally Inclined.

"Well?" she said after a minute. "Are you going to tell me what happened or what? All I could get out of Marvis was that you two were on a job and everything went south."

"That about sums it up," he said, staring out the window.

He didn't have to look at her to see the anger. "Oh, well thank you for clearing it all up, Crowe. I swear you drive me insane sometimes." She sighed and he heard her moving behind him, away from Chester's bed. "You haven't changed a bit."

And then Chester said, "Yeah. He's still a jag-ass."

Crowe turned around and Chester was grinning at him weakly from his bed. Dallas went to him, touched his forehead with a gentle hand. "Chester," she said. "How are you feeling?"

"Right as rain," he said. His voice was scratchy and dry. "Fucking starving, though."

"I'll go get Marvis, have him bring some food."

"Yeah."

She kissed him lightly on the temple, and, with a wary glance at Crowe, left the room.

Chester looked around with bleary eyes. He started to sit up, but winced in pain. Settling back down, he croaked, "You got a smoke? Ah, never mind, I keep forgetting you don't smoke."

"Bad for your health," Crowe said. "Haven't you heard?"

"I think I remember hearing something about that. Thought it was an old wife's tale. Shit, I could use one. What the hell day is this?"

Crowe told him they'd been at the farmhouse for two days now, and what Dr. Maggie had said about his condition. Chester peeked under the blankets at the bandages around his torso, frowning philosophically. "Huh," he said. "Y'know,

I *thought* I felt something like excruciating pain. Now I know." Then, "Looks like you didn't come out so well, either."

"You remember much about what happened?"

He sighed and adjusted his shoulders against the pillows. "Yeah, I think so. Big-ass truck outta nowhere. A bunch of weird cats with guns and what-not. I remember… I remember a guy wearing some metal shit over his face. And... there was some Goth kid, I think. They… they got D-Lux, didn't they?"

Crowe nodded.

"What the fuck?" Chester said, echoing his sentiments from that day. "What… who the hell were those fellas?"

"Don't know. But Vitower was here yesterday, and he wants me to find out. They sprung Murke."

"No shit."

"I'm heading back to Memphis tonight, and tomorrow morning I start asking around."

Chester frowned. "Asking around where? The Crazy-Ass Freako Killer Society?" He laughed at his own joke, but the exertion of it made him groan and wince. He slid down farther under the blankets. "Oh," he said. "Ah, shit. I ain't gonna lie to you, this hurts like a bitch."

Crowe studied him for a moment, thinking about how easy it would be to kill him, right here and now. Just grab one of his pillows, push it over his face, and hold it there for a few minutes. He was far too weak to be able to do anything about it.

"Earth to Crowe," Chester said. "You're looking at me kinda funny."

Crowe gazed back out the window. "Million miles away," he said.

"Yeah? Well, I hope the mattresses are softer wherever you are."

They were dangerously close to small talk, so Crowe said, "I'll see you around, Chester," and headed for the door.

Chester said, "Yeah, okay, I'll see ya," and then, "Hey, Crowe."

Crowe stopped and looked at him.

He said, "Listen, there's something I been meaning to say to you."

"Yeah?"

He shifted painfully under his blankets. "Well, see. It's like this. It's about when you got sent up."

"What about it?"

"I just wanted to tell you, you know. I mean, I know what you must've thought, what with the Old Man not doing anything to help."

Crowe said, "That was a long time ago."

"Yeah, but I think you should know. There wasn't anything I could do, you know what I mean? He was... pissed, right? Pissed that you killed Leon. And the cops had Leon just about cold on a lot of stuff that the Old Man didn't wanna be involved in."

Crowe didn't say anything, just watched him and tried to keep the coldness out of his face.

Chester said, "I reckon you felt... I don't know. Betrayed? But the Old Man had to think about the organization, you know?"

Every word he said was another layer of ice in the pit of Crowe's stomach. Crowe had ideas back then, ideas about loyalty. Ideas about professionalism that almost bordered on sacred. He knew better now, but that didn't stop Chester's little speech from filling him with a sort of ebbing fury.

He took it in hand and said, "Some reason you're telling me all this?"

"Well. I'm thinking about giving it all up. I'm thinking about telling Vitower I'm done. I got some money saved up, you know, and I was thinking about going into business for myself. I mean, a legit business."

"Like what?"

He said, "Heating and cooling. I took a class, you know, and I can fix shit. I'm pretty good at it."

"Heating and cooling," Crowe said.

"Yeah. I mean, just a normal kind of life. I got a kid now. I gotta think about the future. And this whole mess, well… we kinda cut it a little close, don't you think?"

Crowe said, "You finished?"

Chester frowned. "Yeah, I'm finished. I just wanted to tell you that. I don't know why. Never mind."

Crowe nodded and said, "Okay. Be seeing you," and left the room.

15

Faith was drunk when he showed up. She let him in when he knocked, looked at him blankly for a long moment while he eased into the sofa, and with a voice only slightly slurred said, "Well. You look like you could use a drink."

"I wouldn't say no. How do you feel about having a houseguest for a few days?"

She said, "Mixed feelings. You don't look like you're up for nailing me anytime soon."

"Oh, I don't know. It's not as bad as it looks."

"We'll test that out later. For now, though…" Her perpetual rum and Pepsi was on the coffee table, but for him she went off to the kitchen and came back with a bottle of vodka that had been in the freezer and some lime soda and a glass.

For the next three days he didn't do much. He drank more than he should in the evening, exercised half-heartedly to keep his muscles from stiffening up. He thought about Peter Murke, and the bizarre coven of killers who'd rescued him. If Chester hadn't seen the same thing, he might've become half-convinced it was all some crazy dream.

But it wasn't a dream. They'd been stymied by some freak-show posse, and now Peter Murke was free, and all Crowe's plans were teetering on the brink of utter failure.

He and Faith didn't talk much. She was drunk, usually, but on the occasions she wasn't she looked after him pretty well, helping him around in the mornings when the pain was at its worst, feeding him, changing bandages. She even made a trip to the farmer's market downtown and came back with a paper bag full of fresh fruit. On the second afternoon, she went out for a couple of hours and came back with a new overcoat for him, just like the one he'd bought a few days earlier, and which was now blood-stained and lacerated. For his part, he tried at least to clean up after himself, not mention the nauseating smell of rum sweat or the increasingly tedious sex, and in the evenings, when she was at work, he drank and brooded.

He had no idea how to go about finding Murke. But that was what he had to do.

On the third day, he made his way into the bathroom and peeled the bandages off his face and had a sickening minute of incomprehension. Dr. Maggie had warned him, but to see it for the first time was a shock.

From directly above his left brow, a long ugly scar ran over his eye, and ended in a jagged edge at his cheekbone. It was red and raw-looking. His face was the face of someone he'd never seen before.

He was so shocked by what he saw in the mirror that it took a minute before he realized he was seeing the image with both eyes. So at least he still had his vision. But Christ, it was a hell of a scar.

Lucky, he said to himself. Lucky that the blade skipped past the eye. Lucky that he wasn't blinded. Lucky, lucky, lucky.

He grabbed the astringent out of the cabinet and cleaned the wound. It hurt, bad enough that it made him woozy and he teetered back to the sofa and sat down hard and took a few minutes to will the agony away.

So, a slight change of plans. Marco Vitower and Chester Paine weren't the only ones who needed to die.

Faith went gray when she saw it. She came up to him slowly, squat down in front of him and said, "Crowe."

He grinned at her and said, "Don't worry. I'm about to go bandage it up again."

She shook her head. "It's not that. It's just… what the hell are you doing out there that this would happen?"

He didn't know how to answer that. What he did hardly seemed to matter. It could happen to anyone. He'd read about a guy once, just an ordinary every-day sort of fella, who worked in the railroad yards, who fell in front of a rolling boxcar and got himself cut right in half and actually *lived* to tell the tale. Another man got attacked by a grizzly bear and had both his arms ripped off. Another one was walking out of his house one morning on his way to work when a goddamn oak tree fell on him.

Chance. Blind and random. And maybe Crowe did tempt fate a little, but crazy things happened, it didn't matter who you were or what you did.

He didn't say any of that to Faith. He pushed himself up and headed back into the bathroom to put on a fresh bandage.

Later on, with the afternoon sun seeping weakly through the bedroom drapes, and Faith only half-drunk, she said, "Why are you here?"

"I'll leave anytime you want me to."

He felt her head moving against his neck. "No. I don't want you to leave. I just wanna know why you're here. Why are you with me?"

"I don't know. I could ask you the same question."

She laughed, a little derisively. "You mean, why am I in bed with some guy, old enough to be my pop? And involved in some nasty shit, to boot? I don't know. Maybe I'm just fucked up, and you're just the kind of man I deserve."

He didn't know what to say to that.

She propped up on her elbows and looked at him. "I always liked you, even back in the day. And I knew you were wrapped up with some bad stuff. The Old Man and all his people. But I didn't care. I didn't care, and I still don't. I... like I said, I like you an awful lot. Maybe, even... you know."

"Christ," Crowe said. "You're drunk. Knock it off."

He sat up, swung his feet onto the floor. Behind him, she was silent.

She said, "Fine. See, I know you better than you think I do. I knew this was what you were gonna do. I knew this was how you'd react if I said anything. But I don't care. I want you to know how I feel about it."

Not looking at her, he said, "Okay. Now I know."

The last thing he wanted to hear was some raw, uncensored emotion pouring out of the mouth of a drunk. And the thing that doomed them, the thing that she had no way of knowing, was that she was a substitute anyway. When his eyes were closed, it wasn't Faith's face he saw.

Behind him, he heard her breathing go hard and tight, and she said, "You're a bastard."

Someone rapped hard on the front door.

Whatever else she was going to say was swallowed up. They both sat there for long seconds, not doing anything, until whoever was at the door rapped again, a little harder.

She pulled a tee-shirt over her head and stomped out of the bedroom to answer the door.

From the living room, a deep lazy drawl of a voice: "Afternoon, ma'am. I'm Detective Wills, Shelby County Sheriff's Department. I'd like to speak to Mr. Crowe."

16

He must've been about six-three, two-ten, maybe late thirties or early forties. A long narrow face that looked like someone had pressed it between two hot irons, and reddish hair slicked haphazardly back from a wide forehead. He wore an off-the-rack suit and a cheap overcoat with a stain on the lapel. His nose was lined with subtle veins, just a few more bottles away from bursting. His eyes were small and clever.

He said, "I tried you at your flat. Neighbors say you haven't been home in a few days now."

They were sitting in the living room, Crowe in the straight-backed chair near the TV and Wills in Crowe's usual spot on the sofa. After letting him in, Faith had glared at Crowe and barricaded herself in the bedroom.

Wills said, "Well?"

"Well, what? Did you ask me a question?"

He chuckled a little. "Lemme tell you, Crowe, I'm awful glad to meet you. I'm just pleased as punch. I heard so much."

This was the last thing Crowe was in the mood for, some posturing, easy-talking good old boy cop. But it was just one of those things you had no choice about sometimes; cops do what they do. Crowe said, "I heard some talk about you too."

"From Vitower, yeah? Don't pay no mind to any of that.

Really, I'm a nice sort of fella. Vitower and me, we just got off on the wrong foot."

"That amazes me. You make such a good first impression."

He laughed. "Yeah, so do you. My first impression of you was, well, here's a fella been through a blender set on puree. What happened to you?"

"Are you asking me that in some official capacity?"

He shook his head. "Naw. Just shootin' the shit, you know."

"In that case, nothing happened to me. I accidently bit the inside of my cheek while I was eating."

He laughed loudly, even slapped his thigh. "Man, don't you hate when that happens? For a minute there, I thought you was gonna tell me you cut yourself shaving or something."

Crowe nodded, smiling at him. "What brings you around, detective?"

He looked thoughtful for a moment, nodding his head, leaning back in the sofa. "Fair enough. Why don't you tell me, Mr. Crowe, where you were on the morning of January Third?"

"The Third," Crowe said. "What was that, last Wednesday?"

"Last Tuesday, Mr. Crowe. Late morning."

Crowe frowned. "Let me think. I can't be sure, but more than likely I was at home, watching *Oprah*."

"You don't have a TV, Mr. Crowe. I've been in your apartment."

"Oh, *Tuesday*. That's my laundry day. I was down at the Laundromat."

"All day, huh?"

"All damn day."

He nodded some more, and his smile was starting to look stiffer. He leaned forward, clasping his narrow hands together, and said, "I have witnesses, Mr. Crowe, that say you've been making the rounds. Swung by a suspected drug den Sunday morning. Stopped in at The Libre that night. One witness even says you took a little trip to The Libre's backroom, where our friend Marco Vitower keeps an office."

"I don't know anything about any suspected drug den. As

for The Libre, sure, I stopped by there. Wanted to catch up with Faith." He motioned his head toward the bedroom.

"I can't blame you," he said. "That's a mighty fine-looking girl. You're a Detroit boy, ain't you?"

"I haven't been to Detroit in years."

"Yeah. Left when you were twenty-one, or thereabouts. Traded one cesspool for another. Whatever made you come to Memphis?"

"Seduced by the glamour of crawfish and barbeque, I guess."

Wills said, "I been to Detroit. About, oh, five years ago or so. A law-enforcement conference. You know what struck me about it the most?"

"No, Detective, I don't."

"What struck me is how hypocritical and condescending the folks up there are. You tell someone you're from Tennessee, they almost always get that stupid grin on their faces, start saying shit like, oh I just love me that Southern accent, and you folks are just so friendly down there and things are just slower and nicer. Like its still 1870 or something."

"Yeah."

"And then they almost always mention racism. Like we're still lynching niggers off every goddamn tree. And what kills me is, I met more racists up there than I ever met down here. Oh, they almost never say the 'n-word', right. But the way they say 'black', or 'African-American', you know, in that weird guilty little hushed voice, well... it sounds nastier and meaner than any redneck saying the 'n-word' than I ever heard." He shrugged. "What are you gonna do, though, huh? People have their misconceptions, ain't nothing you can do about it."

"I guess so."

He said, "But you, Crowe. You're no racist, are you? You got yourself a fine little black filly just in the next room. And you work for Marco Vitower. Probably the most powerful black man in this goddamn city. Maybe even more powerful than our esteemed mayor Dr. Willie."

"What does any of this have to do with Tuesday, the Third?"

His good old boy mask dropped a bit, and he sighed. "Tell you what, Crowe. Between you and me? Let's not play make-believe, yeah? You may have left Detroit a long time ago, but you still got that northern condescending thing going on. You're gonna sit there and act like you don't know what happened on the Third, and like you don't have a goddamn clue about why I'm here? You're gonna act like I'm some stupid hillbilly cop? It's beneath you. It's beneath both of us."

Crowe was watching him carefully, his mannerisms and speech patterns, and decided he was all colored glass, just transparent enough to show the unbalanced thing beneath it, shifting and creaking. Wills was one bad day—or one stiff drink—away from crossing that thin blue line you always hear about.

He'd seen cops like that before. No one is crazier than a crazy cop.

So he said, "Fair enough."

"I didn't expect you to talk to me, Crowe, not really. But I want you to know. I want you to know I'm here, and you are currently the man I'm looking at. You read me?"

"Loud and clear."

"Good," he said, and pushed a large gnarled hand through his red hair. "That's very, very good. Because *loud and clear* is what I wanna be right now. I want you to know that I have every intention of taking you out of the game at the earliest possible convenience. And just in case you don't know anything about me, I should tell you. I don't let little details hold me up. You know, things like *due process* or *reasonable cause*."

"I've heard that about you."

"Good. So you know. If I can't nail you by the book, Crowe, I will nail you by the balls. You understand?"

Crowe nodded.

Wills stood up with a wheeze, and Crowe could smell the whiskey on his breath from across the room. "I'm glad we had this talk, Crowe. Just so everything's clear."

"Crystal."

"Be seeing you. Sooner than you think."

He grinned the goofy good old boy grin again and headed for the door. He closed it very gently and politely behind him.

17

Faith didn't come out of the bedroom after Wills left. Crowe didn't want her to anyway. He sat around the living room for a while and finally got up, put on his coat and headed out to clear his head.

He walked the few blocks up Madison to Overton Square, where the shops of Midtown lined up in defense of the encroaching ugliness of the city. Just a few short years ago, it used to be fairly Bohemian, with a bookshop, a health food store, a vegetarian restaurant. There would be harmless panhandlers and young hippies in the street, not looking or smelling much different from each other, wearing tie-dies and strumming guitars, just like it was the Summer of Love all over again.

All that stuff was long gone. Midtown was almost as bad as every place else in Memphis these days. A lot of the shops had closed up. For rent signs were everywhere. It was late afternoon, but there wasn't much traffic on Madison and a cold wind skirted along in the wake of each passing car.

He stopped and huddled in the doorway of what used to be a head shop, marveling at the pain in his left shoulder and at his shoulder blades. He'd been stabbed once before, in the side. He was thirty-two when that happened, and he didn't remember the pain of it lingering as long as these new wounds. The cold only made it worse, reaching deep down inside his muscles and clawing them.

He felt old. He felt like a stranger.

Eddie Wills was going to be trouble, that much was clear. More trouble than Vitower or Chester or anyone. It didn't make Crowe's life any sweeter, knowing that the cop would be dogging him. But he'd had cops giving him grief before; it wasn't anything he couldn't handle. And no cop was going to stop him from doing what he had to do.

He was standing there in the cold thinking about Wills and thinking about how damn old he felt when the pimped-out silver Grand Prix pulled up to the curb in front of him. The power window on the passenger side came down, and a handsome black face with a bandage over the nose said, "Crowe. Get in."

He showed Crowe his gun.

Garay got in the backseat with him, sure to keep his gun low. The two others occupied the front. The driver was a big, thick bastard whose hands made the steering wheel look like a toy. The guy in the passenger seat was smaller, with delicate, almost feminine features. Neither of them spoke.

"Found out your name," Garay said. "Didn't even have to ask my sissy."

He seemed proud of that, so Crowe said, "Congratulations."

The car smelled, not unpleasantly, of weed. The driver took a hard left, headed toward downtown. "Yo," Garay said to him. "Go easy on my car, motherfucker."

The smaller guy said, "Stop fuckin' around, Garay. You gotta talk to the man, talk to the man."

Garay looked ready to mouth off to the guy, but then thought better of it. Obviously, he was low man on the totem pole here but didn't want to look too weak in front of Crowe. He leaned back in the seat, gun in his lap, eyed him, his face saying, *who's the bad-ass now, huh*?

He nodded at the bandages on Crowe's face, said, "What the fuck happened to you?"

Crowe didn't answer him. Garay waited a beat, realized he wasn't going to get an answer, decided to let it go. He said, "Well, whatever it was, I'm glad. Makes my little bandage look like nothin', don't it?"

Crowe let him enjoy that for a moment, and said, "You got a reason for plucking me off the street?"

The little guy in front said, "Maybe we gonna kill you. What you think about that?"

"I don't like that plan."

The two in front laughed, but Garay just looked at him warily.

The little guy said, "You don't like that plan. Nice. Naw, we ain't gonna kill you, not unless you get all crazy and shit. Garay, tell your man why we grabbed him."

Crowe looked at Garay, waiting for an answer, and Garay said, "We got a proposition for you. We got a little business arrangement, see what you think about it."

"Is this something just between the four of us? Or are you guys running errands for someone else?"

The driver's huge hands tightened on the steering wheel, and he glanced at Crowe sharply in the rear-view. "What?" he said, his voice rumbling in the confined space. "What, you think we just some motherfuckin' errand boys?"

"I don't know what you are, Fats. You tell me."

Garay looked nervous. He fingered his gun, said, "Chill, bro. Let's just chill, yeah? This don't have to get ugly, right?"

The driver relaxed, taking a deep, resigned breath. His fingers were still tight on the wheel, though. Crowe shrugged and said, "I'm listening."

"You one of Vitower's boys, ain't you?" Garay said. When Crowe didn't answer, he went on: "Marco Vitower, the big fucker. Thinks he's the fuckin' King of Memphis, yeah?"

"What about him?"

"He don't know shit, that's what about him. He don't know,

the game's changin' all around him and he's frontin', actin' like it's still the old days. But it ain't the old days."

The little guy said, "He thinks he's the New Breed. That's what makes me fuckin' laugh. He thinks he's the New Face of Crime in Memphis. But he's DVD, knowmsayin? He's DVD and Bad Luck Incorporated's fuckin' Blu-Ray."

The big bastard laughed, said, "Yeah, yeah! Fuckin' Blu-Ray, motherfucker!"

Garay laughed along with them, and said to Crowe, "He's still playin' the game by the white man's rules, right? He don't know."

Crowe said, "So what does any of this have to do with me?"

Garay smiled slyly, nodding. "You been away for a while. Been in the joint. They be sayin' you're something like a free agent, got no loyalty to Vitower."

Crowe frowned. "Who's been saying that?"

"It don't matter who's been saying what. What matters is that you got no reason to be loyal to Vitower."

"You're suggesting I throw in with you boys."

Again, they all laughed.

Garay said, "Fuck, man, what we gonna do with some old cracker? No, what we got in mind is something more… free-lance, right?"

"You haven't said shit yet, Garay."

The little guy craned his neck around to look at them and said, "The man's right, Garay. You ain't told him nothin'."

"A'ight, a'ight," Garay said. And then, "We want you to cap Vitower. We want you to put a bullet in his fuckin' head."

Crowe said, "What makes you think I'd do that?"

Garay rubbed his thumb and fingers together, the universal sign of cash. "Five large," he said.

Crowe laughed out loud.

Garay scowled. "What the fuck's so funny?"

"You expect me to kill Vitower for five thousand dollars? Are you out of your fucking mind?"

"What, that ain't enough? I know some brothers' would do it for fuckin' five hundred."

"So why don't you get them to do it, then, and stop wasting my time?"

They were coming up on Poplar. The big bastard took a right, cutting off traffic. A lady in a microbus honked her horn but he ignored her. It wasn't quite five o'clock, but already the sky was going gray and the sun was nowhere in sight. The bandages on Crowe's face itched like crazy.

Garay said, "Ain't no one can get close enough, that's why. Fuck, man, how much you wanna get paid?"

Crowe said, "Add another zero, maybe we can talk."

"Fuckin' fifty large? Jesus Christ, mother—"

"Look," Crowe said. "If Bad Luck doesn't have the capitol for something like a hit, who can hold it against them? They have a ways to go yet before they're playing with the big boys, right?"

The big bastard rumbled, "I'm gonna stop this fuckin' car and slit your throat."

"Relax, Fats. I'm just saying, five grand is what I'd get paid just to hear you out. I'm doing you a favor just listening to you."

The big guy calmed down, just a little, but he swerved into the left lane without signaling and touched the gas a little harder.

Garay seemed to be waiting for one of the others to say something, to make a decision, but no one jumped in. Finally, he sighed and said, "Tell you what, Crowe. I'll talk to Falcon, see what's what, and maybe we can—"

The little guy said, "Falcon ain't gonna like it. Falcon ain't gonna pay this cracker fuck no fifty large."

"We'll talk to him," Garay said. "See what's what, and then we'll talk again. How's that sound?"

"Sure," Crowe said. "You know where to find me." And then, because he couldn't resist it, he said, "At your sister's place, fucking her every chance I get."

His face went dark with blood and he gritted his teeth. His fingers clenched the grip of his gun.

The two guys in front laughed, and the big bastard said, "You gotta give this old fucker credit. He got stones."

"Let him off here," Garay said. "Now."

They were still on Poplar, a good four miles from where they'd picked him up. The big bastard pulled over into the parking lot of a strip mall, stopped the car with a jerk.

"We be talkin' to you," said Garay.

Crowe opened the door and started to step out of the car, glancing back just in time to see Garay pulling up his hoodie to put the gun in his waistband. He had a strange tattoo on his washboard stomach, black and red. It was a cross, topped by a blood-red heart.

He reached over and slammed the door shut, and they drove off.

18

He was getting his stuff together to leave that night when Faith finally came out of the bedroom and, without a word, put her arms around him and held on for a long minute. When she looked up, her eyes were clear for a change and she said, "I don't want you to leave."

"I probably should."

She shook her head. "Stay. Please."

So, against his better judgment, he stayed.

Later that night they were out of bed and Faith was stone sober for a change, and they were eating Chinese food in the living room and listening to a CD she had of Count Basie, some cool, loose-limbed thing from when he was on the Okeh label. Crowe was in his boxer briefs, she had pulled a tee-shirt on and was trying to feed him some beef lo Mein, when he said, "I ran into your brother today."

She stopped with the chopsticks halfway to his face, and her eyes went weird. For a second, he thought she might try to gouge the chopsticks into his face. She said, "My... my brother? How do you know my brother?"

"Made his acquaintance a little while back. We've been staying in touch since then."

She put the chopstick back in the carton and set the carton on the coffee table. "Are you fucking with me?" she said.

He shook his head. He hadn't been sure what to expect, but the anger interested him. He said, "Did you know he was a gangbanger?"

She sneered. "Did I know? How could I not know? He always goes around flashing his stupid little gang signs, dressing like a thug. And he always has money, I don't even want to think about where he gets it. If Mama had any idea..."

Her face was set hard, talking about him. She looked at Crowe again, her eyes burning. "How? How do you know him?"

"I told you."

"What is he getting involved in now? Tell me, Crowe, or so help me—"

"I don't know what he's getting involved in. He's with Bad Luck, that's enough, don't you think?"

She shook her head. "Bad Luck doesn't have anything to do with your people. With Vitower's crew. They... they're small-time. I mean... they're street-level. How, Crowe? How did you just happen to run across Garay?"

"Bad Luck's trying to make a play for a bigger share of the city. Garay brought it to my attention."

She stood up quickly, knocking the carton of lo Mein off the table. Noodles and vegetables spilled all over the floor. Cursing, she grabbed a napkin to pick it up, then threw the napkin on the table and stalked off into the kitchen. She came back with a dust pan and a wet towel and started pushing the mess into the pan.

Then she stopped, shoulders slumping, and looked at him. "You don't wanna tell me the details, fine. You know what? I don't even care, okay? I should be used to this shit by now. Every man in my life is on some stupid fucking crusade to prove what a bad-ass he is. My brother. You. Shit, even my pop was a crook. Great role-model for Garay he was. You know what happened to my pop? Did I ever tell you? He tried to rob some guy at gunpoint, and the guy pulled out a gun of his own and shot him. He shot him right in the fucking heart."

"Faith, he—"

"What do you think that did to my Mama, Crowe? How do you think she feels even now? She and Garay live in a nice house, on a nice street in Germantown. Brinkley Drive. Respectable. And there's Garay pulling up in his pimped-out Grand Prix, lookin' like some kind of hood, making my Mama look like a fool in front of all the neighbors. And she doesn't even *know* it!"

She threw the dust pan across the room. It shattered a small vase on the curio by the television. She didn't even look at it. She said, "So you and my brother wanna be tough guys, knock yourselves out. Sooner or later, you're gonna come across someone tougher than you."

She stood up again, glared at him like there was something else she wanted to say. She turned around and marched off toward the bedroom.

In the doorway, she stopped and looked back at him. "You know what, Crowe? I changed my mind. I do want you to leave after all. Tomorrow morning."

He nodded, and she slammed her bedroom door behind her.

19

The next morning, January 11th, Crowe went to work. He'd already packed up his stuff, so he got up before Faith, left, and took a cab downtown. After that, he had eggs and ham and fresh fruit for breakfast at a diner off Union. He lingered over it.

Early afternoon, with the sun trying desperately to break out of the strangle hold winter had on it, he took a cab to the offices of the *Memphis Clarion*.

Lori Cole worked the crime beat for the paper, had since long before Crowe ever came to the Bluff City. Four times in the last fifteen years, the word *Pulitzer* had come up in the same sentence as her name, but so far they had only danced around each other and never consummated the relationship. Probably just as well. Lori hated her job, she hated her bosses, and she hated the people who read her paper. She responded to praise with a disdainful sneer. A Pulitzer would no doubt have sent her over the edge into a total psychotic breakdown.

She saw him coming before he was even halfway across the bustling, noisy newsroom, and something like irritable confusion showed on her face. By the time he made it to her desk, she'd put it together and said, "Almost didn't recognize you, what with all those bandages on your mug. How is it that no one told me you were out of prison?"

"Your source at the joint must be losing his touch."

She scowled. "I'll have to see about that. You here to kill me or something?"

Crowe laughed. "No, Cole. Why would I do that?"

"Because I was the one covered your trial. And I told the truth about you."

"That's your job. Can't fault a woman for doing her job."

She flopped back in her rolling chair and rubbed long fingers across her face. "My job," she said. "Oh, Christ Almighty. Fuck my job. I wish you *would* kill me."

She was about forty years old. Her eyes were Alaskan Husky blue, and the lines on her face formed a perfect frowning mask, like the one you see in posters for drama clubs.

"Maybe someday," he said. "But today, I need your help."

She said, "You need my help, and yet you won't do me a simple favor and put a bullet in my head? Come on, Crowe. It's what you do, right? What do I have to do to piss you off enough to kill me?"

She was joking, but there was a very real despair under her words. Lori Cole didn't really want him to kill her, but if he *did*, she wouldn't have minded too much.

"I want some background on a murder victim from two years ago."

She said, "Patricia Welling?"

"How did you know that?"

She said, "Peter Murke is sprung while in transit to Jackson. Marco Vitower hates Murke's guts. You, who used to run in the same circles as Vitower, show up out of nowhere. The only victim Murke was charged with killing was Patricia Welling. It doesn't take a genius."

Around them, the newsroom whirled and shook. Anyplace else, his bandaged face would've drawn attention, but here no one seemed to be interested. They had their own, more pressing agendas.

It was a large office, almost the entire third floor of the building, but the crush of mad activity and the desks all lined up with only narrow gaps between them made it feel close and claustrophobic. At the desk closest to Cole's, a hard-looking girl was screaming at someone on the phone. A few desks away, a younger reporter with thinning hair and eyes lined with shadows had a phone pressed against his ear, nodding and saying, "Right, right, right" over and over again while jotting notes. The fluorescent lights flickered irritably.

The whole place was a seething, insane cauldron of noise and activity, and Crowe was already feeling edgy. Noise. He really couldn't stand it.

But he smiled at Cole and said, "You never lose those reporter's instincts."

"I reckon not," she said. "Also, the fact that you look like Claude Rains in *The Invisible Man*."

"If he was invisible, how do you know what he looked like?"

She decided, wisely, that the question wasn't worth answering, and said, "So what happened on that day? You wanna give me the scoop on Murke's escape? Whatever it was, it looks like you didn't exactly come out of it unscathed."

"What happened to me doesn't have anything to do with Peter Murke."

"Yeah, okay. That's what I figured. You just wanna know about Patricia Welling because you're a concerned citizen."

"Snag any files you have on the girl, and I'll feed you some info on Vitower."

She sighed. "Ah, Crowe. Honestly, man, I just don't give a shit about Vitower anymore. This city has gone completely to Hell, and good goddamn riddance. Besides, you don't need any files. I've got it all right *here*." She tapped her temple with a long forefinger. "I'm a walking encyclopedia of all the nastiest information this city can offer."

"Hell of a burden."

"Tell you what. Get me the hell out of this office, buy me a drink, and I'll spill my guts."

20

Beale Street was only a couple of blocks from the *Clarion* offices. Natives didn't often hit Beale—it was really a tourist thing—but it was off-season, the weather was bitterly cold, and some of the bars and clubs had half-price drinks mid-day.

They sat by the window in a joint where the walls were covered with glossies of famous and semi-famous blues musicians and rockabilly cats. A genuine Wurlitzer jukebox, retro-fitted for compact discs, grinded out re-mastered blues classics. A beat-up Stratocaster hung precariously over their table.

Cole was already on her second whiskey and soda. She said, "I picked the wrong job. All those years ago, thinking I wanted to be a goddamn journalist. A goddamn crusading reporter. Jesus. If I could go back and talk to that little bitch I used to be, oh, the things I'd say..."

"Naïve youth," Crowe said.

"Amen to that. Say, you don't think I could maybe get a job doing what you do, do you? That sounds like just the ticket. A hired killer."

He sipped his vodka gimlet without enthusiasm. It was a bit early in the day for him. "I'm not a hired killer, Lori."

"Oh, right. You're a handyman, aren't you? Not a killer. A killer just *kills*, but a handyman, well... a handyman does what needs to be *done*. Still… set your own hours, no boss breathing down your neck all the time. Sounds ideal."

"It takes years of training, and the certification's a bitch."

She laughed. "I always did like you, Crowe. You're not very smart, but you're clever enough to know that if you don't talk much people will think you're a genius."

"Tell me about Patricia Welling."

She let out a deep breath, glanced around the bar warily. She said, "Thirteen years old. Family has a home in Bartlett, but since Patricia was killed they spend most of their time away from it, out in some place they have on the other side of the state. The papers never mentioned this, but she wasn't really the sweet little angel she seemed to be. Kind of a wild kid. At that tender age she was already into drugs—nothing major, weed, maybe a little pill-popping—and was in and out of trouble in school. She ran away, had been missing from home for almost a week before they found her body in a vacant lot in the Cooper-Young area.

"I was one of the first reporters on the scene, lucky bitch that I am. And let me tell you, I've seen some screwed-up shit in my life, but nothing really compared to the way that girl was butchered. Equal parts Black Dahlia Murderer and Jack the Ripper. It's hard to explain, but my first impression when I saw the scene… my first thought was *religious*. That there was something religious about it."

Crowe frowned, and she looked embarrassed. Gulping down her drink, she motioned to the bar girl for another, and without looking at him she said, "I mean, her organs. They weren't, you know, where they were supposed to be, right? But the way they were laid out, all around her? It almost looked as if the killer had been sort of *reverent* about it, if you know what I mean."

"No, Cole, I don't."

She scowled. "Oh, fuck you then."

"Sounds like that old sensational journalist chromosome of yours."

"I don't have a journalist chromosome, sensational or otherwise. I'm just telling you the impression I got. And if nothing else, my impressions are always good."

"Okay. So her body was found. How did they link Murke to it?"

"The usual stuff. Just like with Jezzie Vitower, someone saw him hanging around the area shortly before the body was discovered. Mostly, though, it was that new-fangled DNA evidence what you hear tell about." She said that last bit with an exaggerated hick accent; the booze was going to her head a little. Like a lot of people, Cole couldn't talk about ugly things without adopting a distantly humorous tone. If the crime had been much worse, she would've turned into a stand-up comedian. "Sweet little Patricia managed to claw him along his neck at some point, and they got some of him from under her fingernails. Perfect match. It's just too bad, I reckon, they weren't able to link him to any of the other victims."

Crowe said, "It probably wouldn't have made much difference."

She shrugged. "Probably not. But maybe if Jezzie Vitower had some… I don't know… personal justice? Maybe old Marco wouldn't have such a mad-on and you wouldn't be here talking to me right now."

"Maybe."

The bar girl brought her third drink. She looked at Crowe's, still barely touched, and sashayed away back to the bar, where a line of young German tourists with rockabilly pompadours drank beer that must've tasted like watered-down piss to them.

Crowe said, "Was there anything at all that might have connected Murke to her? Or was it totally random?"

"Murke's a serial killer, Crowe. By their very nature, they choose their victims for a reason. You know that, right? I mean, there's often something the victims will have in common, like, I don't know, blonde hair, or thin faces, or one leg shorter than the other, whatever. Like that. But not always. With Murke, none of his victims seemed to have anything at all in common. And they almost certainly weren't affiliated with him at all."

"Almost certainly?"

"I don't like speaking in absolutes, sue me. Unofficially, the cops have lain something like sixteen murders at Murke's doorstep, that's including Jezzie Vitower. See, everyone knows he did them, and the thing is, the only thing the victims have in common is that they're women."

"Well, what about the families of the victims? Anything there?"

Cole drank and said, "What do you think, Crowe? Look at the victims you're familiar with. One of them the wife of our fair city's most notorious gangster, the other the daughter of a modestly prosperous engineer, church alderman, and All-American."

"I don't know anything about Patricia Welling's family."

"Nothing to know. The Wellings are about as 'average citizen' as you can get without morphing into parody. Active in their little community in Bartlett, well-respected as the guy in the Kinks song. It was little Patricia that was trouble, like I said. No one wants to talk about it now, but she was sort of an embarrassment. Running the streets, taking off from home, doing drugs. My colleagues in the media want to whitewash all that now—and I don't blame them, mind you—but before she died Patricia caused nothing but trouble for her parents."

Crowe drummed his fingers on the scarred wooden table and took a drink. Cole watched him, apparently amused at his efforts. Chuckling, she said, "Don't tell me, Crowe. Dead end already? What is you're trying to do anyway? Track down Peter Murke and bring him back to justice?"

"Where was Murke living when they arrested him?"

"Oh, great idea. What you should do, Crowe, is go over to Murke's house and look around. You know, for clues. Because you're certain to find something the cops missed."

"Just tell me, Cole."

She told him—an address off Martin Luther King.

"Good luck with that, Crowe," she said when he started to slide out of the booth. "And thanks for the drinks."

He nodded, tossed a few bills on the table. She watched him with bemused interest as he buttoned up his coat. When he was about to walk away, she said, "Say. There is one thing you may want to look into. One thing that's kinda weird. I mean, it probably won't amount to anything, and I'm sure the cops have already examined it, but it's something."

He looked at her, waiting, and she said, "The Wellings are members of an exclusive little church social thing. In fact, Fletcher Welling, Patricia's pa, is sort of the… chairman, I reckon. The Society of Christ the Fisher, they call themselves, you know, after the idea of Jesus as a fisher of men's souls? Sort of a Christian charity group, except very limited membership. Really secretive about their membership roster, but always doing benign things like raising money for kids with cancer or organizing canned food drives or care packages for our boys in Iraq. That sort of thing."

"A charitable Christian group, Cole? Thanks for the hot lead."

She laughed. "That's the kind of folks you're dealing with, Crowe. Not my fault. When Patricia got killed, I was gonna scoot down to Holly Springs and talk to this writer guy I know, sort of an American theological historian, name of Arley Hampton. When I say he's a theological historian, what I really mean is that he's a nutcase. He knows his stuff, but he's got this idea that the history of the world, the history of religious movements especially, is the history of a vast conspiracy to… I don't know, shackle humanity or something. Subjugate us all. You know the type, right?"

"Yeah, and I know who he is. He wrote a novel, didn't he? Back in the early '70's, I think."

"Late '60's. *All the Flesh*, it was called. Real cult item. One print run, goes for a fortune on EBay. You read it?"

"No, but I heard of him."

"Any case, he said he would give me the lowdown on the

Society. Had plans to visit him again, but my editor put the ki-bosh on it."

"Why?"

"Said I was wasting the paper's money. Said the story didn't have shit to do with some innocuous little church group. But I don't know. I still think, if I'd been able to talk to him, he might've given me some insight into things."

"Maybe you should've done it anyway, on your own dime."

"To hell with that. I'm not that curious about anything anymore. I was relieved, if you want to know the truth." She looked at the table and drank, and he knew she was lying. She was still curious, but she didn't want to be.

She told him where he could find Arley Hampton, if he wanted to, and he left her there with her third drink, and headed back out into the icy cold afternoon.

21

At a pay phone at the corner of Beale and Second Street, he called Vitower's home number. His man answered, and kept Crowe waiting with the bitter cold seeping into his bones while he went and fetched. The cold didn't do anything to help Crowe's wounds. His shoulder was getting stiff and painful again, and the hole in his back screamed at him. He put the receiver down long enough to toss a couple of pain pills down his throat, and picked it up again just in time to hear Vitower say, "Crowe? That you? Where the fuck are you, you piece of shit?"

Crowe told him he was on the job, and the voice that came back over the phone lines sounded like a vengeful ghost. "Good," he said. "We'll get that bastard. You need anything? Money?"

"I'm set on funds, but I need a car. This taxi-cab shit is getting old."

"Where you at?"

He told him, and Vitower said, "Right. Hang tight there, and I'll have someone bring some wheels around. What else?"

"Make sure the car's nothing too flashy. And I could use a cell phone."

"You sure you don't want a smart phone instead?"

"A what? What the hell is a smart phone?"

"Never mind, you been in the joint too long. I'll get you a cell phone."

"And a gun."

"A gun? You get busted with a gun, Crowe, you're no good to me."

"Me having a gun didn't bother you the other day."

"That was before everything went south."

"I need a gun. Just let me worry about getting busted. Oh, and one other thing. I could really use some tools of the trade."

"Such as?"

Crowe told him, and Vitower said, "What the hell, Crowe? You planning on some kind of crime spree?"

"I have a lock pick," Crowe said. "But the electronic device would make my life a lot easier."

"Well, I live to serve," Vitower said. "You get this motherfucker, Crowe, you hear me? I'm not fucking around here." And he hung up.

Crowe found a doorway and huddled there with his coat collar up and his hands shoved in his pockets. The few tourists who decided to brave the weather to soak up some patented Memphis atmosphere gazed at him warily as they passed, making room on the sidewalk in case he leapt out at them.

Forty minutes later, a dark green Jaguar XJS yanked up to the curb and a lanky black guy in a bulky parka stepped out. He said, "You Crowe?"

Crowe nodded and the guy handed over the keys. "Mr. Vitower said you'd drop me back off on Mud Island," he said.

"Did he?"

He got in the Jag. Nothing too flashy, he'd said. He wondered what Vitower considered flashy if the Jag was his idea of low-key.

Vitower's man waited at the passenger door for Crowe to unlock it. A cardboard box rested on the passenger seat. Inside was a sleek little cell phone, a slightly battered electronic lock pick, and a slim hard plastic case. He opened the case. A .45 caliber Colt revolver nestled there next to two boxes of ammunition. That made him happy. Vitower remembered that he preferred revolvers. There was a hastily-scrawled message on a post-it note in the case that read *Try not to leave it on the side of the road this time.*

He turned on the cell phone and it chimed cheerfully. He shoved it in his pocket, started the car, and pulled away from the curb. The delivery guy stood on the corner and watched him go, looking dazed and hurt.

22

Every window in the place was shattered, and glass was strewn all over the bare floorboards. The wind outside whistled through every opening, but there was nothing left in Peter Murke's house to be disturbed by it.

It was a simple, one story home, small enough to feel claustrophobic even without furniture or any signs that anyone ever lived there. Five long strides would take you from one end of the place to the other. Except for near the windows, a thick layer of dust covered the floors, and water stains marred the bare walls. Shadows pooled in every corner where the dim gray light couldn't touch them.

Crowe moved through the house slowly. He wasn't really looking for anything. Nothing tangible, anyway.

In the kitchen, the appliances had been ripped right out, and the empty spaces yawned with exposed plumbing coated with dried sludge. The linoleum had rotted almost completely away, exposed to rain and foul weather through a gaping window.

A small bathroom with nothing but a shattered toilet and a shower stall was just off the kitchen. A dead possum rotted patiently in the stall.

There was no bedroom. He assumed the front room of the house served as bedroom and living room for Murke. On the east wall, someone had spray painted in red MURKE U SYKO FUKK U ROTT IN HELL. On the north wall, in a different hand and partially obscured by water stains, the word HERETIC was written with green magic marker. It was written in neat block letters.

And that was all that existed of him now, in this place. Everything else had been stripped away.

Crowe stood in the middle of the house for a long time, listening to the wind outside and thinking. He thought of the Ghost Cat. He tried to think of Patricia Welling, and Jezzie Vitower, and whoever else Murke had killed, but his thoughts kept coming back to the Ghost Cat.

Heretic, it said. *Syko Fukk*. Two different times, two different people, two different definitions of one man. The '*Syko Fukk*' definition was obvious, once you got past the illiteracy factor, but the 'Heretic' thing… A very religious word, heretic. It made Crowe think of what Cole had said about the impression of *religious reverence* she'd gotten from seeing Patricia Welling's body.

And the darkly holy fear he had woken with after his nightmare about the Ghost Cat.

So. Nothing tangible, right. But something stirred in this house, some deep-seated fear, residual emotion. From Murke? From his victims?

He needed to meet this Arley Hampton guy.

He left the shell of Peter Murke's house, got in the Jag, and drove away.

23

On Highway 78 he headed south, leaving Memphis behind. It felt good to do that. He hadn't been back two weeks and already he hated it. He crossed the state line into Mississippi, kept going past Holly Springs and Cuba Landing. By nightfall he was just north of Oxford. At ten, he stopped off at a roadside motel.

Sleep didn't come easily, and when it did it was fitful and unsatisfying. He half-dreamed about Dallas. It was probably the fact of being in a motel room, just like that night almost eight years ago, or it could have been the persistent pain. He got up twice to swallow a couple of pain pills.

The next morning he changed out his bandages again, using a smaller one on his face. It still covered his left eye, but at least it didn't rub against his jaw. He snagged a cup of coffee and a bagel from the front office and headed out.

Hampton lived just south of Oxford, in a small but tidy one-story house situated on what used to be farmland. Crowe got there just before ten-thirty. An enormous oak tree, about fifty feet tall, dominated the front yard. It fronted a dirt road, with unused fields along one side and thick woods along the other.

Crowe stopped the car halfway up the gravel driveway and got out. It was beautifully quiet. The sky looked metallic blue above, cloudless and cold. There was no wind. He walked up to the house, deliberately kicking gravel, clearing his throat, trying to make noise. Didn't want the crazy writer guy to think he was sneaking up on him.

Stepping up on the narrow porch, he saw a curtain flutter in the window to his right, and a dark shape moving behind it. He rapped on the door, said, "Mr. Hampton."

There were footsteps inside, a chair leg or something scraping along a wood floor. Then a gruff voice, "Yeah?"

"My name's Crowe," he said. "You mind if I talk to you?"

"'Bout what?"

"About God and the universe and the meaning of life."

"That's sort of a broad topic, mister."

"Well, just the meaning of life, then. How long could that take?"

The door cracked open an inch, and a green eye peered out, topped by an impossibly bushy blond eyebrow. "I don't have time for fucking around, son. I'm a busy man."

"I know. I won't keep you long. I want to ask you about the history of… evangelical movements."

"Again, that's a goddamn broad topic."

"The Society of Christ the Fisher."

The eye went wide, then squinty. "Who are you?" he said.

Crowe told him his name again. "Lori Cole, from the *Memphis Clarion*, said you were the man to talk to."

"Cole, eh? Yeah, I remember her. Was supposed to come by, what? Two goddamn years ago."

"She got held up."

Hampton said, "Let me see your stomach."

"What?"

"Your stomach. Lift up your shirt and let me see."

Crowe frowned, unbuttoned his jacket and pulled up his shirt. Hampton squinted through the door at his belly button for a long moment, and then the door opened, and a small bony man with thick white hair streaked with blond stood there in nothing but his underwear. He had a sort of caved-in chest with random strands of white hair, and his belly was small and round. He looked like he'd been on a bender for the last ten years. Even from the porch, Crowe could smell the unwashed booze sweat.

Tucking his shirt back in, Crowe said, "Why did you want to see my stomach?"

He ignored the question. "Crowe, you said? I can give you a little time, but not much. I'm working."

He ushered him in. As ragged as Hampton was, his home was tidy, aside from the books everywhere—they were stacked up in wobbly towers all over the place, flowing off bookshelves and chairs and tables. Some of the stacks nearly touched the ceiling. None of them were on the floor, though; that was swept and clean, the wood worn by long years of traffic.

"You, uh... you want a drink or something?" he said uneasily. He clearly wasn't used to company.

Crowe glanced at the pink neon clock on the far wall, above a battered desk and computer. It wasn't quite ten-thirty yet. He said, "No, thanks. Coffee, maybe."

"Coffee, right," Hampton said. "Offering a man a drink, and here it's not even noon. Stupid." He went into the kitchen and Crowe followed him, careful not to bump into any of the stacks of books.

In the kitchen, there were no books, not even a magazine. After going through the living room, it seemed strangely stripped down and bare. An empty whisky bottle sat on the table next to an empty glass. There were several more empty bottles on the floor next to the table.

Hampton pulled a tin of coffee out of the cabinet and started brewing up a pot in a small coffee maker.

While it brewed, he leaned against the counter and said , "So, you, uh... you're writing a piece on the Society?"

"Yeah."

He nodded doubtfully. "What happened to your face? Did they do that?"

"Yeah," Crowe said again.

"You're writing about them, and they did something to your face. Because you're writing about them?"

Crowe sighed. Hampton wasn't buying it. "I'm not writing about them," he said. "I'm just curious about them. I have my own reasons."

"Right. Well, I'll tell you, Mr. Crowe, I'm glad you came clean about that. You know what Ernest Hemingway said?"

"He said a lot of things."

"He said that a writer has to have a one-hundred-percent foolproof bullshit detector. I may not be a Hemingway, but I do have the required equipment."

"So it seems."

"So you aren't writing about them. What about your face? That still something to do with them?"

"No, probably not. Actually, that's what I'm trying to find out."

Hampton crossed his arms. The fact that he was half-naked didn't seem to bother him. He said, "I wrote an article about them, you know that? Appeared in *Religion & Society*, April '95. Good article, too. They, uh, they didn't like it. Wrote a very pointed response to the editor, and you know what? That editor printed a retraction in the following issue and never returned any of my calls after that."

"Religious groups can be pretty persuasive."

He laughed a raw, phlegmy laugh. "Right, persuasive. It kinda surprised me, tell you the truth, that they cared that much. I mean, in my book I really let 'em have it and they didn't do shit. Course, no one read my book. And my agent dropped me shortly thereafter."

Crowe said, "What did you say about them that got them so worked up?"

"All I did," he said, looking at Crowe levelly, "was tell the truth. That's all I ever do. It's a lot harder than you think."

"Maybe you should try lying once in a while, just for a break."

He shook his head. "No, I'd sooner die."

When the coffee was ready, he found two clean cups and

poured and they sat down at the table. He pushed the empty bottle and glass away, sipped his coffee and looked at Crowe with his frank green eyes. "You're probably thinking, what a sad, washed-up old has-been, eh? Just another writer who never quite made it, killing himself with whisky, distracting himself with myriad conspiracy theories. Is that what you're thinking?"

"I don't know. Is that what you are?"

"No," he said. "Well… yes. But there's nothing sad or washed-up about me. They think they got me licked, but they don't."

"Who? The Society?"

He grinned tightly. "The Society of Christ the Fisher, those sons-a-bitches. The goddamn Society. A Christian charity group, right? Raising money for abused children. Spreading the gospel, curbing hunger. You know their mission statement? *Dedication to Good Works, in the name of Jesus Christ, and the honoring of God in all we do. Working from various communities all over the country and the world, bringing the message of God's Love to a world sorely in need.*"

"Sounds dangerous," Crowe said.

He frowned. "Don't mock, boy. That innocuous mission statement makes my bullshit detector go off like crazy." He scratched his bare chest, and his skin was so dry it left white marks. "We're lucky, I guess, that they only have ten churches, spread out all over the country. Closest one to us is over near Chattanooga, little town called Longbaugh. You heard of it?"

"Longbaugh? No. Why are we lucky?"

He said, "That book I wrote, it's called *The Rise and Fall of the American Evangelical Movement*. Put it out a couple years after my blockbuster novel, *All the Flesh*, and just like everything else I've ever written it sank like a stone. New York Times called it the most ponderous, hysterical diatribe against religion they'd ever seen. I don't know, maybe it was a diatribe, I couldn't say. But everything I said in that book, every little thing, was completely true. I did my goddamn research." His eyes went vacant, and for a moment he looked every inch the sad, washed-up writer he had mentioned. "I did my goddamn research," he said again.

Crowe gave him a minute, not saying anything, and eventually he shook his head hard and said, "What I did, see, was I speculated about the Society being linked to this old church that most theological historians say went under back during the Great Depression. The Church of Christ, Holy Fisher. Holy Fisher sort of splintered off from the evangelical mainstream in the early part of the century. They had more of a... what do you call it... hands-on approach. An aggressive pursuit of what they called Divine Retribution."

"What do you mean?"

"Well, they believed it was their duty, as Christians, to seek out and punish sinners. Harshly. If you read the Old Testament... have you read it?"

Crowe shook his head.

"Ah. Well, you don't know what you're missing. That's some good reading. Anyway, in the Old Testament, it's pretty clear that God isn't all about Love and Peace and all that horseshit. That's happy-crappy New Testament stuff. In the Old Testament, He's all about punishment, see, and extremely harsh justice." He leaned forward, propping his skinny arms on the table, and his voice started to become more animated. "It's like this. You know the Muslims. I mean the Muslim extremists, right, not your average everyday Muslim. The hard-asses, that's who I'm talking about."

"Yeah," Crowe said.

"Well, here's the thing. Those Muslims, if you really want to get technical about it, are the ones who are actually doing exactly what it tells them to do in the Koran. They're the ones who are actually taking their faith seriously, and I do mean *seriously*. The Koran tells 'em to kill some heathens, and so... that's what they do. The Church of Christ, Holy Fisher, was pretty much the same thing. They felt like all the other worshippers of God were half-assing it, or sort of picking and choosing whatever made them feel all warm and fuzzy about their faith. Holy Fisher, they thought, was the only church actually going out and doing the dirty work of Christianity."

Crowe said, "What sort of dirty work are you talking about?"

He grinned, showing a worn-out old picket fence of teeth. "Well, that's hard to say. There was a lot of speculation, you know. But no one had anything solid on them. I mean, you can't go around openly killing folks and expect to stay in business in any legit form. People talked, though. The church fathers of a lot of other Protestant communities along the east coast condemned them as heretical. Said that Holy Fisher was driven by hatred of sinners rather than love of God."

"The Society of Christ the Fisher. This is the same church?"

"No," Hampton said. "Did I say that? I don't think those words crossed my lips. I would never say that. I'm just saying… well, the name is similar, yes? And the secrecy. But the Society has only been around for, what? Twenty years? Thereabouts? And the Church of Christ, Holy Fisher tanked a long time ago."

"How long ago are we talking?"

"Back in the thirties, during the Depression. They really only lasted about ten years or so, but in that time they managed to establish churches in a lot of rural communities along the east coast and into the areas west of the Appalachians. Messages of hate, though, are like sudden fires. They can rage out of control for a while, can burn the fuck out of you, but sooner or later they die out. The message that Holy Fisher was sending didn't catch on in any way that mattered. Hellfire and brimstone in the afterlife is one thing, right, but church-goers didn't want to think that it was their goddamn responsibility to mete out divine retribution to sinners in this life."

Crowe could've argued the point about hateful messages burning out eventually, but he didn't.

Hampton said, "Newspapers uniformly condemned them as dangerous and hateful. A bully in the pulpit urging people to commit monstrous crimes against humanity." He closed his eyes, and quoted: "*The Church of Christ, Holy Fisher, is fit only for simpletons and dangerous psychotics. Quite frankly, they are a church of evil-minded heretics.*" He opened his eyes. "That's from an editorial in 1925. The fire was already starting to sputter by then."

Crowe swished his coffee around in his cup and said, "Hampton. If the Church of Christ, Holy Fisher, has nothing to do the Society of Christ the Fisher, why are you telling me about them?"

He shrugged. "You're going to have to work out some of this shit on your own, boy. What I'm telling you is, if the Society is the same thing as the old church, then, well. I don't know anything about that, do I? If they're just a bunch of yahoos who adopted the name, I don't know about that either. If they have something to do with killing people whom they judge as sinners beyond redemption, well… Let's say someone actually does know the answer to that question. Would that person be wise to go around blabbing about it?"

Crowe said, "Church groups don't go around killing people, Hampton."

"I'm not disagreeing with you. Hey, you showed up at my door. You wanted to know what I know. And now you do."

Crowe stood up. "You don't know anything."

"Suit yourself."

"You're a paranoid basket case."

"Sorry to waste your time."

Crowe clenched his fists. Waste his time… that was exactly what Hampton had done. Crowe came two hundred miles to talk to some raving boozehound with too much free time on his hands and too little grasp on reality.

He gritted his teeth and said, "Thanks for taking the time to talk to me. I'll see myself out."

"Right," he said. And then, as Crowe started to turn away, "Listen, son. The Society, more than likely, is just a savvy Christian charity group, with enough pull to make an old washed-up writer's life miserable. They probably don't have any skeletons in the closet. They probably don't have anything to hide at all. There is nothing, nothing at all, to connect them solidly to the old church."

Crowe looked at him, watched as his face went dark and his eyes vacant again.

Looking at the table, he said, "But I did my goddamn research. I did. They had no right to fuck me. They didn't have any right."

24

The Wellings had a home in Bartlett. Crowe drove all day to get there, and didn't think about what he was doing. He just did it. Non-stop from south of Oxford, and he didn't pause for one second to reflect on what he hoped to accomplish.

Bartlett is east and a little north of Memphis, pretty solidly middle-to-upper-middle class, unlike neighboring Germantown, where most of the real money is.

Finding the place was easy, thanks to the internet connection on his brand new cell phone. Turning into a regular computer whiz, which was funny, because before prison he'd never touched a computer in his life.

Cole had said the Wellings didn't spend much time at their Bartlett home these days, not since Patricia had been killed; most of the time, they were at some other house or cottage or something in the eastern part of Tennessee—Longbaugh, he assumed, where the Society of Christ the Fisher had a church.

That was a good thing. It gave Crowe carte blanche to indulge in some prime B&E.

It was very near full-on dark by the time he got there, shortly after seven-thirty. He was still annoyed about the trip to Hampton's house, but he couldn't shake the feeling that maybe it wasn't quite the waste of time it seemed like.

The cold had eased up a little. Not that it had given way to spring or anything, but at least he didn't feel like the wind was going to freeze his face off. He parked the Jag on the next block and walked over to the Welling house.

The neighborhood was quiet and pleasant, if not sort of bland. The developers had made a point of making sure neighboring houses didn't look exactly alike; there were a variety of houses on the block, ranches and bungalows, Tudors and Cape Cods.

The Wellings place was a Tudor, with pale green vinyl siding and a nice brick front. A light was on in the front window, blurry through some flimsy drapes, but the rest of the place was dark. No cars in the driveway and no signs of life.

A security light, then, probably on a timer. Crowe wondered about their security system.

He glanced quickly up and down the block, saw not a soul, although it was possible someone was watching from one of the many windows up and down the street. It was a chance he'd have to take. He crossed the Wellings lawn, crunchy with clinging ice under his shoes, and went around to the backyard.

There was a small brick patio, and some battered plastic patio furniture. Some of it had been blown over by the heavy winds a couple days before. That was good. It meant that the place was almost definitely vacant. If the Wellings had been home, someone would have righted the furniture by now. He pulled the electronic lock pick out of his inside coat pocket and went to work on the back door.

An electronic lock pick is a beautiful thing. It looks something like a thick, unwieldy pen. You insert the tip of it into just about any lock, press a button, and it agitates the pins several times a second and pops it open in a heartbeat. Perfectly legal, too, unless you happen to have a record, in which case the pick doubles as a 'go immediately to jail' card.

He popped the lock, stepped into the dark kitchen, and gently shut the door behind him. No alarms went off, but he waited for a long minute anyway without moving and let his eyes adjust to the darkness. The house was silent and empty.

The kitchen was very modern, all gleaming silver and spotless white Formica. The pots and pans hung above the stove in a handy space-saving rig. He ran a finger along the countertop. No dust. They probably had a cleaning lady in once a week or so to fend off the unwanted advances of nature. It was a little chilly, which meant they'd probably turned the thermostat down to the low 60's while they were gone. Very conscientious about energy conservation, the Wellings.

He relaxed a little bit and moved swiftly through the kitchen and directly into the living room. This was where the lamp was on, casting an easy light over the comfortable-looking leather sofa and easy chair, enormous wide-screen TV, coffee table and end tables in elegant blond wood. A bible rested on the coffee table. It was the only book in the room.

Down the hall. The bathroom was to the left. He went in and opened the medicine cabinet, found it empty except for a squeezed-out tube of toothpaste. Past the bathroom was a bedroom, and then another bedroom. He went in each one, opened the closets to find them both empty. Good. Just further verification that the Wellings were gone for a while.

At the far end of the house he found the study. He knew it was the study because there was a computer in it, and five or six books.

A colorful life-like painting took up most of the wall, depicting Jesus kneeling amongst a group of modern children, smiling benevolently and resting a hand on one child's shoulder. The children in the painting looked like they were very interested in what he was saying, except one kid in the foreground; he was looking over his shoulder, as if there was a basketball game going on over there and he really wanted to be a part of it.

A fireproof safe sat directly under the painting. He turned on the little desk lamp next to the computer, went to the safe, found it unlocked. He found tax returns, insurance records, yellowed personal correspondence, bills, the usual. Nothing about the Society.

There had to be something, though. If Fletcher Welling was the 'alderman', as Cole put it, there had to be some sign of it in his home.

Crowe sat down in front of the computer and began riffling through the desk. There were five drawers; one long and narrow, and two on each side that were deeper. In the bottom left one he found a stack of pamphlets for the Society. He grabbed one, shoved it in his coat pocket to look at later, and closed up the drawer.

He was about to open the next drawer, when the sound of wood creaking somewhere in the house stopped him cold.

Outside, a car with a bad muffler drove by, echoing up and down the street, and he didn't move.

He strained to hear. He couldn't be sure, but he thought maybe he heard the creaking sound again, under the rumble.

Swiveling quietly in the desk chair, he faced the open door. His hand went to his overcoat pocket for the gun—the gun he realized then that he'd left in the car. *Nice going, Crowe.* He really was out of practice.

He waited and watched the hallway for shadows. Because of the lamp in the living room, if someone was in the house they couldn't come through the hall without Crowe having at least a few seconds warning. He wished he was standing, but moving from the chair would've required more noise than he wanted to make just then.

A tiny digital clock next to the computer said 7:41. It ticked away the seconds, and he listened, and heard nothing. 7:42, and still nothing. No sound, no shadows, nothing.

But he still sat motionless, until the clock said 7:49.

He allowed himself to breath. Okay, so he heard a creaking noise. It was winter, after all, the heat was turned down, and the house was making the usual house noises. He stood up and swiftly crossed to the door and glanced down the hall. The place was empty.

He went back to the desk and resumed foraging through the drawers.

In the top one on the right, he found some official church documents, ledger books and receipts and what-not, and directly underneath those he came across a pile of newsletters that all said *The Society of Christ the Fisher Events and Functions!* along the heading. They were all different, and dating back about four years. Probably being saved to go into a scrap book or something.

He leafed through them briefly, stopped about halfway through when the words *Patricia Welling, daughter of Fletcher and Joan Welling* caught his eye.

It was the caption under a cheerful group photo, taken at what looked like a church picnic. A bright summer day behind them, balloons, streamers, a green park with trees, and children running around. The subjects of the photo were a girl with a distantly bemused smile—Patricia—and four or five other girls. Two adults lingered at the periphery of the shot, but the girls were clearly the subjects. He glanced at the date on the header. June, 2006, it said. That was about two months before Patricia ran away.

She wasn't like the other girls in the picture, that much was clear. They all looked younger than her somehow, even though they were all about thirteen years old. They all had open faces, hearts that shone through in the moment the photographer snapped the button and said cheese. But not Patricia. Her arms were folded across her narrow chest. Her smile was a temporary fixture. Her eyes were guarded and wary. Crowe could almost read her mind; *sure, good times. What are they worth?*

But he could've been reading things into the picture, knowing what he knew about her, knowing about her murder only months later. What kid is that self-consciously cynical? No, it takes a grown man to be that immature.

He was about to put the newsletter in his pocket with the pamphlet, when one of the other faces in the photo caught his eye. He stared at it, the information seeming to take longer than it should have to process. One of the adults, off on the far margins of the photo, smiling beatifically, as if it had every right in the world to be there. It was a face he knew, a face he recognized.

Jezzie Vitower.

He whispered to himself, "Sonofabitch," and then the floorboards creaked in the living room.

25

He dropped the newsletter and stood up and faced the door, heart kicking. It wasn't his imagination, and it wasn't the house settling. It was a footstep, moving stealthily through the living room.

He cast his eyes around for a suitable weapon, spotted a letter opener half-under the computer monitor. That would do. He'd never killed someone with a letter opener before, but he imagined it would do the trick.

He grabbed it and waited, waited for another sound, waited for shadows to spill across the hallway.

And kept waiting. He risked a glance away, at the digital clock. It ticked over to 7:54.

When it hit 7:56 and he didn't hear anything else, he started second-guessing himself, wondering if he really *had* heard someone moving in the living room. That was never good. Before prison, he'd been exceptionally good at his job because he always trusted his gut. But long years away had eroded his instincts, or at least his confidence in them.

But no. He had heard something, He was sure of it, the sort of sound that only a living thing can make. It wasn't just a creak. It was a *stealthy* creak.

Unless the intruder was a complete idiot, he'd have to know

Crowe would see his shadow in the hall if he tried approaching the study. He'd be lying in wait , then, somewhere in the living room or the kitchen, or possibly the bathroom—he could make the bathroom, probably, without Crowe seeing his shadow.

7:59, the digital clock said. So okay. He was waiting. Crowe wouldn't keep him.

He flipped the desk lamp off, counted five, and moved into the hallway. He was very conscious of the bandage over his left eye just then. It severely limited his sight range. If someone came at him from the immediate left, he'd be blind-sided.

With that in mind, he led with his right, holding the letter opener low and ready to thrust upward. He could see part of the living room from where he was—an end table and the stuffed arm of the sofa.

At the first bedroom, he slowed down long enough to close the door. If the intruder somehow managed to make it that far without Crowe seeing his shadow—highly unlikely—he'd have to open the bedroom door again to come out and Crowe would hear him. He did the same with the second bedroom.

Right before the bathroom, Crowe crouched low and moved a little closer to the far wall. From an angle, he peeked in. The light was off in there, but it was small and there was enough light from the living room to show it was empty. The shower curtain was clear plastic, and no boogiemen were hiding behind it.

Crowe straightened up and eased another step or two down the hall.

He could see almost the entire living room now, all the furniture, the lamp, the tables. Nothing moved, nothing made a sound. He could've been lurking right at the doorway, waiting to jump him from there. But, no, Crowe remembered that one of the end tables was in that spot.

So where did he go? Was Crowe imagining things after all?

He took another silent step and the whole living room was visible and there was nobody there. The kitchen, then, just off the living room and on his other side.

Crowe took a step into the living room and looked to his left, where the kitchen opened up. The back door, which he'd so carefully closed behind him, was now wide open.

From the pale light creeping in from outside and the shadowy glow of the living room lamp, Crowe could see every nook and cranny of the kitchen, and the intruder—the intruder besides *himself*, that is—was nowhere around.

Whoever he was, he was gone now, hustled back out into the cold, maybe waiting to jump Crowe once he got outside. But Crowe wasn't particularly worried about that; if he was going to attack, he would've done it in the house. Why take the chance out there, where someone could possibly see or hear?

Crowe relaxed a bit and started for the door.

Just as Crowe's hand closed over the doorknob, there he was, swooping in from his blind left, hitting him with something hard along the upper part of his back.

Crowe felt the stitches in the knife wound between his shoulder blades rip open and he fell into the side of the door and into the cabinet. The attacker kicked the door closed and came at him. It was the Goth-looking guy, with the long black overcoat and dyed black hair.

Crowe lunged at him with the letter opener. Goth-Boy slapped it aside with his weapon—a heavy length of pipe—and with his other fist punched Crowe in the right shoulder.

Crowe's whole right side screamed at him and the letter opener fell out of his suddenly powerless fingers. The pipe came down toward his skull but because he happened to be half-stepping backwards on the linoleum it slammed against the countertop and pieces of Formica scattered all over the kitchen.

Crowe backed into the stove, and the pots and pans above it clattered obnoxiously. With his left hand, he reached behind him blindly and grabbed whatever his fist closed around and swung it at the Goth-Boy.

It was a hefty cast iron frying pan. Not bad. His swing had been sloppy, but he still managed to connect with his temple, and the *thud* sound it made was pretty satisfying.

Goth-Boy choked back a sob of pain and reeled away. Crowe pressed the advantage, fighting through the lancing red agony in his right shoulder and between his shoulder blades. He wasn't impervious to pain, like good old Leon Berry, but he was damn good at working through it. He swung again, catching Goth-Boy on his right shoulder, and Goth-Boy fell back against the counter that Crowe had been against a moment before.

Crowe was ready to finish him off with the patented 'frying pan to the skull' routine, but Goth-Boy had more in him than Crowe reckoned. One clunky black leather boot shot out and nailed Crowe just below the knee. If it had been a fraction of an inch higher it would've shattered the kneecap, but as it was there was enough power in it to halfway drop him.

The lead pipe swooshed, and Crowe pushed himself back and it breezed across his coat collar. He snagged Goth-Boy's arm on the back-swing, jerked it down, and came up with his forehead into his nose.

A crack, a wash of blood across Crowe's face, and Goth-Boy stumbled back stiff-legged, the way someone knocked half-senseless will do. He dropped the pipe. Crowe didn't let up. He jabbed the edge of the frying pan at his throat, heard him say, "*Guh—*," and kneed him as close to his stomach as he could. He gripped the frying pan in both hands and let him have it in square in the face.

There was a wet crunch and Goth-Boy fell back against the kitchen table and chairs clattered across the linoleum and he dropped.

Crowe had learned the hard way that that wasn't the time to stop and catch your breath. The kid looked down for the count, but looks can be deceiving. He bent over him, grabbed a fistful of his black hair, and slammed his head against the floor a few times. Goth-Boy's eyes rolled back and that's when Crowe knew he was done.

Crowe dropped his head, stood up. Blood rushed to his skull and he almost fell down right there next to him. He steadied himself on the counter and let the adrenalin run its course through his body.

His heart rate started slowing and the pain he'd been pushing down flared with every breath he took. He reached into his coat pocket, pulled out the bottle of pain killers, tossed a couple down his throat. His back and shoulder felt hot and sticky. The goddamn stitches.

He went over and kicked Goth-Boy in the head, just to get it out of his system. The kid grunted but didn't move.

Still alive. Good. That meant he could answer some questions.

But that particular plan didn't work out. Crowe had just started to look through the kitchen drawers for some rope when a flashing blue and red light shone through the front window, and the familiar *woop* of a cop car siren disturbed the quiet neighborhood.

26

A neighbor had seen one of them get into the house, or maybe someone had heard the scuffle in the kitchen, or seen the desk lamp burning in the study. Whatever it was, the cops had come quickly and the evening wasn't working out as planned.

Goth-Boy groaned, and Crowe edged away from him toward the door. If the cops were smart, one of them would've been out of the car by now, making his way around to the back of the house before the other one sounded the siren.

Crowe had to bank on them not having that much foresight. He opened the door and stepped out into the darkened backyard, moved quickly across the patio and to the wood fence.

A strip of light from the next door neighbor's rear patio knifed suddenly across the yard, exposing him as thoroughly as a spotlight. At the same second, a cop appeared at the corner of the house. His gun was still holstered, but his hand rested on it, ready. He saw Crowe.

"Freeze!" the cop said, a little predictably, and the gun started coming out.

Behind the cop, Goth-Boy loomed in the doorway, bloody and battered but amazingly still conscious. The cop saw him from the corner of his eye, started to spin, when Goth-Boy slammed the lead pipe across the cop's skull. The cop crumpled, firing off a shot as he fell.

Goth-Boy stumbled over him, carried by the momentum of his swing, and from the front of the house Crowe heard the other cops, doors slamming, someone yelling into a walkie-talkie, shoes pounding concrete and then ice-crunchy snow.

Crowe scrambled awkwardly over the fence and stumbled away.

He'd cleared the next fence and was angling off between two houses and toward the street when he heard one of the cops screaming, "Freeze! Get down on your knees, now!" and for a split second he thought the cop had super-human vision and could actually see him. But it was Goth-Boy he was screeching orders at.

When he made the street, Crowe kept running directly across it and through the next yard. The wound at his shoulder blade was bleeding. He could feel it running hot down his back.

He cut through five backyards, jumped another fence, veered right between two ranch houses. Moving as fast as he could, he crossed another street, passed through another set of backyards.

Behind a modest bungalow, he paused for a moment in the shadows, listening for the cops behind him. Silence. If he was lucky, the cops wouldn't even know he had been there.

He cut through another yard, angled left, made his way silently between two more houses, and came out on the same street the Wellings house was on, Findle Street.

From the shadows between the two houses, he peeked up the block. The Wellings place was about half a block up, and he could see the police cruiser, lights flashing, and the cop who'd stayed behind. The cop stood next to the car door, radio in hand. Waiting for back-up.

Right on cue, another blue light flashed, and Crowe ducked back into the shadows of the house. Another cruiser sped by and came to a quiet stop next to the other one. Two more cops got out. Crowe could hear them talking to each other but was too far away to make out the words. Radios squelched.

Crowe looked up the other side of the street, trying to orientate himself. His car was on the street intersecting Findle.

Right in front of him.

He walked across the yard, got in his car, and drove away.

He made it out of Bartlett without hearing another police siren or seeing any flashing lights. Every muscle in his body ached, and more than once his hand strayed to the pain meds in his pocket. He didn't pop any more, though. He'd decided it was important to keep his head clear for the time being.

Things were going to get worse before they got better. He knew that. He knew it, because the face he'd seen in the photograph, that smiling adult face on the periphery of the happy shot of Patricia and her friends, was a face that meant trouble.

One photo, two victims of Peter Murke. No way that was a coincidence.

Why was Jezzie Vitower in the same photograph with Patricia Welling?

27

When he'd made Memphis, Crowe flipped open the cell phone and dialed Radnovian. Rad answered on the first ring, sounding eager and not at all stoned.

"You expecting someone to call?" Crowe said.

Rad let out a disappointed breath. "You know," he said. "Considering how, according to you, we aren't buddies, you sure do call me an awful lot."

Crowe heard the click of the electric razor, and the whining motor as it came closer to the phone. "Stop shaving for a goddamn minute and listen to me."

"I can shave and listen at the same time."

"I'm sure you can. Turn it off anyway."

It clicked off, and Rad said, "Okay. There. Happy?"

"I need another favor from you. The file on Murke. Get it for me."

"Right," Rad said. "Just kinda… oh, stroll casually into Homicide, pull the file on Murke, smile at the boys in charge of his case and stroll right back out. That what you have in mind?"

"That's about it."

"Crowe, what do you think I am? I'm in Internal Affairs. That doesn't give me authority to do whatever the hell I wanna do, you know."

"It's not your position that gives you authority, Rad. It's how you abuse it."

"You're a sonofabitch," he said. "I really hate you, you know that?"

"Get the file on Murke. Meet me at my apartment tonight."

Rad said, "There's no way I can do that. Not that soon."

"When, then?"

"Tomorrow. Tomorrow night, I can do it by then."

"Fine," Crowe said. "Tomorrow night, seven o'clock."

"Okay, Crowe. But eventually you're gonna have to cut me some slack. I can't keep—"

Crowe flipped the phone shut.

He hadn't been in his apartment in about ten days. There was no mail. Harriston stood just outside his door again, smoking, and when he saw Crowe coming up the steps he said, "Well, hey there, Crowe, long time no see."

Crowe nodded at him and kept moving toward his door. Harriston said, "What the hell happened to you, son? You get in a fight or something?"

"Yeah," Crowe said. "I'll tell you all about it another time, Harriston. I'm beat. I need some sleep."

"Sure, sure. Some sleep. Damn, Crowe, you sure do get yourself in some crazy shit."

Crowe unlocked his door, started to go in, when Harriston said, "Say, I reckon you'd wanna know, you had a visitor a couple-three days back. Said he was a cop."

Crowe looked at him. "Wills?"

Harriston nodded. "Yeah, that's right. Detective Wills."

"I talked to him."

"Okay. But, uh… listen, we don't need any trouble in this building, you know? I mean, cops coming by? Tenants showing up looking like they been trampled by bulls? That's just—"

"No trouble," Crowe said. "It's all a great big misunderstanding. Everything's already straightened out."

"Yeah. Except, you know, with your police record and all—"

Crowe went in his flat and shut the door.

The garbage can was starting to smell bad with apple cores and orange peels. Crowe ignored it, and stumbled into the bathroom.

A hot shower took the edge off his pain but brought the fuzziness to the surface. He changed out his bandages and dropped into bed naked.

But as tired as he was, he couldn't sleep. He lay there, looking up at the dark ceiling, hearing the noise of traffic outside, the ticking of the clock by the bed, the sounds of the building straining against the earth.

Jezzie Vitower and Patricia Welling, in the same photograph. The Society of Christ the Fisher. Peter Murke.

He was too tired, too tired to make sense of any of it. He was no goddamn detective. When he needed to know something, he beat it out of the person who could tell him. But that wasn't going to work this time; the sources who could tell him anything were either dead or missing.

Or not even real. Like the Ghost Cat. It could tell him something, he thought, if it actually existed.

But that was his exhausted brain, scrambling around in his head and grasping at phantoms.

He eventually started to drift off, and his half-awake thoughts turned to Dallas. They were dark thoughts, full of flesh and sweat and heat, and they kept him from falling asleep completely.

He got up and made some coffee.

He sat at the window and drank coffee and thought about how he needed to stop thinking. It was one in the morning. He had another cup of coffee, got up, got dressed, left the apartment.

He drove to Dallas's house.

28

"Crowe," she said, blearily. "What are you doing here? It's one-thirty in the morning."

He looked at his watch and shrugged.

"What… what are you doing here?" she said again.

"I don't know."

She opened the door and let him in, peeked outside to see if any neighbors were around, and closed it behind her. She wore over-sized men's pajamas. Her mascara was smeared down her cheeks.

"You shouldn't be here. Are you drunk?"

"No, I'm not drunk."

"It's one-thirty in the morning."

"We've established that. Chester still at Dr. Maggie's?"

"Yes."

"What about the boy?"

"His name's Tom, and he's asleep. What, did you think he'd be up this time of night?"

"No."

She stood there looking at him, and finally sighed and said, "You wanna drink?"

"Yes."

"I don't have any vodka. Only whisky. But it's good whiskey."

"Fine."

She frowned at him and went into the kitchen. He sat on the sofa. The living room was tasteful and only slightly bohemian. The furniture was standard tan and black, the walls a muted lime green. There were knick-knacks in gleaming silver, a few art deco type pieces, and a slim curving lamp that lit the whole room. It smelled very delicately of Dallas, as if she'd scented the place lightly with her own perfume.

She came back in carrying a bottle and two tumbler glasses. "It's been in the fridge," she said. "You don't need ice." She sat down next to him and poured drinks.

He tossed his back, grabbed the bottle and refilled his glass. She sipped hers, and said, "So. I reckon I should say Happy Birthday."

"What?"

"Today's your birthday, isn't it? Don't tell me you didn't know. You're fifty today, Crowe. That's a big deal, right?"

He shook his head. Was it his birthday already? And more importantly, who gave a shit?

He said, "Okay. Thanks."

She said, "I didn't get you anything."

"That's fine."

"A card or something would've been nice, though, huh? Maybe sometime today I'll pop down to the Hallmark and—"

"Dallas," he said. "Shut up."

She frowned. "Right," she said. "You never liked it when I made a big deal about your birthday. I forgot." Then, "Chester isn't home yet, but if anyone saw you here there'd be huge trouble."

"Yeah, I suppose so."

"But you came anyway."

"Why not? You took the chance of coming to my place a couple weeks ago."

She said, "Well, you got me there. It couldn't be helped, though. I really needed your help."

"So what if I need *your* help? What if that's why I'm here?"

"My help? With what?"

He looked away from her and took a drink. "I don't know," he said.

"Look. Obviously, you're having a bad time right now. I don't think—"

"Scratch that. I don't need help. I just came to give you this." He reached into his coat and pulled out some of the cash he had left over from Vitower. It was about two grand. He shoved half of it in her hand.

She looked at it blankly, and said, "How much is this?"

"Enough to get you out of Memphis. You go somewhere, we'll work out a way for you to contact me, and I'll meet up with you."

"Meet up with me? Crowe, why?"

He hated that she asked that. He took another long drink and said, "Why do you think, goddamnit? To… to give you more money."

Her hand dropped to her lap, still clutching the wad of cash. Very quietly, she said, "I shouldn't have come to you in the first place. It was stupid of me."

"Yeah, probably."

"You… you obviously still have feelings for me."

He stood up. "You're crazy. I don't have feelings for you. I hate your guts."

She looked up at him. "Is that right? Then why are you helping me?"

He set his teeth and snarled, "That's a goddamn good question," and started for the door.

Halfway across the living room, she caught up with him, put a hand on his arm, and he turned to look at her, ready to put his fist across her face or shove her away or something, he didn't know. But when his eyes met hers, something else happened and he grabbed her by her shoulders and pulled her to him.

She didn't stop him from kissing her, but she didn't kiss back either. He tried to pretend he didn't notice. He kissed her harder, moving his hand up and under her pajama top and squeezing her breast.

She was breathing hard and her eyes were closed, but with his mouth pressed against hers she managed to say, "Crowe, no. No."

He stepped back from her, and she looked up at him. She was breathless and her face was flushed. Her voice, though, was steady and controlled. She said, "That's a mistake. I'm sorry, but it's a mistake."

He didn't say anything.

"What we had, Crowe… it's gone." Then, "No, that's a lie. It's not gone. But it should be. We were weak then, that's what we were. But it's different now."

"Yeah," he said.

"I'm… well, the things I told you about the other day? I've been reconsidering them."

"Reconsidering."

"Yeah. I mean… I don't know. Maybe leaving Chester isn't such a good idea."

"Oh, for fuck's sake."

She said, "It's Tom. He needs a father. And Chester has been talking lately about—"

"About giving it all up. Changing his ways."

"Yeah."

"And you believe that?"

"I feel like I should at least… I don't know, give him the chance to do that. He's not a bad man, really."

He wanted to tell her that it didn't matter what sort of man Chester was; in another week, maybe less, he was going to kill him, so it didn't matter. But he didn't. Instead, he said, "Right, Dallas. Give him a chance, sure."

"You're clearly exhausted," she said. "Why don't you sleep here tonight? On the sofa. We can talk more in the morning."

"No thanks. I'll get going."

"Please? We'll have a couple more drinks, and then you can

get some sleep, and everything will seem clearer in the morning. Okay?"

He sighed. "Okay," he said.

29

It was still dark when he opened his eyes, the only light streaming in dimly from a security light outside in the building's parking lot. He was sprawled out on the sofa, a throw blanket draped over him and his shoes off. The boy was sitting on the edge of the coffee table, staring at him.

Crowe looked at him and the boy cocked his head. "Hello," he said.

Thin, pale like his mother. In the darkness Crowe couldn't tell what color his eyes were. His disheveled hair was light, maybe dirty blond or brown. He seemed to be glowing.

The boy said again, "Hello. Who are you?"

"Nobody," Crowe said.

"You're somebody."

"Okay."

Crowe sat up woozily. He was still drunk. "What do you want?"

"Nothing. I got up to get a drink of water and I saw you. Are you a friend of my mom's?"

"Yeah."

He nodded. "My dad's at the doctor's house. Are you here to do dad stuff until he gets back?"

"No. What? No. Go away."

He frowned. "This is my house, I don't have to go away." Then, "You smell like alky-hol."

Crowe rubbed his temples, thought about getting up and leaving, but the idea of moving at that moment was too daunting. Instead, he lay back down.

"Are you an alky-holic?" he said.

"No. I hardly ever drink," Crowe said, and then wondered why he bothered explaining it. He didn't want to see this kid. He didn't want to talk to him, drunk or otherwise.

"My name's Tommy. Tom. I was named after a famous American. What's your name?"

"Crowe."

The boy smiled. "Crow, like the bird? Crows eat dead stuff off the road. Why do you have a bandage on your face? Did you hurt yourself?"

"You need to go back to bed. Your mom would be mad if she knew you were up."

"No she wouldn't. My mom doesn't get mad about stupid stuff like that."

"Kid," Crowe said. "Go away."

"But—"

"Go away!"

The boy jumped, surprised, and looked at him. For a second Crowe thought he was going to burst into tears, but instead he shrugged. "Fine. Be a jerk, see if I care." He stood up and walked with as much dignity as a seven-year-old could back to his room.

Crowe had a hard time getting back to sleep after that. He kept seeing the boy's white face, glowing in the soft light. Eventually, though, he slept.

30

It couldn't have been more than three hours later he sat up, head pounding and muscles screaming.

The money he'd given Dallas was tucked in one of his shoes. The bottle was almost empty on the table, and he realized that he drank most of it; he didn't remember Dallas having more than two drinks.

Stupid. His tolerance for booze wasn't up for that sort of challenge.

He threw a couple of pain pills down his throat, forgetting all about his resolve to stay clear-headed, and in the next room he could hear activity—the sounds of the household coming awake. Through the bedroom wall, he heard Dallas saying, "Well, good morning, sleepyhead," and the muted giggling of the boy.

He couldn't see him again. He stood up quickly, grabbed his overcoat, and headed for the door.

Fast food for breakfast, a greasy sausage and egg combo, and as soon as he finished it he was in the restaurant's bathroom, throwing it back up. He needed some goddamn aspirin and another ten hours of sleep.

His place was too far away, so he got back in the Jag and headed for Faith's, in Midtown. It would be hard, explaining what he was doing back, but he needed a place to be for at least a couple of hours.

There was no answer when he knocked. She usually worked until two in the morning, was in bed by three, and slept until ten-thirty or eleven. She was a light sleeper, so he knocked again, a little louder.

Still no answer. He tried the door, and it was unlocked.

That wasn't like her at all. Checking to make sure the place was locked up before she went to bed bordered on being a compulsion with her.

He went in and said, "Faith?"

Nothing. He made his way through the living room, saying again, "Faith? It's me."

The living room looked normal, nothing disturbed, no signs of visitors, legitimate or otherwise.

Except for one thing: a shoe-print on the carpet, just outside the bathroom. A fairly large print, edged in dark red.

He'd remembered his revolver this time, and his hand went into the coat pocket and rested on the butt.

The bedroom door was open, as usual. He went in and stopped just inside the doorway.

Faith was in bed.

Most of her was, anyway.

31

The bed was soaked with blood and the carpet around it stained a dark ugly red. She'd been opened up from throat to pelvis, and the gaping hole of her torso was like a giant red mouth, half-open. It smelled like an abattoir.

Pieces of her had been arranged on the bed next to her. Some other pieces were on the floor at the foot of the bed, like bedroom slippers. They were organs, but Crowe couldn't tell which ones.

He stood there for a few seconds. And then he went back to the front door, made sure it was locked. He did a quick sweep of the apartment, checking behind the sofa and in the hall closet and anywhere else someone could hide. He looked in the bathroom, being careful not to step on the bloody shoe print. Then he went back in the bedroom and, not looking at the thing on the bed, checked the closet there.

He thought about looking under the bed, but it would have required slinking through the mess of blood and gore and he wasn't sure he was up for that. There was less than four inches between the floor and bottom of the bed anyway.

He stepped back and looked at Faith. Her eyes were open, staring blandly at the ceiling.

He felt a lot of things all at once, but pushed them away.

There was no time for any of that. Faith had a small vanity table next to the bed, and he pulled the chair over from it and sat down and thought.

Opened up, parts of her pulled out. Just like Patricia Welling. Just like Jezzie Vitower. And just like fourteen other women he didn't know, would never know. Victims of Peter Murke.

But it didn't have to be Murke. Just because the MO was the same wasn't evidence that Murke had done this. He had buddies, old Peter did, buddies that rescued him from the transport van and Vitower's wrath. Buddies that went after anyone who got too close. Maybe one of them did this.

Crowe wondered if Faith was being slaughtered at the same time he was fighting Goth-Boy. He couldn't see or smell any signs of decay, so it had to have happened fairly recently.

He stood up, took a step toward the bed, and placed his fingers on Faith's eyelids. He gently closed them.

Her face was clean and unstained by the blood that covered everything else. Which was lucky, because otherwise he never would have noticed the symbol carved into her temple.

He bent over to get a closer look, being careful not to touch anything.

It had happened after death, and hadn't bled much. A small cross, it looked like, small enough that a regular knife wouldn't have been able to slice it in such detail. A razor blade then, or an exacto knife, something like that. The arms of the cross bent downward, and it was topped by what looked like a heart-shape, balancing at the top of the cross like a fat man on top of a pole.

It nagged at the back of his brain. He'd seen that symbol before, he was sure of it. But he couldn't remember where.

He let his anger take charge then, if for no other reason than to smother the guilt. In the closet, he found a large wool comforter and took it to the bed and covered Faith's body. He'd have to call the cops. After he'd gotten far away from there, of course.

Someone pounded on the front door, hard.

He went cold and his hand reached for the revolver in his coat pocket. He didn't move.

There were a few seconds of silence, and then more pounding. "Open the door, Crowe," Detective Eddie Wills said. "I saw you go in, you sonofabitch. Open the goddamn door."

32

Crowe went silently into the living room, eyes peeled on the front door. He heard Wills in the hall outside, huffing impatiently, and could see him in his mind, that long sad horse face, that booze-ruined nose, and big gnarled hands ready to knock the goddamn door down if he had to. Like he'd said, he wasn't the sort to worry about due process.

Crowe could let him in. Close the door to Faith's bedroom, act like everything was normal, play it cool. But Wills was an observant bastard, and if Crowe could spot the bloody shoeprint outside the bathroom, he could too.

Wills pounded again. "Crowe, I will knock this fucking door off its fucking hinges if you don't open it right now."

He would've known Crowe had nothing to do with this: it was the kind of work that took time. But Crowe didn't trust him.

He went back into the bedroom, closed the door behind him. Despite his best efforts, it clicked shut audibly and Wills pounded harder on the outside door.

Crowe moved across the bedroom to the window, opened it up. Faith lived on the second floor. There was a drop of about fifteen feet to the icy grass below.

Normally, Crowe wouldn't have had any qualms about it,

but in his current state it made him nervous. No matter what, the landing would hurt.

But what the hell. He had a pocket full of pain killers, may as well use them.

He could still hear Wills through two closed doors. "Fine, Crowe, that's how you wanna play it," he said, and then he was smashing at the door. Crowe heard the lock rattling hard, the muted sound of Wills' shoe kicking the wood.

Crowe eased himself through the window, and heard the front door giving way with a terrific crash.

"Crowe!" Wills said, and Crowe heard him storming through the living room.

Crowe jumped from the window.

He landed on his feet and rolled left, trying to minimize the damage to his right shoulder. It hurt like a bitch regardless, and so did the wound in his back, and he had a split second of not wanting to move once he'd come to rest on the cold earth.

But he made himself stand up and risked a glance up at the open window. From the bedroom, Wills voice boomed, "Jesus fucking Christ!"

Crowe ran. From the corner of his eye he saw Wills' head sticking out the window and Wills screamed, "Freeze, Crowe!" but of course Crowe didn't.

He scrambled around the side of the building and toward the parking lot where he'd left his car. A young couple pushing a baby stroller got in the way, and Crowe shoved the man aside, causing him to nearly fall into his wife.

"Hey, what the hell, man, take it easy!" the man said, and the baby started screeching. The wife yelled at Crowe's back, being pretty creative about his anatomy and what he could do with it.

He had his keys out when he reached the Jag, started to unlock it, when the side view mirror shattered and the crack of a gunshot echoed across the parking lot.

Wills stood at the far end of the lot, just in front of the apartment building, about fifty feet away. He was in classic shooting stance, the kind they teach you in police training, and his pistol was leveled at Crowe. It surprised Crowe that the cop remembered anything from his training.

"Don't move, Crowe, or so help me I'll put the next one in your head!"

The woman stopped yelling at Crowe and started yelling at her husband and they grabbed the baby out of the stroller and ran in the other direction.

Crowe got in the Jag, started it up. Another bullet shattered the glass in the rear passenger window.

He ducked low, threw the Jag into gear and pushed the gas. The tires screeched on the blacktop and the Jag shot forward. Wills fired again, but if the shot went anywhere near, Crowe couldn't tell. He jumped the median that separated the two sections of parking lot, jerked the wheel to the right and between two other parked cars, and accelerated toward the street.

Wills was running hard toward him, gun out, firing. Crowe heard two bullets hit metal before he made the street, took a left, and sped away. He glanced back just once, saw Wills shoving his gun back in its holster and making a break for his car. As big a loose cannon as he was, he'd still call for back-up on this one, and Crowe knew he could expect cops to swarm any minute.

He hit Union Avenue, merged his way into traffic heading west, back toward downtown. His fingers were tight on the steering wheel. He pushed the Jag up to forty-five, as fast he could risk it, weaving in and out of slower traffic like one of those assholes you see during rush hour who think shaving a few minutes off the drive-time is worth risking lives over.

But in this case, it was definitely worth it.

A police cruiser sat at the corner of Union and Manassas, and just as he passed it he saw the driver eyeing him, talking into his radio, and starting his engine in a hell of a hurry.

The cop hit his lights and siren and pulled out after him.

Crowe banked hard to the right, cutting off a Honda Civic, barreled into the mouth of a narrow alley. He kept it at about forty miles an hour. If someone decided to pop out in front of him, that would be pretty goddamn unfortunate for them.

Nobody jumped in front of the car, though. He cleared the alley, cut right again, and wound up on Madison.

He cursed under his breath. Madison wasn't a straight shot; it angled off and bled right into Union, where he'd just come from. He had to stop driving randomly, work out some sort of plan. He'd been away too long and didn't know the lay of the land as well as he should have.

More sirens wailed from somewhere nearby, but he couldn't see them. He got stopped at the light, just in time to see another police cruiser speed by, heading west. The light turned green and Crowe turned left, back in the direction he'd come from. There was a chance that the first cruiser hadn't seen him cut into the alley, although how the cop could have missed it was beyond him.

Maybe, maybe, maybe, the fumble would actually buy him a little time.

He drove fast up Union, risked staying on it for two miles. He didn't see any cops, didn't hear any sirens. It was a lucky break, but the luck wouldn't hold. He had to get rid of the Jag, right away.

At the next light, he took a right, and then another right, and a left through another alley and wound up on Sam Cooper, heading north. A sad-looking strip mall occupied the next intersection he came to. He pulled into it, found a parking spot between two SUV's, and cut the engine.

For about a minute, he sat there and listened for sirens. Didn't hear any.

He got out of the car, tossed the keys on the seat. The strip mall parking lot wasn't exactly heavy with pedestrians. An old man was just coming out of a Greek restaurant, jingling his keys. He nodded at Crowe as he passed and Crowe nodded back. A group of teenagers, being rowdy and hilarious, were getting out of a tan Ford Taurus and heading toward the video game store. They didn't look at him.

Crowe waited for the old man to get in his pick-up truck and pull out, and then he started perusing the parking lot for a suitable vehicle.

He settled on the Ford Taurus. It was a pretty inconspicuous car, and he had the advantage of knowing the teenagers wouldn't be coming out right away. They'd even very thoughtfully left the door unlocked.

He got in, popped the ignition, got it going in about twenty seconds. He put the car in gear, backed out of the space, and headed for the road. After driving the Jag around for a couple of days, the Taurus felt stiff and unresponsive, but beggars couldn't be luxury car drivers.

He turned onto Sam Cooper and headed north, not feeling near as anonymous as he wanted to be.

33

When he was well into the suburbs he found a quiet residential street and pulled into it. It took only a couple of minutes to find a suitable car parked at the curb. Feeling conspicuous as all hell, he glanced up and down the street, took a screwdriver to the parked car's license plate, and switched it with the Taurus'.

So that was one precaution seen to. The other one: the bandage on his face. The cops would be looking for that. He wasn't certain the wound was ready to go without bandages, but he didn't see any other options.

A grimy service station restroom served as medical station. In the smudgy mirror, he carefully pulled the bandage off, washed his face as thoroughly as he could with the pump soap, and examined the wound.

The scar didn't look as swollen or traumatic as before, or maybe he was just more prepared this time. In the strange fluorescent light it looked gray and unreal, as if his face was made of clay and someone had furrowed a line right through his left eye.

He'd have to get used to it. No use moaning.

Hello, Crowe. How you liking Memphis so far? Time of my life, brother, time of my life.

It wasn't quite noon yet, which meant he had more than

seven hours before he had to meet Radnovian. The apartment was out, obviously. And he couldn't contact him by phone to set up a new meeting place—whether he liked it or not, Rad would be part of the effort to bring Crowe in now.

Fine, Crowe thought. He'd just have to set up a more *spontaneous* meeting.

By twelve-thirty, he checked in at a mid-line motel, one of the chain places, clean and nicely bland. He took a long shower, shaved, cleaned out and changed the bandages on his other wounds. He swallowed another pain pill. He made a point of not thinking, not on any conscious level.

Not that he was entirely successful. Little things kept nagging at the back of his brain, things like the strange symbol carved in Faith's temple—for some reason he couldn't put his finger on, that bothered him more than what the killer had done to the rest of her.

But he pushed it back down whenever it popped up. Better to let it simmer, let his subconscious work it out. He set the little digital alarm clock on the nightstand for 5:00 pm, not really thinking he would fall asleep but just as a precautionary measure. He stretched out fully clothed on the bed, arms behind his head, and stared at the ceiling. He felt something in his jacket pocket, something crinkly. He pulled out a crumpled piece of paper—the Church pamphlet from the Welling's house.

He crumpled it up into a ball and tossed it across the room. It bounced off the wall and rolled to a stop near the nightstand.

Fuck it, he thought. He closed his eyes, and within minutes he'd fallen asleep.

The dreams that played out in his head were scattered fragments. But the Ghost Cat wandered through them, the way a real cat wanders from room to room. In some rooms, the Cat was whole, it was alive and healthy, but in other rooms it would come through the door and pieces of it would be gone, blood would be matted in its fur, bits of bone would be sticking out of it.

He was a boy again in the dreams, but not *himself* as a boy. He was someone else. He was a boy who was afraid and elated and shamed all at once. He was a boy holding a kitchen knife, and blood, someone or something else's blood, was hot on his face.

The beeping of the alarm clock woke him and he opened his eyes and stared at nothing for a full minute before reaching over to slap the clock quiet.

34

Radnovian lived in a refurbished old apartment building on a pleasant little street near the University campus, and by five-thirty Crowe was in his neighborhood. The sky was already going pale but the temperature didn't seem to be dropping much. This whole winter business was starting to get to him; he couldn't remember Memphis ever being quite this bleak and cold and gray before. Or maybe it was just him.

He cruised up and down his street a couple of times, and for a half-hour or so drove around the neighboring streets. He kept his eyes open. There were a lot of young people around, late 'teens and early twenties, students. Crowe would have expected that, since the campus was only blocks away, but none of them seemed in any particular hurry to get to classes or anywhere else for that matter. Young neo-hippies mostly, with a few jock-types mixed in to soften the flavor. Some of them were on the sidewalk, coming to or from the campus, but most seemed to be just hanging around. They all eyed Crowe with absolutely zero interest as he drove past.

At around six, he parked in the lot of an apartment building on the next block over from Rad's place. Through a row of cherry trees that had shed their leaves, he had a good view of the building and its parking lot. He shut off the engine and waited.

He'd had the cell phone off, but now he flipped it on and saw that Vitower had called three times in the last four hours. Only one message, though: "Crowe, call me as soon as you get this. I haven't heard from you. That Wills bastard was here, and I need to know what the fuck is going on. Call me post-fucking-haste."

Crowe turned the phone back off.

After twenty minutes, Rad came out of the building, bundled in a thick black winter coat and wearing a ski cap over his balding head. He twirled his car keys on his finger as he trotted over to his car, a deep red Pontiac G6.

He was alone.

Crowe watched as he got in the Pontiac, started it up, and pulled out. He kept watching as Rad stopped at the intersection, then took a right onto the main road, heading in the direction of downtown.

He waited for a full minute, scanning up and down the street for any sign of cops tagging along behind him. If they were there, they were too good to be spotted. Crowe keyed the ignition and headed out.

His place was just off Front Street, but Crowe pulled up to the curb on Front itself, switched off the car, and got out. Pulling his coat collar tight around his neck, he trotted up to the corner and stopped. His building was half a block up, and he could see it clearly from where he stood.

Rad's Pontiac was parked across the street from the building, wedged between a beat-to-shit Cavalier and a dirty white Nissan. He'd be in the building now, maybe knocking impatiently at Crowe's door or yakking it up with the ever-present Harriston. *He was here late last night*, Harriston would be saying. *Thought I heard him leave again real early in the morning. Haven't seen him since.* And, blowing cigarette smoke from out of his lungs, *Say, what's going on anyway? We don't want no trouble in this building, y'know?*

Crowe leaned against the lamppost and waited. At five after

seven, with the gray finally giving in to night, Rad came out of the building and walked to his car. He got in, started the engine. He sat there for another ten minutes while Crowe's bones got steadily stiffer and stiffer in the cold.

Finally his taillights flashed as he put the car in gear, and Crowe hurried back to the Taurus.

Rad came out onto Front Street just as Crowe started his car. Rad passed him, heading toward Union, and Crowe had to do an illegal U to catch up to him. Rad took a right on Union, heading east again, and Crowe followed, being careful to keep two or three cars between them.

There was a barbeque joint a few blocks up Union, on the right. Rad pulled into it without using a turn signal. Crowe passed it, turned down the next street, and made a big square through the subs to get back to Union again. A minute and a half had gone by; plenty of time. He pulled into the barbecue's lot and parked next to Rad's car, where he had a good view in the rear view mirror of the inside of the restaurant.

Rad was sitting in a booth by the window. He was giving his order to a pretty young waitress, who smiled at him very professionally. After a few seconds, she left him, and he stood up and made his way across the restaurant toward the restrooms.

Crowe grinned and got out of the car and went inside.

The aroma of cooking pork and tangy barbeque sauce set his mouth watering. He wished he had more time; he could've killed a pork barbeque sandwich just then. "Evening, sir," the hostess said. "How many?"

"I'm meeting a buddy," Crowe said. "Is he here yet? Thin guy, sorta balding on top?"

"Yes, sir, he sure is." She indicated the booth Rad was using. "I think he just went to the restroom."

"Oh, good." Then, smiling, "Actually, that sounds like a good idea."

She smiled dutifully and Crowe winked at her and walked to the men's room.

It was small, but clean and well-lit, with two urinals and one stall. The stall door was closed. When he walked in, he heard Rad clear his throat—the universal heads-up sound to indicate someone was present.

They were alone in there.

Grinning, Crowe rattled the door to the stall. In a small voice, Rad said, "Hey, oh. Uh. Occupied, friend."

Crowe pounded on the door, hard.

"Hey, what the hell?" Rad said, more nervous than pissed.

Crowe took a step back and kicked the door open with his heel.

It banged hollow against the stall, and Rad, sitting on the closed toilet lid, stared up at him blankly. He had a rubber tourniquet around his arm and a needle half in a vein. His kit had fallen to the floor.

"Crowe?" he said dumbly. "Hey, what…"

Crowe grabbed him by his neck and yanked him up, slammed him against the wall. He said, "What's the news, Rad?"

"What do you… what do you mean?"

"I mean, how hard are they looking for me? They got you involved yet?"

The needle fell out of his arm and clattered on the floor. He said, "Listen, man, listen. I have nothing to do with any of that, right? I mean, yeah, they're looking for you, but that doesn't involve me. You know that."

"You didn't tell anyone you were meeting me?"

"No, man, I promise!" he said. "Why would I do that? Jesus, that would be stupid, wouldn't it? Why would I incriminate myself like that?"

Crowe loosened his hold on Rad's neck a little, and Rad said, "Christ, Crowe, what the hell did you get yourself into? They say that woman was butchered. Why? Why would you do something like that?"

"I didn't. And Wills knows I didn't."

"Whatever, man, they still have every intention of bringing you down hard. Don't be surprised if they decide to just shoot you on sight. I mean, that chick was carved up like a turkey, from what I heard."

"Her name was Faith," Crowe said. "Faith..." He wanted to say her last name, but he didn't know what it was. That bothered him. He gripped Rad's throat tighter and, choking, Rad clawed at his fingers.

Crowe said, "You brought what I asked you to bring?"

Rad nodded, face going red.

"Where?"

He said, "C... car... in my...car..."

Crowe let go of him, and Rad nearly collapsed, clutching his throat and coughing. "Jesus!" he said. "Crowe, for Christ's sake, you... you don't have to..."

"Come on," Crowe said. "Pick your stuff up off the floor. We're gonna take a ride in your car."

35

"Where are we going?" Rad said, weaving through traffic on Union. He had his electric razor in one hand but hadn't turned it on.

"Just drive."

The accordion file on Peter Murke rested in Crowe's lap, and while Rad drove he opened it up and started leafing through it. It was moderately thick, about one hundred pages, mostly pertaining to the murder of Patricia Welling. Some of it, though, involved the murders he was suspected of, or the murders they knew he'd committed but had nothing solid for. There were about ten pages of information about Murke himself.

Rad took a left on Fourth Street, his fingers tight on the wheel. He finally put the electric razor down on the seat between them and said, "I should tell you, Crowe, just to be fair… I, uh, just had a hit—part of one, anyway—and I maybe shouldn't be driving."

"You can handle it," Crowe said, barely looking at him. He was actually thankful Rad had a little dope in him. It made him far less likely to try anything brave.

He pulled the info about Murke out and slid the rest back into the accordion.

Peter Murke, 24 years old when he was arrested two years

ago. Five foot seven, 168 pounds. Sandy blond hair, brown eyes, no distinguishing marks. Born in Biloxi, Mississippi, to a single mother whose police record included prostitution, possession of cocaine with intent to sell, and child endangerment.

Murke was already off to a beautiful start.

By age ten, he was seeing a child psychologist twice a month. Acting out in school, getting in fights, skipping. He was the stereotypical quiet kid, picked on, disliked, teased. At sixteen, he got in a fight with the local bully and wound up breaking both the kid's arms, knocking out half his teeth, and wouldn't stop kicking the kid in the head until a group of teachers pulled him off. He was expelled for that. But the bully's parents didn't press charges, amazingly enough, and Murke didn't get sent to juvie.

Later that same year, Murke approached a policeman on the street and said, *"Please lock me up. I'm going to kill someone. I'm going to kill myself."*

By that time, his mother had taken off with a man, leaving young Murke to fend for himself. Attempts to track his mother down met with failure. They put Murke in front of a psychiatric board, found enough proof that he was a danger to himself and others, and had him committed for a period of three years.

He did well in the psychiatric hospital, according to the records. He took his pills and he attended group therapy and one-on-one sessions with a shrink, and by the time he was released he seemed a different person entirely. He smiled a great deal. He shook hands with people. He engaged in small talk.

And, police suspected, he started killing women within a week of his release.

The first victim that they suspected might have been his work was found just off I-40, midway between Nashville and Chattanooga. A '91 Ford Explorer was sighted in a ditch, and police found Julie Stanton, age 33, in the backseat, her throat sliced open and several bones broken. They decided that Julie Stanton had picked up a hitchhiker, who somehow got her to pull off on the side of the road, where he beat her nearly to death before cutting her throat.

Later investigation found that a man fitting Peter Murke's description had been spotted at a roadside convenience store in the area earlier that day.

Officially, Julie Stanton's murder was an open file. But unofficially, it was case closed. State police knew she was Peter Murke's first victim.

Crowe, on the other hand, knew that she wasn't. Peter Murke's first victim wasn't even human. Peter Murke's first victim haunted Crowe on a regular basis.

Rad said, "Hey. Hey, man."

"What?"

"I need to pull over, man. I'm... I'm getting drowsy."

Crowe looked at him and saw that his eyes were half-lidded and dark. His face had gone slack. Goddamn junkie.

"Fine. Pull into that drug store."

Rad did as he was told, finding a place to park outside a Walgreen's. He kept the engine running, mumbled, "Really tired, man. Feel good, though, you know?"

"Yeah."

"Gonna just chill awhile, right?" He leaned his head back on the headrest and looked at Crowe, smiling. "Tell you the truth, Crowe, you should try it someday."

Crowe ignored him, put the info on Murke back in the file and pulled out the reports on Patricia Welling, Jezzie Vitower, and three or four other suspected victims.

The first thing he saw in the coroner's report on Patricia Welling made him stop cold.

There were the usual ugly close-up photos of the corpse, accompanied by detailed descriptions of each and every wound. Each laceration on her body was catalogued and numbered, each bruise given special notation. But the photo that happened to be on top was a close-up of young Patricia's back, near her left hip.

Murke had carved a symbol there in the soft flesh. A cross, with descending arms, topped by a bloated-looking heart-shape.

Crowe flipped quickly to the photos of Jezzie Vitower. Buried within all the other post-mortem photos was one of her abdomen, just below her belly button and slightly to the right. The same symbol. The same carved cross with lowered arms and a heart for a head. Just like on Faith's temple.

He'd seen it before. He'd seen it on Garay's stomach. Faith's brother.

And he'd seen it one other place as well.

The accordion file resting in his lap, he looked out the window at the flashing lights of the Walgreen's and muttered to himself. He'd very nearly forgotten that Radnovian was even in the car.

And that was a huge mistake, because Rad chose that exact moment to act like a cop, probably for the first time in years.

From the corner of his eye, Crowe saw Rad's left hand dip down below the car seat and come up with a standard police issue .45. He swung it around in Crowe's direction, aimed, so close the barrel touched Crowe's jaw, and said, "Don't move a muscle! Don't even breathe!"

Crowe breathed—no real option on that one—but didn't move. He stared straight ahead.

"This bullshit ends now," Rad said. "This pushing me around. I'm a goddamn cop, Crowe, and you act like I'm some kinda punk."

Crowe didn't say anything.

"You think just because I like to shoot up a little, I'm some kinda push-over, man? I don't know how to do my job? Well, I got news for you. I'm completely straight right now. You bust into that bathroom stall before I had a chance to dose myself. I reckon I should thank you for that."

Crowe shrugged. "Think nothing of it. But what now?"

Rad tapped the gun barrel against Crowe's jaw, hard. "What do you think? I'm gonna arrest you."

"You sure that's such a good idea?"

He sneered. "Yeah, I'm sure. Why the hell wouldn't I be sure?"

"Considering the way we ran into each other today—you

know, you with a needle in your arm and all—I just thought it might not be such a great idea."

"That has nothing to do with anything. Like I said, I'm straight right now. I can arrest you, bring you in, and it has nothing to do with anything else."

"If you say so. It's just that…" Crowe shrugged again.

"It's just that what?"

"Well, if I start talking about what you were doing in that bathroom stall, they may want to give you a drug test. You think you'd pass it? I mean, a lot of your fellow cops know you shoot smack, yeah? What would happen if they had something to substantiate it? How do you think you'd stand?"

Rad said, "They wouldn't do that," but he looked a little uncertain. "They wouldn't make me do a drug test, just on the word of some scumbag murderer."

"You're probably right," Crowe said. "Odds are, they won't even listen to me. I figure, what… about a twenty percent chance? You're probably safe. Yeah. You should just arrest me. It's worth the risk, isn't it?"

His face twisted, but the gun barrel didn't move from Crowe's jaw.

He said, very quietly, "I know something that's even less risky. You could wind up dead, resisting arrest."

Crowe frowned. "Yeah. There's always that."

"I saw you in front of the Walgreen's. I tried to arrest you. You shot at me. And I had no choice, I had to gun you down."

"That sounds pretty good."

He nodded. "Get out of the car," he said.

Crowe laughed. "No."

"Get out of the goddamn car, Crowe!"

"If you're gonna shoot me, Rad, you'll have to do it right here. Right in your passenger seat."

He said, "You dirty sonofabitch, get out of—"

Crowe jerked his head back, out of the line of fire, grabbed Rad's wrist with his right, and hit him in the nose with his left. The space was too close so there wasn't much power in the punch, but it managed to bring blood. Rad made a startled grunting noise, hitting the back of his head on the driver's side window, and his gun went off.

The front windshield cracked into spider-webs on the passenger side as the bullet plowed through it. Crowe twisted his wrist hard, and the gun fell to the floorboards. Not letting go, he elbowed Rad hard in the throat, grabbed the back of his neck with his left, and slammed his face into the steering wheel.

Nose cartilage cracked, blood spattered on the dashboard. Crowe smashed his face against the steering wheel twice more, just to be certain, and let him go.

Rad slumped back against his seat and his head tilted and came to rest against the window. He was out.

Amazingly, the gunshot hadn't attracted any attention. The parking lot had been mercifully empty when the gun went off. And in this part of Memphis, guns going off weren't exactly big news anyway.

That didn't mean it was time to take it easy. After a few seconds of catching his breath, Crowe picked up Rad's .45, shoved it in his coat pocket, and stepped out of the Pontiac. He went around to the driver's side, and pushed Rad's limp body out of the way until he was half on the seat and half on the floorboards on the passenger side. Crowe climbed in and shut the door behind him. The engine had been running the whole time, and the car was almost too warm now. The smell of gunpowder and fresh blood was overwhelming.

Crowe's cell phone buzzed in his coat pocket. He pulled it out and looked at it. Vitower again. He put it away.

The windshield was only cracked and spider-webbed on the passenger side, so he had no problem seeing through it. He drove away from the parking lot.

They were just north of the industrial section. He drove until they were in the heart of a particularly dank industrial park, pulled around behind a gray and lifeless warehouse, and got out of the car. He opened the passenger door and Rad almost fell out. Crowe righted him and got a grip under his armpits and pulled him out. There was a pick-up truck by the Dumpsters, so he hauled Rad over to it and dumped him in the truck's bed.

He would be stiff and cold as hell in the morning, but the temperature wasn't expected to drop too low so Crowe felt sure he'd survive the night. He checked his pockets to make sure he still had his heroin kit on him; he did. That made Crowe laugh a little. If the cops found him before he woke up, he'd have some serious explaining to do. It might even mean the end of his career.

Good luck, Rad. Crowe got back in the car and checked his watch. Eight-thirty. The night was still young, and he still had a lot to do.

36

The timing couldn't have been better. The mall's shops closed at nine o'clock; by nine-thirty even the latest of stragglers was gone and by a quarter to ten only the employees were left, ragged and weary after a long day of forced smiles and brittle politeness.

At nine-thirty, Crowe pulled in near the employee parking area on the lower level of the concrete parking structure. Her car was a sporty dark blue GTO. It was parked near the entrance to the mall's anchor department store. He parked a few empty spaces down, turned off the ignition, and waited.

She came out a few minutes later. A mall security guard wished her a good evening and locked the mall employee door behind her. Crowe half-expected him to offer to walk her to her car, but he didn't. Probably she'd said no enough times that he didn't bother with it anymore.

Her heels clicked on the concrete as she bee-lined for the GTO. He got out of the Pontiac and started toward her. She was so focused on getting out of the cold that she didn't even notice him. She had her key in the lock when he said, "Dallas."

She jumped, dropped her keys, whirled to face him, looking like a cornered animal about to attack. It struck him again, that strangely feral look she had, with her dark eye make-up and red mouth and wild red hair. When she saw who it was she relaxed and said, "Jesus Christ, you scared the shit out of me!"

He kept walking toward her.

"What the hell are you doing here? Christ! You don't just creep up on someone like that."

They were alone on this level of the parking structure. From above, a car engine revved, and a faulty suspension squealed, and whoever it was pulled out and drove away.

When he was right in front of her he grabbed her by the shoulders and shoved her back against the door of the GTO. She said, "Hey—" and he shook her, hard, his fingers digging into her shoulders.

"Crowe, what are you—"

"Shut up," he said. "You'll talk when I ask you a question."

"Crowe—"

Holding her against the car, he ripped open her coat, started pulling her blouse out of her skirt. She said, "Jesus, Crowe, no," and started struggling to get away from him. "Please don't do this."

What she was thinking hadn't even occurred to him, and when it finally did it just irritated him. He said, "Knock it off," and continued pulling up the blouse until her midriff was bare.

He took a step back, one hand still holding her shoulder, and looked down to see the tattoo on her stomach, right next to her belly button. He'd only caught a glimpse of it before, up at Dr. Maggie's farmhouse, when she'd stood up and stretched.

A small cross, arms descending, crowned by a simple heart.

She saw her chance and took it. The second he looked away from her eyes, she swung at him with her right, nailing him good in the jaw. He stumbled back a step and she turned to run, back toward the mall entrance. He grabbed her arm and spun her around.

"The tattoo," he said.

She tried to jerk her arm away, and then tried to punch him again. He caught her fist with his other hand and pushed it down to her side. "Let go of me!" she said.

"The tattoo," he said again. "What is it?"

"You sonofabitch, let me go!"

"Dallas, don't think I won't hurt you. I'm going to ask you one more time. What is that goddamn tattoo?"

She snarled and glared like a wild animal, but stopped struggling. "What do you care what my tattoo is? Have you lost your goddamn mind?"

He put some pressure on the arm he was holding, and she winced.

"Maybe," he said. "Maybe I'm a complete raving lunatic. And maybe that means you should answer my question before I break your arm."

"It's just a tattoo, Christ!"

"When did you get it?"

"I don't know. About… about three years ago, I guess."

"Where?"

"At a goddamn tattoo parlor, Jesus!"

"What is it? What does it mean?"

"Crowe, it's just a tattoo."

He twisted her arm a little more, pressing up against her, and she hissed painfully through her teeth. "Don't lie," he said. "Or the next sound your body makes will be a snap. Do you understand me?"

Her breath came hard and ragged, and she nodded.

He said, "Do you know how many have died already? Do you know how many corpses have that same symbol on them? Exactly the same, but not in ink."

"What are you talk—"

"Not in ink, but in blood, Dallas. Carved, right into their flesh."

"Jesus," she said. "I don't know what you're talking about…"

He let go of her, and she slumped against the GTO, rubbing her shoulder and glaring. He said, "You told me, a few weeks ago, that you got religion for a while, but that it didn't take. You remember you telling me that?"

She nodded sullenly.

"You gave it a go, but decided it wasn't for you. That's when you got the tattoo, isn't it?"

"Yes. So what?"

"What does it mean?"

She said, "It's just a symbol, is all. A sign of faith."

"For the Society of Christ the Fisher?"

She blinked, surprised. "How do you…"

"Is that the church you went to?"

She nodded. "Yes, but how did you—"

He said, "It's no ordinary church, is it?"

"What do you mean? Of course it's an ordinary church."

"People are dead, Dallas. People are dead, and that symbol you have tattooed on your stomach is carved right into them."

She didn't say anything for a moment, only looked at him blankly. Her eyes were wide and dead-looking. When she finally spoke, her voice was a whisper. She said, "Carved."

"With a razor blade."

Her lower lip quivered, very slightly, and her dead eyes went watery. "With a razor…" she said. And then, "You… you're all over the news, you know that? They're saying you killed a woman."

"You think that's true?"

"I don't know. No, I don't think it is."

"Her name was Faith. She was a friend of mine."

"A good friend?"

For a beat longer than it should have taken, he hesitated. He said, "No."

Dallas nodded. Behind them, the mall employee entrance opened again, and two men came out, laughing and carrying on.

"Come on," one said to the other. "I'll buy ya a beer."

"Naw, I gotta get home. Wife'll be pissed if I show up late tonight."

"Jeez, who wears the pants in your house?"

They both laughed and, walking past them, nodded. One said, "How ya doin'?" He got no answer, shrugged, and the two of them walked on to their cars.

When they'd pulled out and left, Crowe said, "Tell me about the Society."

Dallas shook her head, said, "They're an ordinary church. Completely. Except…"

"Except what?"

"Except that, well… there's a select group of them, some of the longtime members, or the ones with money. The hierarchy, I guess you'd call them. A church within the church. They have a more… specific… agenda."

"What is it?"

"They… sorta play dirty, if you know what I mean. They expose, in the press, anyone they judge to be sinners." She laughed, without humor. "And that's a lot of people, you know."

"How did you get involved with them?"

She said, "Through Jezzie. She… she and Marco were members."

"Was Chester involved, too?"

She shook her head. "No. They didn't tell him about it. Just me. I think… well, they sorta… wanted me."

"Wanted you?"

"You know, for… well, they liked to swing on occasion. And I think Jezzie had me pegged."

"Wait a minute," Crowe said. "That's not exactly behavior suiting someone in that group, is it?"

"I suppose not. But Marco Vitower sort of fails that test on quite a few levels, doesn't he? They only reason they were members was because of the influence the group has. Why do you think Vitower is practically untouchable? They have a lot of members, Crowe, and some of them are pretty well-placed."

"What are they called?"

She said, "They don't really have a name. But, amongst themselves, it's a little different. Jezzie told me once that, in the past, their ideas were considered heretical, and so that's what they call themselves. The Heretics."

"The Heretics," Crowe said. "Goddamnit."

"They mean it ironically, of course. As far as they're concerned, it's everyone else who are heretics, not them."

Crowe said, "Why did you leave the group?"

She shrugged. "It started feeling… weird. Especially after Jezzie was killed. Fletcher seemed almost—"

"Fletcher? Fletcher Welling?"

"Yes. He seemed almost glad Jezzie was dead. He and Vitower had an argument about it, and Vitower left the group. It was just me then, and the only reason I was there to begin with was because of Jezzie. I left the same day Vitower did."

"Dallas, the Heretics killed Jezzie."

She shook her head. "No. They never killed anyone. They just did things like… exposing people in the media. You know? Calling them out. In a way, I kinda like that part of it, even though the whole God-bothering part started seeming more and more ridiculous to me. The stuff where they would call out the bad guys, reveal their cheating or lying or stealing, I really liked that part. They really let a lot of bad guys have it right in the ass."

"Right," Crowe said. "All the bad guys, except the ones who were members."

"Well, I guess you can't nail everyone."

"You can't be that blind, Dallas. Jezzie was killed because she was a sinner. A fornicator."

"Fornicator? Oh, for God's sake—"

"And Patricia Welling was killed because she was a drug addict. Or maybe it was because she didn't respect her parents. I don't know. It doesn't matter why. They were both murdered by the Heretics."

An icy wind cut through the structure, flailing at their coats, messing up her already crazy hair. She stiffened against the cold and shook her head. "No, that's not true. It was Murke who killed them. Peter Murke."

"Murke is one of them."

"That's insane."

"Both of them have that symbol, Dallas, carved right into their flesh. The symbol of the Heretics."

She was still shaking her head. "No," she said. "No, that can't be true. It can't."

Crowe laughed. "Christ, Dallas. Only you. Only you could be a member of a secret society and not even know it. A bunch of lunatics masquerading as a religious group, its numbers filled up with the rich and powerful. Meeting in secret. Getting tattoos. Are you that naïve?"

"It's not a secret society," she said. "For God's sake, you make it sound like some sort of conspiracy or something."

"It is a conspiracy, you stupid bitch."

"No," she said, although she didn't sound quite as certain anymore. "No, Crowe. It's nothing at all."

"Right," he said. "Nothing at all. Just ritual murder."

She said, "Are you telling me that Fletcher Welling had his own daughter killed, Crowe? Do you realize how crazy that sounds?"

"That's exactly what I'm telling you. And Patricia's murder was the one they screwed up on. Murke left too many clues behind, and they finally caught up with him. The Heretics had to scramble to cover their tracks. They're the ones who sprung him."

She looked at him, doubt playing across her face, her eyes blinking rapidly. She said, "If you're quite done, I'm leaving now. I think I've heard all I need to about this."

He stepped away from her. There was no reason to stop her from going, but he felt a strange sense of disappointment. What had he been hoping for? An ally? Someone who could help? But that was ridiculous, of course. He was in this alone.

She opened her car door, making sure to keep one eye on him in case he went spontaneously psychotic. She slid into the car, started it. Before she closed the door, she said, "You should never have come back to Memphis."

He said, "Don't talk to anyone from the Society."

She shook her head, slammed the door shut, and backed out.

He watched her drive off. The wind funneled through the parking structure, and little cold fingers clawed at his face and hands and plucked at his coat.

The sound of her engine died away, and the structure was quiet except for the plaintive moaning of the icy wind. The naked yellow lights flickered. Somewhere in another part of the structure, a chain was banging against the concrete, and it echoed dimly through the empty levels.

He stood there for a long minute, letting the cold work its way into his bones. Dallas. She always did exactly what he expected her to do, and yet, every time, he was disappointed.

He sighed and shoved his hands in his pockets and turned to walk back to the Pontiac.

There were four of them, all standing in front of the car, waiting for him very patiently.

37

There were no other vehicles on this level, and he hadn't heard them approaching. Sneaky bastards. The two guys dressed like businessmen from the '70's stood smiling at him, flanked on the right by the muscular James Dean wannabe, wearing his jeans and tee-shirt and a leather jacket, and on the left by the older man with the red cowboy hat.

"Mr. Crowe," one of the businessmen said. "It would probably be in your best interests to go along with Mrs. Paine in this matter."

Crowe didn't say anything.

The businessman said, "It's good to see that you're recovering from your wounds."

Crowe felt the metal of the gun in his pocket. Could he take out all four of them before they got him? Not likely; there was only a distance of about ten feet between them, and he'd seen how fast these bastards were with their knives.

The other businessman said, "I hope someone is taking notes regarding Mrs. Paine. I consider this reasonable evidence that she's an adulteress."

His partner said, "Why, Stone? Because she talked to Mr. Crowe here?"

"And, last night, yes? He showed up at her home very late and stayed until morning."

"It bears looking into."

Crowe said, "You people killed Faith."

"No, that wasn't us. It was Peter. He… he was there to see you, of course, but you were nowhere around. So he took out his frustration on your female."

"What do you want?"

They didn't seem to be armed at the moment—or at least they didn't have their weapons in their hands. The thinner of the two businessmen said, "My name's Eckstine. And this is my associate, Stone."

The other businessman nodded and straightened his tie.

"The hooligan in the leather jacket," Eckstine said, "is Nick. And this is Larry."

The cowboy said, "Howdy, Crowe."

"Well," Crowe said. "Now that we're all friends. What can I do for you?"

"You can start," Stone said, "by removing your hand from your pocket. Removing it without the gun in it."

Crowe let go of the gun and pulled his hand out.

Eckstine said, "We're not here to kill you, Mr. Crowe. Not this time."

The 'hooligan' called Nick said, "That's a fuckin' shame, too. I voted for slicing you into little tiny pieces."

"Me too," said the cowboy, Larry. "Nothin' personal-like, mind ya. It just woulda been a helluva lot easier. Path of least resistance, and all that."

"See," Eckstine said. "It's like this, Mr. Crowe. You really shouldn't even be here. You know? You've sort of found yourself involved in matters that don't really concern you directly. Mr. Vitower can't seem to find the wherewithal to fight his own battles—which I personally find rather cowardly—and so he's sent someone he doesn't mind seeing die."

"Vitower just wants Murke," Crowe said.

"Yes, that's true. Really, he should know better. He had a

complete falling-out, you see, with some of our associates. It goes way beyond a spat between him and Peter."

"A spat," Crowe said. "Funny."

Eckstine nodded. "Funny, yes. I guess so, depending on one's sense of humor. Yes, I guess I can see the humor in it. But honestly, I wasn't trying to be funny."

Stone, losing patience with his partner, said, "The point is, none of this really involves you, Mr. Crowe. A council was held, and killing you was voted down. They just don't know enough about you to determine whether or not you would qualify as being sanctified."

"Sanctified?"

"Well, despite the differences of opinion amongst our brethren of late, we can't just go around killing whoever we want to, can we? That's what got Peter into such trouble. We have to be careful. And let's be honest—you're not long for freedom anyway, are you? The police are going to catch up to you very soon, and take the burden out of our hands."

"Who are you people, exactly?"

Nick said, "That don't concern you."

Crowe nodded. "Let me guess. Basically, you're all a bunch of psychos. Yeah? A bunch of nut-cases who, for whatever reason, are particularly susceptible to religious conversion. The Society gathered you all up from various pits around the country, gave you some sort of purpose, made you feel like you were part of something bigger and better. Am I on the right track?"

The businessmen just smiled patiently. Larry the cowboy turned his head and spat on the concrete. Nick glared.

Crowe said, "You all hooked up with a group of fanatics who think that the only way to save the world is through… what? Killing sinners? Or rather, they have *you* lot kill them. Because, really, only a bunch of raving lunatics would think that's a good idea."

Nick said, "We ain't raving lunatics, motherfucker. We're Sacred Executioners."

Stone said, "Shut up, Nick."

Crowe laughed. “Sacred Executioners. Well, that’s something, isn’t it?”

Nick said, “I don’t have to stand here and listen to this cocksucker insult me. I’ve cut men’s heads off for less than that.”

“Nick. Shut it.”

Nick shut it, but a long exotic-looking blade, about twelve inches, had appeared in his fist, and he looked ready at that moment to give up his religious conversion entirely just to see Crowe’s blood.

Crowe said, “So you Sacred Executioners can’t kill me? Unless I’m sanctified?”

Eckstine said, “I wouldn’t put it into those exact words, Mr. Crowe. We are authorized to kill you if you display an unwillingness to let this matter rest. Which, if you don’t mind me saying so, you seem to be doing. But it would be a regrettable situation.”

“I don’t think your boy Nick there would regret it.”

Nick said, “Not one bit.”

Stone said, “Enough of this. Are you going to drop this matter, Mr. Crowe?”

“You’ll kill me if I don’t?”

Stone said, “You’ll be… sacrificed.”

Crowe nodded. “Okay, then. I’ll drop it.”

“And leave Memphis?”

“And leave Memphis.”

Larry the Cowboy chuckled. “Well, that was just too easy, wasn’t it? Fellas, I think maybe ole’ Crowe ain’t bein’ straight here.”

“You boys have orders not to kill me if I tell you I’m going to drop the whole thing. Yeah?”

Eckstine frowned. “Yes. That’s right.”

“Okay then. Consider it dropped. I’ll see you around.”

He waited for them to move away from the car. They didn’t. He took a step toward them and another, fishing the keys out of his pocket. When he was right in front of Eckstine, Crowe looked at him and said, “Anything else?”

Eckstine said, very quietly, "You're lying. You have no intention of dropping this."

Crowe shrugged.

Nick said, "This is fucking stupid. We should just kill him. He refused to back off. He tried to put up a fight, said he'd give up over his dead body."

Larry rubbed his jaw. "That sounds about right. The fella just don't have the sense God gave a monkey. He pulled out his gun, was fixin' to shoot one of us. We didn't have no choice but to kill him."

Eckstine eyed Crowe, but spoke to the others. "Is that the way it happened?" he said.

"I reckon so," Larry said.

"That's what happened," Nick said.

Eckstine glanced at Stone. Stone looked thoughtful for a moment, then nodded. He said, "Regrettably, yes. We had to kill him."

Eckstine said, "What a shame," and pulled his machete out from inside his coat.

Crowe had his keys gripped in his fist, protruding through his fingers like claws. Before Eckstine's machete had cleared, Crowe lunged at him with the keys, gouging him in his right eye. He grunted in pain and fell back against the hood of the G6. Stone was next closest—he already had his knives out, one in each hand.

Larry was just pulling a revolver out of a holster under his jacket. Nick was moving in from the left with his blade.

With his right Crowe yanked the .45 out of his pocket, and with his left grabbed Eckstine by the hair and pulled him up and threw him stumbling into Larry. Stone's knives flashed, and one sharp edge sliced through Crowe's coat sleeve as he stepped back and raised the gun.

Larry had pushed Eckstine out of his way and had his revolver cocked and ready to shoot. Crowe fired first, and got him in the wrist. The shot echoed through the parking structure like an explosion.

Larry said, "Arrrh!"—more pirate than cowboy—and his gun flew out of his hand. It was a goddamn impressive shot, or would've been if Crowe had actually meant to do it.

While Larry grabbed his shattered wrist and dropped to his knees, Stone had taken another lunge at Crowe, cutting him along the top of the left hand. Crowe tried to elbow him in the throat, but he sidestepped and the blow skittered along Stone's shoulder. He slashed again with the knife in his right hand, cutting straight down through Crowe's coat and almost snagging the blade on the seams.

Crowe took advantage of the second-long hang-up and punched him in the face. The knife came free and Stone stumbled back a step or two.

All of this had taken something like five seconds. Crowe knew it would be a miracle if he survived another five.

From the corner of his eye he saw Nick moving in, his exotic blade flashing in the yellow light, and threw himself back against Eckstine. Nick's lunge missed by about a foot. From the hood of the car, Crowe kicked out blindly and caught him in the stomach. Nick huffed air but didn't drop his knife.

Crowe swung his gun around and shot Nick in the chest. It was at such close range that it literally knocked him right off his feet, and he flew back a good distance before his lifeless body hit the concrete.

Stone was coming up on him again, but Crowe swung the gun in his direction and fired blind. Stone dove out of the way, and Crowe fired again, kicking up concrete inches away from his shoe.

Stone ran, making it around the corner to the level below just ahead of another bullet.

Eckstine was on the concrete in front of the G6, clutching his face and moaning. Blood poured out from between his fingers. Crowe glanced around. Larry was gone.

"My eye..." Eckstine said. "My eye, oh Christ."

Crowe frowned at him. "Hurts, doesn't it?" I said.

"Oh, Jesus, help me. Sweet Jesus in Heaven..."

Crowe pointed the .45 at his head, and Eckstine's one good eye grew wide between his fingers. He said, "Crowe, you don't… you don't have to kill me. I'm no threat to you now. Please. I'll go… I'll go away and you'll never see… see me again…"

Crowe was in no mood for mercy at the moment. He shot Eckstine in the head.

38

It took ten minutes to get to Germantown from the Mall of Memphis. If Bartlett was where the middle-to upper class working stiffs of Memphis went at the end of the day, Germantown was the place they never left. It had a reputation for being lily-white and completely removed from the city. That reputation wasn't entirely true, but it was true enough.

Brinkley Drive was a short block, maybe six or eight houses on each side. Mostly Colonials with large front lawns and well-tended landscaping, the occasional ranch. Crowe drove up and down it five or six times but didn't spot Garay's Grand Prix. Finally he parked at the end of the block where he had a good view of the whole street and waited.

He was tired, dizzy, and in a lot of pain, and it was all he could do to keep from falling asleep in the cold. There was only one streetlamp, way down at the other end of the street, and the spot he'd parked in was pitch dark. He put a new clip in the .45, checked the action, and stuck it in his waistband, under the coat.

He waited.

It was a quiet street. For over half an hour, not a single car came through. Some lights came on in the upstairs window of a house on the left side, then went off again. In the house next to it, he saw the shadows of people moving around, but they too disappeared after a moment.

He fell asleep, but woke up when a car rumbled past, its headlights cutting a slice out of the darkness. Heavy bass thumped dully from inside the car, loud enough that Crowe could hear the dashboard rattling. It was Garay.

The Grand Prix pulled into the driveway of one of the ranch houses, about halfway up the street. The porch light came on. Garay cut the engine and the rumbling bass stopped. He got out of the car and trotted up to the house.

Crowe could see another figure in the doorway, waiting for him—his mother. Faith's mother. Crowe wondered if they knew about her already. How could they not? If it was already on the news, the cops were obligated to tell the immediate family first. But he didn't know if they'd released the victim's name yet. Should've been listening to the radio, Crowe thought. Again, he was going into something unprepared.

One thing was for certain: if they knew Faith was dead, then they knew Crowe was the one the cops liked for it.

Another thing he was certain of: Garay knew full-well Crowe didn't kill his sister. He had the tattoo, the mark of the Heretics. He knew.

When the porch light went off Crowe got out of the car and walked to the house. His head spun. His back and shoulder screamed for mercy. He ignored it all and kept walking.

He came up the driveway, half-expecting the porch light to come on, but it didn't. He tried the knob. The door was unlocked. Typical Germantown behavior, forgetting to lock the goddamn door.

He wondered if Garay's crew knew he lived in a nice house on a nice street, away from the squalor and degradation of Memphis. He wondered how they'd feel about it, if they knew. It couldn't be good for his cred, living in a neighborhood where you didn't even bother to lock the door.

The foyer was dark, the only light coming from the far end of the hall. Crowe closed the door gently behind him and, without moving, gave it a quick look-over. There was a sitting room immediately to the right, filled with the kind of overstuffed furniture that no one sits in and a walnut Grandfather clock that ticked away the seconds of life with all the compassion of a killer. To the left, a carpeted staircase leading up to the second floor.

Straight ahead, where the light came from, shadows moved and someone sobbed very softly. Garay was saying, "It's okay, Mama. It's gonna be okay," and the sobbing broke off a little, just long enough for her to say, "Oh my baby, my poor baby," before starting up again.

There was a door just under the staircase. Crowe moved quietly along the carpeted foyer, opened it. Linoleum-lined steps led down to a pitch-black basement. He stepped down onto the first stair and closed the door behind him, leaving it open only a fraction of an inch.

"Why?" the woman cried. "Why would somebody kill my baby? She never hurt no one."

"I don't know, Mama. I don't know."

"Oh God, oh God, my poor baby girl…"

"Shh, shh, Mama. I came as soon as I heard. I'm here now, Mama."

It felt strange, listening in on their grief, muted through the basement door. It made Faith's death more real, somehow. More real even than seeing her mutilated corpse. Crowe don't know why. Something like regret surged through him, and his body sagged a little.

He pushed it out.

It went on for a few more minutes, the old woman's crying getting softer and softer, and Garay doing his best to sooth her. Finally, Garay, "C'mon, Mama, let me help you upstairs. You gotta get some rest, okay?"

"No, I don't wanna sleep, I can't sleep."

"You need to, Mama, okay? Let me help you upstairs."

Crowe heard them shifting, standing up, and then moving

toward the foyer. They passed the basement door, inches away, the woman stifling now. Her feet shuffled on the carpet.

The stairs groaned above as they went up, and then Crowe couldn't hear anything.

He waited. About ten minutes went by.

The stairs groaned again, softer this time, and he heard Garay pause at the foot of the stairs. He sighed, muttered to himself, "Christ. Jesus Christ." The front door knob rattled briefly as he locked the door, and then he was moving through the foyer again, back toward the rear of the house. Peeking through the crack in the door, Crowe saw his shadow on the wall. He pulled the gun out of his waistband.

He opened the door just as Garary was passing it and placed the barrel against his temple.

"Not a sound," Crowe said. "Unless you want to involve your mama in this."

To his credit, Garay didn't jump or even flinch. He went stock-still, and, without even looking at him, said, "Crowe. You sonofabitch. You come into my goddamn home, you sonofabitch—"

"Shut up," Crowe said. Then, "Downstairs."

He flipped on the light switch and got behind Garay as the kid led the way down the steps. He was wearing a Chicago Bulls jersey, faded loose-fitting jeans and a pair of well-tended Timberland's. He kept his hands out, where Crowe could see them, doing the drill like an old pro.

The basement was partially finished, with an old well-used sofa facing a 52-inch flat screen and a fairly impressive sound system. There was a mini-fridge next to the sofa. On the far side of the basement was a workbench with all the tools carefully displayed on the wall. There was a length of heavy twine next to a box of nails.

They stopped in the middle of the basement and Garay said, "Well?"

Crowe motioned to a wooden chair near the workbench. "Sit down."

He did, looked up at Crowe with a pretty good impression of impatience. He said, "My sister died today. But you probably already know that."

"Reach over and grab that twine on the workbench."

Garay looked at it, and then back at Crowe. He actually smiled. "You gonna tie me up? How you plan on doing that? You'll have to lower your gun, and the second you do that, motherfucker, I'm gonna be all over you."

"That's a good point, Garay," Crowe said. As a solution, he took a step toward him and whacked the gun hard against his temple.

Garay slumped out of the chair, out cold.

39

He was awake five minutes later. By then, Crowe had him back in the chair, tied securely with twine, his wrists tied to arms of the chair and his ankles bound tight. After he was tied, Crowe pulled up his jersey to get a look at the tattoo on his abs; it was still there, of course. A simple black cross, topped with a slightly misshapen blood-red heart.

Securing Garay took a lot out of him, and Crowe was still breathing hard and fighting dizziness when Garay came to.

It took Garay a few moments to get his head together. Crowe gave him the time, saying nothing, until finally Garay peered up at him with bleary eyes and said, "You… you sonofabitch… if I get outta this I'm gonna kill you, I'm gonna rip your goddamn lungs out."

Crowe put away the gun and found a soiled cloth and a solid hammer on the workbench. Sears & Roebuck. The right tools for the job. He said, "Here's how this is gonna work, Garay. I'm not gonna get cute about it, and I'm not gonna engage in any banter with you. Understand? It's gonna be simple."

"You motherfucker—"

"I'm gonna ask you questions, very specific questions, and for every answer you give that makes me unhappy I'm going to smash one of your fingers with this hammer. Is that clear enough?"

Garay eyed the hammer, and finally some of the fear he'd been feeling began to show on this face. But he still had some bravado left. He said, "I ain't scared of you, Crowe."

"Not yet," Crowe said.

This was Crowe's element, hurting people. It was what the Old Man had paid him for, back in the day, and he was good at it. It was simply a matter of shifting perspective, shoving all the human aspects of mercy and compassion to another part of the brain and just going on machine-mode. He didn't get any pleasure from it, but he also didn't suffer remorse. It helped, too, that Crowe was exhausted beyond caring.

Garay clenched his fists, hiding his fingers, and it was all there in his eyes now, the knowledge that bad things were about to happen to him and there was nothing he could do to stop it.

Crowe said, "Keep your fingers out. If you don't, I'll just have to smash your hands first and believe me, that'll make things much worse."

Garay just looked at him, sweating now, teeth clenched and something like the shakes coming over him. He kept his fists tight.

In a quiet voice, he said, "You… you ain't any different than them. You think you're better? You ain't any different than them."

"Okay," Crowe said, and shoved the cloth in his mouth.

He smashed the hammer down on Garay's left hand.

Garay screamed against the cloth and his body spasmed, straining against the ropes. His fingers shot out like ten exclamation points against the chair arm.

Crowe brought the hammer down again, crunching his left little finger to a pulp.

Five minutes later, Garay had told him everything Crowe

needed to know, and it had only cost him his one hand and the pinky finger attached to it.

Crowe left him still tied to the chair, barely conscious and muttering to himself. Upstairs, he half-expected to see the mother, since even with the cloth in his mouth Garay hadn't been exactly quiet. But she was nowhere around. Grief must have sent right into the deepest of sleep; that's how some people deal with it.

Garay had some interesting things to say, things about the Society of Christ the Fisher.

"It's like… like I told you," Garay had said. "Vitower is old news. Bad Luck, they… they're the New Breed. Welling knew it. And it made a… it made a split in the Society."

"What kind of split?"

"Some of the others in the Society, they didn't wanna do deals with Bad Luck. But Welling trumped 'em… he wanted to get Vitower outta the picture. Vitower knew it. I don't know how, but he knew it. That's… that's why your man Vitower wants to kill Murke… it ain't got nothing to do with his dead bitch. Well… not much, anyway."

"I don't understand. Talk sense, Garay."

Garay was crying, looking at his mangled little finger and his flattened hand. "'Cuz, man… 'cuz Murke would be on Welling's side. And now… now that Murke is out, the others in the Society, they'll be, what, over-ruled."

So Bad Luck, Inc, were the Society's new first line of defense in the city now, doing the dirty work that didn't relate specifically to the Society's agenda. They'd been ordained. They'd been taken into the fold and given tattoos and the Word.

Vitower and his wife and certain select others—like Dallas—had been welcomed into the Society. And then Murke killed Jezzie: the beginning of the end for Vitower's future with them. If he'd been the kind of guy to shrug off his wife's murder, things might have taken a different turn. And Vitower probably knew that. And yet… and yet he'd decided his course, and to hell with the repercussions.

Crowe almost admired him for it.

Head spinning, Crowe left Garay's house and the cold night air didn't help clear things.

He was beyond exhausted. He remembered climbing behind the wheel, popping another three pain killers. The stitches between his shoulder blades had busted again and blood ran warm down his back. His right shoulder ached fiercely from exertion, and even the scar on his face felt as if it had been lit afire.

Somehow, some time later, he was at the motel, pulling up in the space in front of the room. He got out of the car and nearly stumbled on the walkway, and was dimly aware that it wasn't just the wounds; he was dangerously close to putting himself into oblivion with the pills.

It seemed like a minor consideration, though. In fact, it almost seemed like a goddamn good idea.

He managed to unlock the door after what seemed like a very long time, nearly fell inside, and slammed it shut behind him. Sleep, he thought. Some sleep, some oblivion, and he would be fine.

He leaned against the door, eyes closed, trying to will the strength in his legs just to make it to the bed.

When the bedside light snapped on and he heard the voice, he wasn't even surprised.

"Well, look what the cat dragged in," the voice said.

Crowe opened his eyes and saw Detective Wills, reclined on the bed, his gun leveled at him.

"Try to resist arrest, Crowe," he said. "Try it. 'cause there's nothing I'd rather do than shoot you down right here and now."

40

There was a bottle of whisky on the nightstand, and the bedside lamp shined through it and showed it nearly empty. The room reeked of it. Crowe willed the fuzziness in his head away, off to the corners, and tried to focus. Wills smiled at him and crossed his legs and wiggled his toes in his socks.

Crowe said, "Whisky and firearms don't mix."

"Are you kidding?" he said. "When I'm drinking whisky, that's when I like my gun the best."

"Probably," Crowe said, "that's the only time you can actually feel good about it. Right?"

Wills frowned briefly before understanding dawned and then a slow grin spread across his face. "Oh, right. That was Freudian, yeah? Ain't you the clever boy?"

His coat was draped over the little writing desk by the front door, and his shoes were arranged nicely at the foot of the bed. Crowe sighed and leaned back against the door, feeling all his muscles screaming. "Are you gonna shoot me, Wills? Or arrest me, or what? Because whatever it is, let's get on with it."

Wills sat up, stretching, and grabbed the bottle. With the gun still trained on Crowe, he took a long pull of whisky, finishing all but a nip of it. Burping, he tossed the bottle over his shoulder, where it bounced on the bed and rolled off to thump on the floor.

"Truth is," he said, "I haven't really decided yet, Crowe."

"Well, then. You care if I sit down?"

He motioned to the floor. "Go right ahead. Right there on the carpet, in front of the door."

Crowe slumped down carefully until he was sitting, legs splayed and hands on the carpet. It didn't feel any better than standing.

"You wanna know how I found you?" Wills said. "It was amazingly easy."

"Not really interested."

"Aw, come on. Don't you wanna hear about how the dumb-ass redneck cop tracked down the oh-so-clever crook?"

Crowe thought for a moment, and said, "Rad's Pontiac. GPS device or something, yeah?"

Wills looked disappointed, and Crowe couldn't help but laugh. "Yeah, Wills, that's really clever, boy. You sure did outsmart me."

He stood up, took one long stride across the room, and kicked Crowe in the gut with his bare foot. Crowe doubled up on the floor, not able to breath, and everything went dim around the edges.

While he struggled for breath, Wills said, "The stroke of genius was in knowing *who's* car you'd be in. Get it? You and Radnovian, you been like pigs in a poke. I figured you'd turn to him eventually. So after you killed that little piece of ass of yours, I—"

"Didn't kill her," Crowe said. "You know… you know I didn't…"

"What? I didn't hear you, Crowe, on account of I was talking. As I was saying, while everyone else in town was scouring the streets for you, I just turned my attention to Radnovian. And you didn't disappoint. You turned up there in no time at all."

Crowe managed to sit up straight again. The room was cool, almost cold, but sweat ran down his face and pricked under his arms. His perspective was off; Wills looked like a long, narrow giant looming over him. Crowe was getting vertigo looking up at him.

"Okay," Crowe said. "Hooray for the cop."

Wills laughed a sort of throaty, sick laugh and turned around and went to sit down on the bed again. He perched on the edge, legs splayed, so Crowe could see the bad cut of his slacks stretched along the thighs. There was a hole in one sock, and his little toe stuck out of it. He said, "I was thinking that maybe you were my ticket to seeing Vitower locked up. I've been waiting for a long time for that, you know. Something, anything, to pin on that bastard. And the minute you came back to town… scratch that. Not the minute you came back to town, but the minute you showed up at Vitower's club, I started getting my hopes up. Crowe, I thought, wouldn't be seeing Marco Vitower without a good reason. And the fact that ole' Peter Murke was about to be transported to Jackson, well… it just all came together, didn't it?"

Crowe didn't answer, and Wills didn't look as if he really expected him to. He set his gun on the bed next to him, reached for a pack of cigarettes sitting on the nightstand, lit one up, and, sucking smoke, gazed at Crowe thoughtfully. Finally, he grinned again and said, "But it didn't really. It didn't come together at all. You haven't given me anything, Crowe. Nothing to pin on Vitower. Oh, sure, I could take you in and the prosecution could work up a good case against you on something—if not your bitch's murder, then something else—but what good would that do me? I still wouldn't be any closer to Vitower."

"See, now you're making me feel bad."

Wills snorted. "Yeah."

"What's your mad-on with Vitower anyway?"

"He's a crook. I'm a cop. Do the math."

"There's plenty of crooks. You've made it your private mission to take Vitower out. It's not just the job. There's something personal there. Right?"

Wills' face went dark, and his eyes glittered with alcoholic fury. He said, "You need to mind your own business."

"Yeah, okay. Sure. But you know, if you really want Vitower, you could always try to convince me to turn state's evidence or something."

"You seen too many cops and lawyers shows. There's nothing you could give me."

Crowe drummed his fingers on the carpet. "Maybe, maybe not. But as it happens, I was at the scene when Murke got busted out. It's possible that I could tell you a thing or two about that."

Wills shook his head. "You really are a major league dumbass, Crowe. You think I don't know you were there? But lucky for you, there was nothing at the scene that could officially connect you or any of Vitower's people to it. And even if there was, it still wouldn't do me any good. The state cops are handling that investigation now. If you got busted, it would be *their* break, not mine."

Crowe laughed weakly. "Well, that's some hard luck, Wills. You got me, but now you don't know what to do with me. Like a dog chasing a car."

"Oh, I got some ideas about what to do with you, Crowe. Don't you worry none about that." He took a last long drag on his cigarette and flicked the butt in Crowe's direction. It bounced off Crowe's leg and on to the carpet, where it immediately started burning a hole.

Crowe picked it up and crushed it out between his fingers and tossed it away. "When did you become such a bad cop?" he said.

Wills stood up very suddenly, gun back in his hand, and for a second Crowe thought he was going to shoot him right then. His face tight, Wills said, "I'm not a bad cop. I'm the good guy here, Crowe, you understand that? I'm the one trying to stop the bad guys."

"Well, you haven't done such a hot job so far, have you?"

"It's not my fault that the system works in their favor. People like your boss, they're well-protected in this fucking city. They know the ins and outs. They know the right people. It makes my job goddamn difficult."

"So what's your solution, Wills? You gonna shoot me and leave me for dead here?"

"You wouldn't be the first gangster found in a seedy motel room, killed under mysterious circumstances."

"There wasn't anything seedy about this room before you got here, Wills."

Teeth clenched, Wills pointed the gun at Crowe's head and Crowe forced himself to not look away, to stare him right in the eyes. Seconds went by that felt like minutes, and Crowe's heart pounded.

After an eternity, Wills lowered the gun and said, "Boy, have you got some kinda death wish? Or are you just stupid? You don't talk like that to a man with a gun. Especially a man who already wants desperately to just kill you and be done with it."

"If you really wanted to kill me, Wills, you'd have done it by now. As lousy a cop as you are, you're still not good with killing a man in cold blood, are you?"

"I wouldn't presume so much if I was you."

Crowe shook his head. "It's not in you. Or rather, it is in you, but you don't want it to be. This city has made you sick, Wills. Sicker than the bad guys."

"You don't know what you're talking about."

"I think I do. I think Vitower did something to you, something that hit you in the guts, and you haven't been able to think straight about him since. What was it? What did he do to you?"

For a long moment he looked torn—Crowe could see all of it in his face. Wills may have been a tough one, but booze makes even the toughest bastard a weakling. An open book. Anger flickered through his features, then doubt, and then fear, the kind of fear a little kid has, unreasoning and panicked. He said, "You… I mean, you don't…"

Crowe waited him out, and finally Wills took a deep breath. When he spoke again, his voice was softer. "The Old Man…

your old boss, I mean… he and I had an understanding. He wasn't a bad guy, not like the gangsters now."

"You mean he wasn't black."

Wills shook his head hard. "No. That's not it. Typical stupid Northerner assumption. You think I hate Vitower 'cause he's black? No, I hate Vitower because he…"

"Because he what?"

"Because he killed the Old Man. It wasn't no heart failure. Vitower killed him as sure as I'm standing here."

"What do you care?"

"What do I care? That's a helluva question. What do I care, he says. Goddamn sonofabitch."

"The Old Man was just another gang boss. No better or worse than Vitower."

Wills' face twisted and he spat, "That's a lie. You say that again and I will shoot you, Crowe. The Old Man was decent."

"Yeah. The most decent guy who ever ordered a hit. The most decent guy to ever sell drugs to kids or pay strong-arms to break people's legs."

"Shut your mouth."

"What a sweetheart he was."

Wills screamed then, and it surprised Crowe so much that he jerked his head back and hit it on the door. "He raised me, you smart-mouthed punk! He was like a father to me!"

"What?"

"He treated me like his own flesh and blood, and you think you can bad-mouth him, can defile his memory?"

"What?"

Wills was breathing heavily, the gun still gripped tight in his fingers. His face had gone purple, and the broken capillaries in his nose showed white. He said, "My father… my real father… died when I was a kid. He worked for the Old Man, and he… he tried to go behind the Old Man's back and do some drug deals on his own. He got killed by a bunch of dealers from Nashville. You'd think the Old Man would say 'good riddance' to a guy who tried to double-deal him. But he didn't. He… he took care of me and my mom. He gave her money. He made sure I went to school. He—"

"He did this," Crowe said, "without anyone knowing?"

"He wanted me to be a cop. I don't… I don't know why. But that's what he wanted. And so that's what I did."

Crowe threw his head back against the door again, on purpose this time, and laughed out loud.

"What the hell's so goddamn funny?"

"You, Wills. You're killing me. That's the sappiest story I ever heard in my life."

"It's not sappy!"

"The benevolent old gangster, taking the poor widowed mother and little boy under his wing. Honestly, tell me you're pulling my leg."

"You motherfucker."

"Your real dad died when he went against the Old Man, yeah? But the Old Man didn't have anything to do with it. Please, brother. You really believe that?"

"He never would have lied to me."

"All he ever did was lie to you, Wills! Any moron could tell you the real story: the Old Man had your dad killed, and took your mom in because… well, I don't know. Was she hot? Did he wanna fuck her?"

Wills took a step toward him and whipped the gun against his skull. Red light exploded behind Crowe's eyes and he fell to the floor. Blood poured down his forehead and across his cheek, but he laughed.

"You filthy sonofabitch," Wills said.

"And he… he wanted you to… to be a cop… because that would be just the funniest punch line ever…"

Wills glared, and Crowe saw it finally happen, saw the tether finally snap. Wills extended his arm so that the gun barrel was pushed up hard against Crowe's head, and his finger tightened on the trigger.

Crowe stopped laughing and kicked out with his left leg and got him hard, just below his right kneecap.

It snapped, an ugly muted sound in the little motel room, and Wills fell to his right, still gripping the gun. It went off, and the bullet kicked up plaster from the wall about six inches from Crowe's head, and Wills' skull hit the edge of the little writing desk by the door and the sound that made was even uglier than the snapping bone of his leg.

He dropped on the carpet and was still.

For a long time, neither of them moved; anyone looking in from outside would've thought they were both dead.

Crowe kept telling himself he should get up, get out, but he couldn't will it. The carpet against his jaw felt nice and cool, and even the blood dripping from his scalp where Wills had pistol-whipped him didn't trouble him much.

He drifted off for a few minutes, and woke up very suddenly, close to panicking over some real or imagined threat. Wills was still where he had fallen. Crowe could see the pulse in his neck, and that surprised him; he'd assumed Wills was dead.

That meant he had no time. Wills would either lapse into a coma and die without ever waking up, or he'd come to, get up, and kick the shit out of Crowe before putting a bullet in his head. Crowe didn't want to wait around to find out.

Pulling together the little strength he had left, he dragged himself laboriously to the bed. It took about five minutes, according to the little bedside clock on the nightstand. Another four minutes, and he'd pulled himself up and was sprawled with his face in the sheets.

It was comfortable there, and he didn't move for a while.

When he looked back at the clock, ten minutes had gone by and he said, "Shit. Shit, shit, shit," and pushed himself up and to his feet. He wobbled a little, but standing helped to clear his head and he went toward the door. Blood dripped in his eye from the fresh wound on his temple; he swiped it away and nearly stumbled over Wills.

Wills groaned, and the fingers of his left hand moved. The gun was still in his right. Crowe thought about leaning over to get it, but the idea of bending down and back up again was too daunting and he let it go.

He opened the door and went out into the cold night.

The Pontiac started up easily and he pulled out without smashing into anything and drove away from the motel.

41

The Ghost Cat rubbed against his hand and purred. He scratched it behind the ears. The cat liked that. It pushed its head against his hand, arching its back, tail up, and he felt for the first time what it was like to have a friend. The Ghost Cat didn't hate him because he was skinny and ugly, not like the other kids, not like Mom, who thought he was stupid and worthless. The Ghost Cat liked him.

The cat started to move away, done for the moment with the boy's attentions. But the boy wasn't done with it. He grabbed its tail and pulled it back. It dug its claws in the dirt, but the boy pulled harder and grabbed it around the middle and squeezed it to his chest.

Ghost Cat struggled against him, clawing and scratching, and the boy said, Shh, shh, it's okay, I love you, I just want to love you, but the Ghost Cat wouldn't listen, was being foolish and obstinate. Shut up, the boy said, and hit it in the face. It hissed, ears back, and that made the boy madder. He hit it again, and again, and one of its teeth broke away in the boy's knuckles. He gripped it around the neck and threw it against a tree and when it hit the ground it wasn't moving but the boy was still mad, was still furious at the betrayal and wasn't done with it yet.

He pulled out his knife and walked toward it.

42

Crowe woke with a cry on his lips.

It was night still. The driver's side window was rolled down and cold air rushed in. He had the usual moment of anxiety, not knowing where he was or how he'd gotten there—this time it was even more pronounced because even after a few seconds he still didn't know.

He was in the car, pulled off on the side of the road on a long empty stretch of two-lane highway. He craned his head around, looking for any other signs of life, but he was completely alone.

No memory of how he'd gotten there.

His heart rate slowed down eventually and he rolled up the window and sat there shivering.

"Jesus Christ," he said. "Jesus fucking Christ."

The nightmare was vivid in his mind. He could still feel the sensation of fur on his fingertips, could still taste the copper tang of adolescent rage.

His muscles ached horribly. He fumbled around in his pockets until he found the pain pills. He popped them open, shook two of them out onto his palm. He stared at them. Then he slid them back into the bottle and closed it and put it back in his pocket.

Go with the pain, he told himself. Go with it, let it keep you focused. Let it guide you right to the Ghost Cat. And let it be the power that puts a bullet in Peter Murke's heart.

He drove the rest of the night, east on 40 again but this time past Germantown and Bartlett and well away from Memphis. At a little town about sixty miles west of Nashville he stopped for gas and coffee and a couple packets of little chocolate donuts.

He remembered the GPS in the car then, cursed himself for letting his brain get so foggy, and stopped at a rest station until a blue Saturn with Ohio plates pulled in. A lone guy, probably a salesman, piled out and hurried to the restroom. Crowe got out of his car, unscrewed the plates, switched them, and then got the Saturn going. Within four minutes, he was off again, heading east.

The sun was coming up, gray and cold, when he finally stopped at a motel just east of Murfreesboro. He got the key to his room from an old geezer who looked as miserable as Crowe felt, made it into the bed, and fell asleep still dressed.

It was icy in the room when he finally woke up, a good ten hours later. He lay there for a long time, studying a long crack in the ceiling that ran from one corner to the other. In the room next to his he could hear a woman saying something, a man laughing in response. Their TV came on, but he couldn't make out what program it was.

Getting up was harder than he'd expected. Ten hours of sleep, unmoving, had stiffened his abused body, and every step toward the curtained window sent shimmers of pain up his back and through his shoulders. He made it to the window, peeked out through the curtain at another gray evening. It was just after six, and the sun had already disappeared.

The battery in the cell phone Vitower had given him was dead, had been for a while without him noticing. He tossed it in the little plastic trash bin in the bathroom.

His temple throbbed where Wills had smashed him with his gun. Gingerly touching his head, he flipped the dial up on the thermostat to get some heat, hobbled to the bathroom, peeled off his clothes and took a long shower. He cleaned his wounds and the effort of it took away the little reservoir of strength he had left. Naked, he crawled back into bed and fell asleep again.

He didn't leave the motel room for another two days.

All sorts of ugly thoughts played through his head during that time. The Ghost Cat was a recurring visitor in his nightmares, leaving a stain of guilt on that really belonged to someone else; but maybe it belonged to him after all, maybe it belonged to everyone, everyone who could let a monster like Murke live.

Or maybe the guilt was simply for being what he was. *You're no different than them*, Garay had said. *You think you're better, but you ain't.*

Well, no kidding, Garay.

Crowe hated Vitower enough to want to kill him, and really, he'd done nothing to him and Crowe knew that and it still didn't matter.

He hated Murke too, that was the thing. He hated him and that hate felt different, it felt a bit closer, a bit more real. He'd killed Faith.

But when Crowe contemplated that, lying there in bed in an anonymous motel room, he could feel his face flush with the lie of it. He didn't hate Murke because he'd killed Faith. Crowe had hardly thought of Faith at all since finding her body.

No, he hated Murke because his first victim was haunting him and forcing him to see the world through the warped eyes of an angry, screwed-up boy. He hated Murke for making him recognize the similarities between them.

It could've been Crowe. That's what the Ghost Cat was telling him.

So he stayed in that room for two days and told himself he was recuperating. Longbaugh, that was where this would all end, and he didn't know what the ending would mean and he was no longer sure he wanted to know.

43

Crowe called the desk clerk to bring a travel kit with a toothbrush and a razor, but he didn't use either. The first night he ordered delivery from an awful Chinese place next door to the motel and the second night a pizza. He kept the heat turned up and didn't wear clothes and was in constant pain but didn't take a single pill. He kept the TV on all the time, even when he was sleeping, which was often.

On the third morning, about four AM, he woke up knowing that the time had finally come and he got up before giving himself a chance to change his mind. He showered and got dressed and finally used the toothbrush and the razor. He looked at his face in the mirror, examined the ugly scar that ran from temple to jaw, and thought about how it changed his whole face and made him look more like the scarred man he was inside, and that little bit of melodrama made him laugh.

Losing it, he thought. Getting soft or something.

He checked out of the motel, bought a roadmap of Tennessee from the display stand in the office, and started the long drive to Longbaugh.

The flatlands of western Tennessee had given way to hills

and woodlands and twisting road long before he'd made it to Nashville, but the farther east he went the more pronounced the differences became. It was already spring here, the trees sprouting new leaves and the world turning various shades of green. He drove past great sloping slabs of red clay that loomed over the highway. He drove through dark narrow tunnels that opened out onto curves, clinging to the edges of startling drop-offs into deep valleys. Pine trees and kudzu everywhere, mountains in the distance and little towns far below. The smell of wet earth. It couldn't have been more different from Memphis.

He stopped for gas at a lonely little station isolated by the woods just outside some Podunk town off the freeway. While he was there he bought a gallon gas can made of bright red plastic, filled that up too. He put it in the trunk of the Saturn. Then he drove without stopping, and by early evening he'd reached the outskirts of Longbaugh.

It was south of Chattanooga, a good twenty miles off the highway. A long two-lane road wound through woods so thick with new spring-like growth they formed a canopy over the road and it was like driving through a silent cathedral. The setting sun cast rippling shadows on the path ahead of him.

At first, Longbaugh was nothing but a few meager houses hiding behind the trees, but soon little signs made themselves known, one by one—a gas station/auto repair shop, a bait store, a couple more houses, a package store, a shoddy-looking motel. The road curved sharply to the left, and there was downtown Longbaugh.

There wasn't much to it. Crowe drove right through the heart of the place in less than three minutes. A few minor streets leading off left and right, and between them a dry goods store, a video rental place, a bar. Down the side streets he saw modest houses, economy cars, battered pick-up trucks and SUV's. On a street to the left, he saw the tall spire of what could only be a church.

Could finding the Church of Christ the Fisher actually be that goddamn easy?

He drove past it, wanting to get a look at the rest of the town first. There were a couple of women standing near the road, in the wide gravel parking lot in front of the bar. A little farther down, a young man with a Buffalo Bill beard and a tee-shirt braved the cold weather with stoic idiocy, loitering in front of his pick-up truck. A few other people were around, and they all stopped and stared as he drove past.

Driving, it took him a minute to realize he'd actually been through Longbaugh and out the other side. The buildings thinned out and next thing he knew he was surrounded again by the forest.

He managed to turn the car around on a wide spot in the road and headed back.

The same people who'd eyed him before eyed him again. The two middle-aged women who'd been in the bar parking lot approached the road as he pulled near and one of them waved for him to stop.

He stopped, rolled down the window. The woman who'd waved leaned down to get a look at him. She smelled like rum and cigarette smoke. She said, "Hey."

"Hey," he said.

"You lost or somethin'?"

"No, I don't think so."

"I only ask 'cause you was driving back and forth and all."

"No, not lost. I'm heading back to that motel I passed."

She looked in the direction he'd indicated, like she wasn't aware of any motel. She said, "Oh. No kidding? I don't know that anyone's bedded down there in a while. Maybe it ain't even open."

"Guess I'll find out."

"Guess you will at that," she said, and smiled. All her bottom row of teeth were missing. "That's some scar you got, mister, if you don't mind me saying."

He said, "Is this bar the place to be in Longbaugh?"

"If it ain't, no one gave me the good word." Her friend leaned in closer, trying to get a look at him, and the one at the window pushed her away, saying, "Geddoff, you drunk bitch," and then, "It's the bar or the church, and the church ain't open 'cept on Sundays. You thinking of coming by for a drink?"

"Thinking of it."

"I'll be around. Buy me one, I'll spend some time with you."

Her friend pushed her back enough to share the same space by the car. She was a little younger, a little easier to look at, but not by much. She said, "Willie's such a slut, don't pay her no mind."

"You bitch! I ain't a slut!"

"Every time some man comes through town, she just loses it."

They started giggling and pushing each other around, like two teenage girls, and then the one called Willie decked her friend hard with a balled-up fist and a full-on fight had started.

Crowe pulled away, glanced in the rear-view to see them fall to the gravel, punching and kicking. Two men came rushing out of nowhere to break it up and Crowe took the right toward the church and couldn't see anymore.

44

Church of Christ the Fisher, the sign on the sparse lawn read. *Services Sunday 8-11 AM & Wed 7-9 PM*. The letters were neat and blocky, the sort that can be changed periodically, but these didn't look like they'd been changed in a long time. Plexi-glass covered the sign, held in place with a simple lock. In smaller letters on the bottom it read *Society of Christ the Fisher*.

The church itself was unremarkable. Aside from the spire that rose up in front about two stories, it could've been an industrial building— tan slabs of painted wood, small windows, battered steel door. Crowe pulled into the small empty parking lot and got out of the car, muscles aching from the long drive.

From the front of the church, he could barely see the main road he'd just left, and the far corner of the bar's parking lot. But for the most part the church seemed pretty well-secluded; woods on both sides and behind, and only a single modest house directly across.

He could probably break in to the place without raising an alarm.

The idea juggled around in his head for a minute or two, until he set it down and opened the trunk of the Saturn. He pulled out the plastic gas can, closed the trunk and walked back to the church. He set the can at the corner of the church, hidden by a ragged shrub, well out of casual sight. He got back in the car. It could wait another couple of hours, until dark.

Back at the main street, a bunch of men had broken up the fight, and a crowd of about eight people had gathered. They all stopped to look at Crowe again when he paused at the corner, and continued to stare after when he headed back toward the motel.

Wouldn't it be just my luck, he thought, if every single one of these bastards knew the truth about the Society? If every last man, woman and child had been initiated into its bloody rites?

That was a ridiculous thought, of course, he knew that, but the idea of an entire town full of religious fanatic murderers, surviving in this strange and remote town far off the grid, sent a chill of apprehension down his spine.

Motels had become a way of life for him this last week, and this one was the worst yet. The door to the small lobby was off its hinges, resting against the outside wall, and the battered screen door creaked when he entered. The lobby was close and icy cold, bare wooden floor unswept, and instead of a counter there was a beat-up metal desk next to the entrance. The place smelled wet and musty, like rot.

From the next room, he could hear a TV show. Dr. Phil, it sounded like. Someone said, "Hey, yeah, hold up a minute, here I come," and a second later a man showed up in the doorway. He wore a ratty bathrobe and a baseball cap and hadn't shaved in a good long time. He had a bowl of cereal in his hand, and milk dribbled down his chin.

"Oh," he said. "Hey."

"Hey," Crowe said. "Can I get a room?"

He giggled. "I dunno. Can you?" Then, "Just kiddin'. My old English teacher, she used to do that. I'd say, can I go the bathroom, and she'd say I don't know, can you? Like that. Trying to tell me, you know, I meant to say *may* I go to the bathroom."

Crowe said, "*May* I get a room, then?"

"Right," he said. He ambled over to the metal desk, set his bowl of cereal down and pulled a ledger out of one of the drawers. "Yeah, right, a room, sure." He sat down, flipping through pages of the ledger. "Ain't had nobody here in a while, sorry if I'm not lookin' too presentable-like."

Crowe didn't say anything.

"I just poured me a bowl of cereal, too. Now the flakes are gonna get all mushy before I can eat it."

"Yeah."

"Ain't no biggie, though. I got plenty of cereal. Hey, you want some?"

"Just a room."

From the next room, Dr. Phil was telling someone they just needed to get their lives straight and stop being such a burden to their loved ones. Cereal man pushed the ledger over, saying, "Just, you know, the John Hancock there. It'll be, uh… say, fifty dollars?"

Crowe signed, handed him a twenty. "Let's not say fifty," he said.

The guy took the twenty, shrugging. "Okay, twenty's fine, I reckon." He reached in another drawer and pulled out a key and said, "Room two. You need anything, you lemme know, all right?" And then, "Say, buddy, that's some scar you got there, you don't mind me saying."

Crowe took the key and went back outside. There were only five rooms along the side of the building. He made his way to the second door—none of them had numbers— and went in.

The room lived up to the promise offered by the rest of the place. A small, grubby bathroom immediately to the left. Not a window anywhere. The room itself small and boxy, nothing but a bed with ragged sheets and a wooden chair in the far corner. No television or phone. It smelled strangely of rotted fruit, as if someone had stashed a bunch of banana peels under the bed a month ago.

But it didn't matter. He didn't plan on staying long.

He left the door open to keep from suffocating in the awful stench. Cold air swept through, seeming colder somehow than it had been outside. Crowe sat on the edge of the bed and thought.

What he knew: the Society of Christ the Fisher had split into two factions. Welling wanted to deal out Vitower and start working with Bad Luck. Another faction, led by who knows who, wanted to maintain the status quo. Welling had the final say, though, and he had Murke sprung to help him.

And Vitower… well, Vitower had more than one reason to want Murke dead. There was revenge for the murder of his wife, yes, but also… also, he would have to know that Murke could easily be Welling's tool for killing him.

Crowe wracked his brain, trying to think of some way he could use this rift in the Society to his advantage. But he couldn't think of an angle. Strategy was never his strong point.

He'd just have to bull his way through it. Rack up a body count.

He went back outside, and paused in the gravel parking lot. His was the only car, except for a heavy-duty pick-up in the far back of the lot, loaded with an industrial-size lawn mower. Big letters on the side of the pick-up said *Star-One Lawn Mowing, Landscaping and Gen. Maintain*. Crowe figured it belonged to the slob who owned this place. There was no way he made any money running the motel.

It was getting darker, a sort of gray, despondent darkness that smothered out the landscape. Directly across the two-lane road, heavy woods. Even with most of the leaf coverage just coming in, they were still thick with layers of branches and a low, dark gloominess. Crowe figured about a half-mile walk straight through them would take him to the church, angling off just a little to the right.

Or, straight down the road a considerably shorter distance, the bar.

He buttoned up his coat, squared his aching shoulders, and started walking.

45

The place was a little busier than when he'd driven by earlier. They had the neon going, *Bud Lite* and *Pabst Blue Ribbon* and *Miller's High Life* all competing for attention in glaring red and blue. There were a few more vehicles in the lot, mostly trucks. From the road, he could hear music playing inside. A female vocalist was saying something about her *humps*, over and over again.

The music, so alien, combined with the constant flow of pain in his muscles, made him feel the weight of all his years. For a long moment he stood there on the road outside the bar, like some dazed and dumb old man. A dinosaur. A relic.

He crunched across the gravel parking lot and went in the bar.

It took a moment for his eyes to adjust to the gloom, but when they did he saw it was bigger than it looked from the outside, and with only a modest crowd of good old boy types and sloppy-looking women. Mostly in their twenties, but a few older even than him and some of an indeterminate age. A long bar stretched along the left of the place, and a lone bartender served beers to the men who perched there. To the right, tables and booths, two pool tables, where four or five guys in jeans and work shirts and baseball caps played.

Cigarette smoke hung thick in the air, mingling with the raw scent of stale beer and unwashed flesh. The music throbbed painfully in his ears and now the singer was saying something about her *lovely lady lumps*.

All eyes were on him, and the ebb and flow of various conversations, the rattle of phlegm-y laughter and stupid jokes, stopped cold.

He was overdressed for this joint.

He went to the bar, took a stool. The bartender eyed him from the far end for a moment, then drifted over. He looked as if he expected trouble. His eyes were hooded and wary.

"What'll it be?"

Crowe ordered a bottle of Bud. The bartender served it up, said, "That'll be four bucks, mister." Crowe dropped a five on the bar, picked up the bottle, and turned away from him.

A few faces were still set in his direction, but mostly everyone had gone back to whatever they had been doing when he came in. Crowe marked two guys at the pool table; if there was going to be any trouble it would be from them. Open hostility there.

"Hey!" A slightly slurred female voice, from his left. "It's the Scar-Man! You said you might stop in but I didn't think you really would."

It was the middle-aged rummy with bad teeth—Willie. She pushed in close to him, grinning, the glass in her hand sloshing rum and coke over her fist. Her friend wasn't with her.

Crowe said, "What else am I gonna do in this town?"

"You got that shit right, babe," she said, and threw the drink down her throat. She set the glass down on the bar and said, "Buy a girl a drink, why don't ya?"

Crowe motioned to the bartender and he brought another one for her. She took the glass, nodded in what he could only assume was supposed to be some sort of toast, and drank.

"You are a gentleman," she said. "A true gentleman. Even with that fugly scar, you're a gentleman. You don't see a lott'a gentlemen round about these parts. I like it."

Crowe nursed his beer. The song about humps and lumps ended, and another came on that sounded like a cross between "Werewolves of London" and "Sweet Home Alabama". It was awful, but it got a positive reaction—there were several woops and *hell yeah*'s.

"You don't talk much, do you?" Willie said. "I like that, too. These boys here, all they ever do is talk. Talkity talkity talk, drives a girl fuckin' crazy, all that talkin'."

She'd already downed half her drink and now she'd started rubbing up against his arm, so close that when she spoke he could feel her hot boozy breath on his neck. She said, "What say you and me get outta here, huh? You got a room at that fleabag place up the road, don't ya?"

"What's the hurry? I just got here."

She frowned, made a peeved sort of huffing noise, shrugged. "Suit yourself. I'm just sayin', don't think I'm gonna be available all night."

They sat there at the bar for a while and she talked and drank and he bought her another while he nursed his beer. The awful song on the jukebox ended and another one came on, another female vocalist saying that *man, she felt like a woman*. The singer after that was proud to be an American. Crowe never really had much of an ear for music, but it seemed that while he'd been in prison music had only gotten more inane and vapid.

The bartender was starting to look annoyed that he was taking up space. Crowe finished the Bud and ordered another and that pacified the bartender for a little while. Willie was getting drunker and making less sense all the time. She was saying, "—and so I tol' the bitch, I tol' her, you think you're sumpin' other than a cheap fuck to him, you stupid bitch? Don' make me laugh! 'sides, I seen what he's packin' in them jeans and it ain't nothin' to get worked up about, believe you me!"

When she shut up for a minute, Crowe said, "You go to that church?"

"What?" she said.

"The church over there, Christ the Fisher. You go to it?"

She scowled. "What the fuck does that have to do with what I was sayin'?"

"Nothing. I just want to know."

"What are you, some kinda… some kinda church guy or somethin'?"

"I just want to know."

She shook her head. "Fuck no, I don't go to the church. Jesus fuck, man. What kinda weird question is that? What are you, some kinda… church guy or somethin'?"

"I was just curious."

The bartender had heard part of their conversation. His jaw was set hard, and his flinty eyes shifted from Crowe to the pool players and back to Crowe.

Willie said, "Just 'cause half the town goes there, there ain't no law sayin' everyone has to. So the Bible-thumpin' fuckers run the town, so fuckin' what? I don't gotta do shit, do I?"

"No," Crowe said.

"You some kinda church guy? Jesus, what a question."

In the mirror behind the bar, Crowe saw them approaching. Four guys. One carried his pool cue, all of them carried bottles.

Before he'd even turned around to face them, Crowe had run through several different scenarios—without a weapon he couldn't take all four of them, not without breaking a bottle of his own and slashing some faces. He would do that if he had to, but it would probably be better to cut and run: hurt one of them, make an exit.

But he kept his options open. He'd left the .38 in the Saturn, but the .45 was still in his coat pocket. He hadn't come here to go on a shooting rampage, though.

As he turned on the bar stool, one them said, "Hey, old man. What's with the monkey suit?"

It was the Buffalo Bill jackass he'd seen on the road earlier. He leered, tongue sticking out and touching his chin. The other three guffawed, sipped their beers, and Buffalo Bill said, "I been watchin' you since you walked in here, old man. I gotta tell you… there's just somethin' about the way you look, makes me wanna fuck you up."

Crowe looked at him, waited, bottle in his hand. There was no question, this was going to come down to bottles and faces. Just like a goddamn Western.

The one with the pool cue said, "What's the matter, you deaf? My boy's talkin' to you. Don't you hear good? He asked you, what's with the monkey suit? You a monkey?"

Another laugh all around. From the corner of his eye Crowe saw Willie edging away, drink still in her hand.

The boys were laughing and making monkey sounds now, and Crowe thought *this is getting idiotic—time to make something happen*. He stood up quickly, telegraphed it like crazy, the beer bottle in his right fist and ready to smash against Buffalo Bill's face—

--and someone said, "You boys need to step down. What kind of image of Longbaugh are you giving?"

A man, mid-forties, with a plump friendly face and immaculate reddish-blond hair. He was fit and trim for his age, except for a slight paunch, wearing khakis and a cord-knit sweater. He wore simple frameless glasses. He stood with his hands in his pockets, smiling. He looked like the nicest guy on Earth.

"Well?" he said. "I'm sure there's nothing going on here that has to be resolved with violence."

The boys had gone all wishy-washy. They stood there looking at him like a bunch of puppies who'd just been scolded for pissing on the carpet. "Mr. Welling," one of them said. "We, uh… we didn't know you was in town."

Mr. Welling. Fletcher Welling, in the goddamn flesh.

"Well, I am," he said, smiling. "I just got in, as a matter of fact. I come in here for a refreshment, something to fortify myself, and what do I find? Members in good standing of the church, acting like a bunch of teenage hooligans. For shame, boys."

Crowe couldn't place Welling's accent, but it sounded Northern or maybe Midwestern. Buffalo Bill actually blushed.

"We didn't mean nothin', Mr. Welling. We was just havin' some fun."

Welling pushed his glasses up on the bridge of his nose. "Fun, right. At this poor gentleman's expense? I think you owe our visitor an apology."

They all mumbled shame-faced apologies, and it was all Crowe could do to keep from laughing out loud. But he nodded at each of them sternly and sat back down.

Welling said, "You boys go on back to your game now, hear?"

They did.

Welling turned to Crowe, said, "Mister, if you don't have too bad a taste in your mouth, will you let me buy you a beer?"

Crowe shrugged. Welling sat next to him, where Willie had been, and showed two fingers to the bartender, who instantly put a bottle in front of each of them.

Sipping his beer, Welling said, "My name's Welling. Fletcher Welling. I'd like to apologize myself for those rowdies, Mr....?"

Crowe said, "You know who I am, Welling."

He frowned. "Sorry?"

"You know who I am. Let's not play this game."

He mulled it over, and said, "Okay, fair enough, Mr. Crowe. No games. But what I said before, about there not being any need for violence... I meant that."

"We might differ on that point," Crowe said.

Welling shook his head. On the jukebox, an old Steve Miller Band song came on, the one about liking your peaches, wanting to shake your tree. Crowe didn't like it any more than he did the others, but at least he knew this one.

Welling said, "Mr. Crowe. Why have you come to Longbaugh? What, exactly, are you trying to accomplish?"

"I'm here to find Peter Murke."

"And then what?"

"Kill him."

Welling chuckled, sipped his beer. "No, Mr. Crowe, I can't let you do that. Peter is protected by the Society, you understand?

You can't touch him, not without bringing down the wrath of Christ the Fisher on your head."

"I haven't been particularly impressed with your wrath so far, Welling."

"You haven't seen but a faint glimmering of it yet, Mr. Crowe."

They both let that one hang out there for a moment, sipped their beers. Side by side, like they were pals.

Crowe said, "I've seen some dirty fuckers in my time, Welling, but you take the cake. This guy, Murke... he kills your daughter, your own daughter, and you're rescuing him, protecting him. And for what? Power? In one lousy, stinking city that's already rocking on its heels and ready to hit the mat. That's pretty pathetic."

If he was mad, Welling didn't show it. He played with his glasses, said, "I hate to sound as if I'm spouting off clichés, Mr. Crowe, but really... who are you to judge me? Your whole life has been nothing but one long, ugly bout of senseless violence. Do you suppose God approves of what you do? Do you think He'll forgive you for the people you've hurt or killed?"

"I'm not interested in God's forgiveness."

"I thought as much. The man who doesn't stop to contemplate God's wisdom is a man whose life is—"

"Welling," Crowe said. "Shut up. If this God of yours actually approves of what you do, or even what I do, then I don't want anything to do with Him."

For the first time, Welling showed some spark of anger. He gritted his teeth, looking at his bottle of beer, and said, "Blasphemy is a sin, Mr. Crowe."

"Fuck you, Welling."

His eyes snapped around and locked on Crowe's, and there was rage there, finally. But in a second it was gone again, and he smiled politely. "My father always told me," he said, "when you're having a drink, never talk about politics or religion. Good advice, huh?"

He laughed and drained his beer, ordered another.

For two or three minutes they sat there in silence, drinking.

When he was halfway through his second beer, Welling said, "I understand where you're coming from, Mr. Crowe, I really do. Peter killing your girlfriend, Faith, was unfortunate. We didn't really plan that, I promise you. It's just that sometimes Peter is a little… hard to handle. You understand?"

Crowe didn't answer, and Welling said, "This is a trying time for everyone, you see. Your employer, Vitower, is not… what's the expression? Not going gently into that good night. He doesn't understand that he has nothing to offer us anymore, that the real power on the street now belongs to Bad Luck, Inc. The death of his wife, Jezzie, has made him less than useful to us, you know? I've been trying for some time now to cut him loose, but… well, I may be the top dog in the church but I'm not a dictator, if you know what I mean. Other members want to keep Vitower. These disagreements have forced me to take drastic measures."

He looked at Crowe. "You were sort of… pulled into all this, I'm afraid. None of it has anything to do with you. But I'm afraid that if you keep poking your nose in, it's going to get cut off. Really, it'll be out of my control."

"I'll keep that in mind."

Welling frowned, seeming for all the world like the pastor who tries without success to get through to the young heathen. Sad, quiet disappointment in his sensitive eyes.

"You don't understand what the Society of Christ the Fisher is all about," he said. "But I'm not surprised. Most people don't. You seem to think it's all about power, about manipulating things behind the scenes, and while that may be a part of it it's only so that we can accomplish bigger things."

"Bigger things," Crowe said.

"Yes. You see, when the Society first formed, in the early part of the last century, it had a simple mission: to punish sinners. To eradicate sin, as God would desire. Such a simple, obvious mission, one that couldn't be clearer in the Good Book. But the world is filled with hypocrites and liars, Mr. Crowe—as I'm sure you know—and the Society's work was condemned and cursed by man. The Society took on the task God Himself had given, but other religious groups had grown too soft, too corrupted by the world. And so the Society was forced underground."

He paused to sip his beer, and push his glasses back up on his nose. They seemed to keep sliding. He continued, "But we never went away. We continued our work. And we found others... lost souls. And we saved them and honed them to use their natural gifts for a greater purpose."

"Lost souls," Crowe said. "I assume you mean psychopathic killers."

"What is a psychopath? He's merely a candle without a flame. A vessel waiting to be filled with glory and purpose. And as far as the... less savory types we are forced to deal with—like your Vitower, or Bad Luck, Inc—well, I'm sure you understand that sometimes one has to bend in order not to break. It's an unfortunate but sad truth of this corrupt world."

"You're absolutely breaking my heart, Welling."

"I wish, Mr. Crowe, that I could make you see things my way. I'd love to count you among my friends." Then, "I believe you'd fit right in with us."

That got under Crowe's skin. He snarled, "Welling, I'll see you dead before this is over."

Welling looked slightly taken aback by that, blinked behind his lenses. Then he sighed and finished his beer. He stood up, said, "Well, I suppose you're going to make your mistakes, no matter what I say to you. I hate it, Mr. Crowe, I really do. But ultimately, you're responsible for your own actions."

He started away from Crowe, but stopped very suddenly and faced him again. He said, "Oh, and Mr. Crowe, about my daughter?"

Crowe looked at him, waited.

"I miss her every day. My wife never recovered from it, you know, and I don't suppose I ever will either. But we all must make sacrifices to glorify His name, and my daughter in her childish zeal lost her way." He paused, smiling sadly. "Suffer the children, as the Good Book says. Suffer the children."

And then he turned and walked out of the bar. As if that explained everything.

46

It was full-on dark when Crowe left the bar, and so cold it bit straight through his coat like a razor blade. He stopped just outside the door, half-expecting to be ambushed before he'd taken three steps, but no one was around.

Whatever. It was going to happen tonight, he was sure of that. This dancing around they'd been doing with each other had to end, and they all knew it.

He walked back up the road, being careful to stay in the shadows as much as possible. Every sound he heard from the woods was a legion of murderous nut-jobs, every branch shifting in the woods a guy with a machete.

He had a pretty bad case of nerves going, which was a strange and foreign feeling. He played it through his head, examining it, wondering where it came from and why.

But then it dawned on him: he'd had bad nerves all along, ever since he'd come back to Memphis. It had been in his guts, seething around impatiently. In the day, before prison, he'd never experienced nerves because he had no expectations, no anxieties.

Now, though, now that he had a clear goal in mind, the nerves had been eating away at him without him even realizing it. He'd heard someone, a Buddhist maybe, say that expectation is the source of all misery. Peace of mind could only come with letting go of all that. Like the junkies at Jimmy the Hink's place, human dregs who'd abandoned all ambition and with it all anxiety.

Now that he understood where the nerves were coming from, he told himself he felt better about it and kept walking.

He was on his guard to the point of being jumpy, so how they managed to get the drop on him was a mystery for the ages. It happened fast. He heard a noise in the woods off to his left, dry wood cracking, and as he stopped, eyes peeled in that direction, a blob of shadow swooped onto the road from the other side. He spun to face it, caught a glimpse of a yellow parka, a baseball bat swinging.

He raised his arm to block the blow, but too late. The bat hit him along the side of the head, and he fell to his knees. He couldn't see anything but shuffling shadows. Heard nothing but roaring air and ringing in his ears.

The second blow from the baseball bat hardly registered, but it was enough to drop him far, far down into a red-tinged night.

47

First, a vague, purple-y mist and it started to shift and change to a dark, dark red, and at the same time he began to feel and hear a tremendous pounding at his temples. Blood shooting through his brain, reviving, torturing.

He was aware, peripherally, that he was coming out of it, but he didn't want to. He wanted to stay in the dark. He wanted to bury himself in the cold dirt, away from the burgeoning pain of consciousness. But it insisted. It pulled him up, up and out of the blood-red mist and into a world of bright agony and pinpoints of sharp light.

He could hear voices, but couldn't understand what was being said. He didn't care. He squeezed his eyes shut and his head throbbed and he felt horribly sick. The voices kept talking, though, and he began to catch words here and there that he understood but that didn't have any real context.

His eyes opened and he saw a single dim florescent light, buried in the ceiling. It wasn't bright, but it still hurt to look at it and he turned away. Moving his head made the sickness come rushing up and out of him and he vomited all over himself.

Someone said, "Oh man, that's gross!" and then laughed.

He forced his head around to look at the speaker. It was Cowboy Larry. He was grinning down at him.

Down at him. Crowe was lying on a cot, in a cold dank room.

Next to Larry, another figure took form and said, "Get a wet towel and clean him up."

Larry said, "What? Why me? I'm not the fucking janitor."

"Just do it, Larry. Show a little respect for the man."

It was Welling. He smiled down at Crowe, like Crowe was a loved one just coming out of a long illness and Welling was overjoyed to see he was feeling better. Larry grumbled and left the room.

"Glad you're back," Welling said. "Do you need anything? Some water, maybe?"

Crowe couldn't answer him yet. Welling yelled over his shoulder, "And Larry, some water as well!" and then, "For a while there, I was sort of worried we'd hit you too hard."

"Fuck... off..." Crowe croaked at him.

He ignored that, said, "I want to make absolutely certain you recover, you know. We have a great deal to talk about."

Crowe turned away from him, looked at the bare wall that the cot was pushed up against. He wasn't tied or bound-- conceivably, he could jump Welling right now and escape. But the thought of even moving-- let alone jumping-- was far too daunting.

They'd stripped him down to under-shorts and tee-shirt and the room was freezing. The only furniture was the cot and a beat-up wooden chair. Above the bed there was a small casement window, closed and locked tight.

Larry came back with a wet towel, tossed it on Crowe's chest. The cold of it shocked him into a sharper degree of awareness and he flinched. Larry said, "There's his stupid wet towel. He can clean his own self off."

Welling frowned but didn't argue.

Slowly, Crowe sat up, placed his bare feet on the cold floor, and began gingerly cleaning the filth off. When he was as clean as possible, he tossed the soiled towel in the middle of the room and looked up at them. "How about that water?" he said.

Welling said, "Larry, would you mind?"

"Hell yes I would mind! You want him to have water, you get it yourself. You seen what this fucker did to me." He held up his right arm, showing the bulky cast around the wrist.

Crowe laughed, although he was still too weak to put much into it.

Larry scowled angrily.

From a doorway behind them, someone said, "You got off lucky, Larry." He came into the room carrying a plastic jug of water. Stone, the businessman. "Our Mr. Crowe killed Nick. And… my associate, Mr. Eckstine."

There didn't seem to be any malice in his voice. He handed Crowe the jug. Crowe swigged a huge gulp of water, felt his stomach consider rebelling against it before settling down. He set the jug carefully on the floor between his feet, closed his eyes, took a deep breath. The throbbing in his head relented a little bit.

When he opened his eyes again, the three of them were standing there staring at him-- Welling with studied kindness, Larry red-faced and furious, and Stone completely impassive. Crowe managed a grin, said, "So. The Whole Sick Crew. Except… except Metal Face. And the guy who bashed me with a baseball bat… Parka Kid."

Welling said, "They're around, don't you worry about that."

"Oh, and Murke. Where's Murke, Welling?"

Welling didn't answer. The others looked at him with more than a little disdain, and it was obvious trouble had been brewing in the ranks, like Garay had said. Welling was dangerously close to losing control of his God-bothering psychos. Crowe wondered if he knew that.

Welling said, "Larry, Stone… would you mind leaving me alone with Mr. Crowe for a moment?"

They started out, and Stone said, "We'll be just on the other side of the door, Mr. Welling. I'd advise you to watch him very carefully."

"No worries. Mr. Crowe isn't in much shape to do much damage. And I think he knows that. Right, Mr. Crowe?"

Crowe didn't answer.

Stone and Larry shut the door behind them, and Welling pulled up the wooden chair and sat facing him. The room was close and cold. The light in the ceiling cast a dim glow that felt sickly and surreal. It bathed Welling's face piss yellow and colored the lenses of his glasses.

"You see, Mr. Crowe?" he said. "We could've killed you any time in these last two hours. Believe me, they all wanted to, and it was all I could do to stay their wrath. But you're alive. What does that tell you?"

"That you're an idiot."

He shook his head. "No. I'm not an idiot. I'm merciful. Don't you get it? The Church is not what you think it is. Earlier, in the bar, you said that you'd see me dead before you'd consider my position. Or something to that effect. But I really believe that, if you hear me out, you'll come around to my point of view."

Crowe picked up the water jug and had another swig. He set it back down, looked at Welling. Welling's face was so earnest, so benevolent, Crowe had to laugh.

"Welling," Crowe said. "Pay close attention this time, will you? I'll try to spell it all out very carefully, so that even your pathetic mind can grasp it, okay?"

"Mr. Crowe--"

"Shut up and listen. It's like this. Those mental deviants you have doing your dirty work? The only reason you've snagged them away from their true calling of being stupid sick fucks is that they're weak-minded. You get it? They have no will of their own. Probably never did. Hell, that's probably why they became crazy to begin with-- lack of any real... what?... personalities of their own? They were all powerless little shits, afraid of their own shadows, and so they picked up guns or knives or machetes and started killing the things that scared them. They're pathetic. Don't you see that?"

Welling started to interrupt, but Crowe said, "Wait, I'm not done. They're scared little boys, looking for meaning. And so you show up in their lives and tell them that God Himself thinks they're special. God Himself has a plan for them. And they behaved exactly like any armchair psychiatrist could've predicted. They came running to your side. And now, instead of acknowledging that somewhere deep down inside they're actually sub-human scum, they get to pretend that they're---" Crowe started laughing, "-- Sacred Executioners."

The little speech had tired him out, and the laughing didn't help. Welling watched him, the benevolence on his face tightening into barely suppressed anger, and Crowe grabbed up the jug again and drank.

Welling stood up very quickly and slapped the jug out of Crowe's hands and across the room.

Crowe looked at him dully.

Welling's fingers were balled into fists and his face was red. In a clipped tone, he said, "And you, Mr. Crowe? Just how are you any different from them?"

Crowe said, "I'm not afraid."

"Everybody is afraid, eventually."

"Maybe. But..." and he laughed again, "... I'm not there yet."

Welling struggled to control his temper, said, "All I have to do, Mr. Crowe, is call out for Larry, or Stone, or any one of them, and they'll come running in here to kill you. They'd love to do that."

"So why don't you?"

He licked his lips. With forced calm, he sat back down, adjusted his trouser legs. He said, "Because I'm trying to save you. I'm a man of God. And I see such... potential in you."

Crowe sighed and lay back down on the little cot. He was tired and hungry and cold as hell.

Welling said, "Those men you dismiss so easily are much more than you think they are. Stone, for instance? He and his partner, Eckstine, once cut a swath of blood and vengeance through the Pacific Northwest, back in the '70's, that would amaze you. They were corporate executives, once, before losing their jobs and... losing their way. Individually, they committed murders of no importance or imagination, but once they met--

quite by accident, actually-- they realized they had a bond, and the friendship they formed was remarkable. Together, they killed over sixty people. Just… random people. Until the Church of Christ the Fisher found them, about ten years ago."

"Now they kill sinners," Crowe said, looking at the wall.

"Exactly. They serve a divine purpose. You can imagine how lost Stone feels, now that his friend and confidante is dead. And Larry? He worked in the Southwest. Was a hired killer, much like you, for many years. Reliable and steady. Until he began losing sight of his motivation-- which was profit, initially-- and began killing because it made him feel better. The Church found him about four years ago, and turned him into an instrument of God."

His voice was making Crowe sleepy. Crowe closed his eyes.

"And the same is true of Nick, poor tortured Nick, who you killed. And also Kondrashev and Nathan."

Crowe mumbled, "Who?"

"Kondrashev, the one you referred to as Metal Face. And Nathan is the young man in the parka."

"The one who hit me with the baseball bat. Gonna have to remember that."

"And, of course, there's Peter," Welling said.

Crowe opened his eyes, turned his head to look at Welling. He said, "Peter. You know, Murke is all I want from you. You realize that, yeah? You give me Murke and this could all be over."

Welling shook his head.

Crowe forced himself back up, sat on the edge of the cot. Welling watched him very carefully. Crowe was feeling better, stronger, with each passing minute, but made a point of still seeming weak and sick.

He said, "If it was Larry I wanted, or Nathan, or Metal Face--"

"Kondrashev."

"--you'd hand them over, wouldn't you? Just to get rid of me. But not Peter Murke."

"I wouldn't betray any of them."

Crowe smiled. "Yeah, Welling, you would. But not Murke.

He's the only one still completely loyal to you, isn't he? The others are losing confidence in you, they don't like the way you're handling things in Memphis, and they're ready to jump ship. But not Murke. He still worships you, doesn't he? And you can't let that go."

"They are all my flock," he said. "I love them all. None of them are more important or more valuable than any other one."

"Has it really come to that, Welling? Are you really that ridiculous and insecure?"

The anger in him flared again. "You want ridiculous and insecure, Crowe? You want to see how ridiculous and insecure I am? I'm going to have Larry come in here right now and slit your fucking throat."

"Sure, call Larry."

He jumped up. "Better yet, I'll do it myself!"

Crowe looked up at him. "Sure," he said. "But you can't. You've never killed anyone in your whole life. You've had your 'flock' do it for you. You don't have the guts to kill me, Welling."

Welling glared, trembling, and Crowe knew he was right. He decided to press it home a little more.

He said, "God's wrath is… well, it's just too big a job for a little man like you."

For a long moment, Welling stared, eyes bulging behind his glasses, and then he spun on his heel and stormed for the door. He jerked it open, barked, "Larry!"

Larry was waiting. "Kill him?" he said.

Welling glanced back at him, seething. He struggled with himself for a second, and said, "No. But… hurt him. Hurt the cocksucker," and was gone.

Larry rushed into the room, swinging his good fist, and clocked Crowe in the right temple. Crowe dropped back onto the cot and was out.

Again.

48

Natural light was streaming in through the little casement window when he came to. His head and his eyes ached, but it wasn't nearly as bad as the first time. He wondered if he was getting used to being knocked fucking senseless.

Peter Murke was sitting on the edge of the cot, watching him.

They stared at each other for long seconds, Crowe baffled and Murke shy or something.

Finally, in his croaking sick voice, Crowe said, "What… the fuck… are you doing?"

Murke's fishy face turned pink with embarrassment, and he said, "Wha? Nothing. I ain't doing nothing. I'm just sitting here, man, that's all." His voice was nasal and whiny and strangely child-like.

Crowe managed to push himself up and slightly away, toward the wall. "Well," he said. "Back the fuck off a little, will you?"

Murke stood up and took a step away from the cot. "I didn't mean nothing. I'm not gay or nothing like that. I was just, you know, sitting there."

Crowe rubbed his right temple, felt dried blood caked there. He felt awful, but at least he was fully aware of his surroundings and didn't feel like throwing up.

It was still cold in the room, and he was still in his underwear and tee-shirt. A fresh jug of water was on the wooden chair. He slid over to reach it, had a long drink, while Murke watched uneasily.

Crowe burped and looked up at him and said, "Thanks for the water."

He nodded. "No sweat, man, no problem. How you feeling, bro?"

"All things considered..." Crowe shrugged.

Murke frowned, and Crowe realized Murke didn't know what he meant.

Not a bright boy, Peter Murke.

He sat up and looked around the room. The old plastic jug that Welling had knocked out of his hands was still there, in the corner. The towel he'd used to clean himself up was also still there, stiff and disgusting, in the middle of the room. The only thing different was the light in the ceiling-- it was off now, replaced by gray daylight.

Crowe thought about standing up but couldn't muster the energy. He said, "How long do you folks plan on keeping me here?"

Murke said, "I don't really know. Sorry. I think Mr. Welling is figuring out what to do with you or something."

"Deciding whether or not to kill me?"

He shrugged. "I reckon so."

"And what are you doing here, Peter?"

Murke said, "Well... I asked Mr. Welling if it would be okay if I talked to you, like."

"About what?"

He shrugged again. "I dunno. Stuff. You know. Is that okay? I mean, is it okay if we talk?"

Crowe sighed. "Sure. Talk away."

Murke licked his thick wet lips, scratched his belly. "I kinda wanted to ask you, Mr. Crowe. I wanted to ask you why?"

"Why what?"

"Why you... why you want me? I mean, what do you want

with me? Mr. Welling told me you came here for me. Is it because of your girlfriend?"

"Why do you think, Peter?"

"I'm sorry about her, I really am. I just got… I got carried away. But it's okay, you know. She's with Jesus now. I did a good thing, when you really think about it, right?"

Crowe didn't know how to respond to that one, so he didn't.

Murke said, "Our world is a veil of sorrows, right? That's what the Bible says. I think. Or that's what Mr. Welling says the Bible says. I don't really know, but I believe him."

Crowe said, "I don't know either. Sounds about right, though."

He perked up a little, hope gleaming in his bulging eyes. "So… so you aren't mad at me, then? For killing her? You understand, don't you? I mean, I had to do it. The… the Holy Ghost took over my body and I couldn't… I couldn't stop cutting."

Crowe's stomach twisted and he had to look away from him.

He could hear the disappointment in Murke's whiny voice when he spoke again. "You are mad at me, aren't you? Please, please don't be mad."

Crowe made himself look at him again. Tears glittered in Murke's eyes. Crowe said, "I'm not mad at you."

"Really?"

"Really. I don't see any reason you and I can't be friends, Peter."

Murke's face lit up. "Wow, that's so cool of you. I really, really appreciate it."

Crowe forced a grin. "So what's next, Peter? Is Welling going to have you kill me now?"

Murke turned red, looked away. "I… I dunno, Mr. Crowe. I surely hope not. I wouldn't wanna kill you."

"No? Why not?"

"Well… cuz. Well. I sorta… you know, I sorta admire you. I always have."

Crowe felt his grin drop away. "What?" he said.

"Don't take it the wrong way, Mr. Crowe. I'm just saying, you know? I mean, I knew all about you, from the people I…

from the people I ran into, you know? I heard about you and everything."

"What the fuck are you saying?"

Murke took a step toward the cot, his hands out in a sort of pleading gesture. "I know it sounds stupid. Ha. I just mean that... well, when I was... what you call, researching, before Mrs. Vitower and everything, I heard a lot about you. How you were so cool, right? And how you could hurt people just as much as you wanted and no more, and how you could even kill people sometimes and get away clean. You had, like, a reputation and everything."

"Jesus," Crowe said.

"And I remember thinking, right," he said, stumbling over his words now, "I remember thinking, ha. Wow, that Crowe guy, what a bad-ass, right? What a cool customer. I wish I could be that cool, right?"

Crowe couldn't meet his gaze anymore. Again, he looked away.

Murke said, "Stupid, right? I know it sounds retarded. But it's not, like, gay or nothing. I don't want you to think I'm a fag or something. I'm just saying--"

"Shut up," Crowe said.

"I just mean--"

Crowe stood up and screamed at him, "Shut the fuck up! Just shut up! Get out!"

Murke jerked away, startled, but didn't move for the door. Crowe said again, "Get out!" and Murke started shakily for the door, saying, "I'm sorry, Mr. Crowe, I didn't mean to offend you," and then he was out and Crowe fell back on the bed, holding his aching head in his hands.

49

Crowe slept for a while. When he woke up, the room was just going dim and the ceiling light snapped on, cold yellow light pushing against the gray.

He sat up in the cot, feeling cold and miserable. The jug of water was still there. He took a long sip of it, and the feel of it sloshing around in his stomach reminded him of how hungry he was. Did they plan on starving him into submission?

For a long time he only sat there, shivering and thinking. When the sliver of sky outside the casement window had gone completely black, he stood up and stretched.

Everything hurt. Not just the wounds in his back and shoulder, but his head and every muscle in his body. The pain killers would've been extremely welcome right then.

He started examining the room. Aside from the cot and the wooden chair, it was completely bare. He picked up the chair, examined it. It would make a decent weapon if the room was a little bigger and he actually had room to swing it around. As it was, though, it wouldn't do him much good. He set it back down and started pacing around.

He went to the door and gently tried the knob. Locked. From the other side he could hear someone moving.

The ceiling light was recessed. He looked up at it.

Conceivably, it could be yanked out and… he didn't know… thrown at someone.

Yeah, that would help.

He climbed up on the cot and examined the casement window. It was locked tight, but even if it had been open it was way too small to get through. No escape option there.

Another drink of water, another tight stroll around the room. No ideas. He sat on the wooden chair and looked at the casement window.

He stood up again, walked around some more, sat back down.

After what seemed about two hours, he climbed back in the cot and went to sleep again.

The next time he woke, it had all come clear.

He got up and went as stealthily as he could to the door and put his ear against it. Someone was snoring, very lightly, which meant that there was only one guard. If there had been two, one of them would surely have kept the other awake.

The disgusting towel still lay there in the middle of the little room, getting stiffer and more disgusting all the time. Crowe was almost glad it was so cold in the room, otherwise the thing would be smelling pretty bad by now. He picked it up, unmindful of the vomit smeared all over it. He bundled it up over his fist as well as he could so that his knuckles were well-padded.

He climbed up on the cot and faced the casement window. Tentatively, he pushed his towel-padded fist against it.

Took a deep breath. Slammed his fist as hard as he could against the glass.

It shattered, and jagged edges of glass fell to the cot and the floor. A couple pieces shattered loudly, loud enough to wake up the guard outside the door.

Crowe heard his sudden commotion, heard him fumbling with keys, heard him sliding one into the door lock. Crowe jumped down off the cot, found one vicious-looking piece of glass about the length of his hand. He grabbed it up, unmindful of it slicing into his palm.

The door burst open and the Russian guy with the metal

mask, Kondrashev, came rushing in. He had a .45 in one hand, Crowe's .45, it looked like, and keys in the other. The fucker was also wearing Crowe's overcoat.

Crowe came at him. Kondrashev dropped the keys, started to grip the gun in both hands and get a bead. Crowe threw the towel at his face and even though it was only a towel he reacted as if Crowe had sicced a mad ferret on him and took a split second to swipe it away.

In that split second Crowe stepped in close, slicing with the piece of glass. It tore open Kondrashev's throat and blood sprayed out thickly, making a sound almost like a solid object as it hit the floor and the wall.

Choking, the freak dropped the gun and stumbled backwards, clutching his throat. Crowe wasn't ready to take chances. He slashed at him again as he half-turned, and cut open a gash along Kondrashev's neck that opened up and spilled blood everywhere. The freak fell into the open doorway, gurgled, and died.

Crowe dropped the piece of glass and snatched up the .45, backing up into the room quickly in case there were more coming and checking the clip.

The clip was full, and no one else showed up.

After a few seconds, he came out, gun ready. He was in what looked like a long basement room, with a churning furnace going at half-power in one corner and exposed pipes overhead. At the far end of the room, stairs led up.

He bent over Kondrashev, examined him. He was pretty dead. Roughly, Crowe picked him up enough to peel the coat off him. Then, while he was at it, he yanked off his pants. They looked roughly the same size.

Crowe pulled on the pants. They were maybe an inch too short, but he wasn't complaining. The overcoat felt great after having spent the last who-knew-how-long freezing his ass off. Crowe looked at his shoes, but could tell at a glance they were too small. He'd have to barefoot it.

He started toward the stairs, but on a sudden whim stopped.

Bending over the freak again, he worked at the straps on his mask and pulled it off.

It wasn't the face of Freddy Krueger or Michael Meyers. It was just a face. Boyish, a little. Normal. Crowe felt oddly disappointed, as if he'd expected some sort of monster under there.

But no worries, there were still plenty of monsters to be dealt with.

50

Up the stairs, cautiously, and into a short hallway. He could already tell it was the church-- there's something about the atmosphere of a church, even a Protestant one, that's unmistakable. They feel like elementary schools, thick with the smell of floor wax and oppression. And he felt reasonably certain that they wouldn't have locked him up in the basement of an elementary school.

The short hall opened up into the church proper, where a few modest rows of wooden pews were lined up facing the podium. A gigantic portrait of Jesus standing in front of a shimmering waterfall dominated the room.

The wide double doors that led out were opposite Jesus. Crowe headed for them. Shutting the doors behind him, he heard the lock click.

Outside, it was as cold as ever, and his bare feet against the gravel started aching immediately. He tried to ignore the pain, headed around to the row of shrubs where he'd hidden the gas can earlier. It was still there.

He started through the woods, heading in what he hoped was the direction of the motel. There was no sense in staying here now, trying to take them on. The only chance he had was to get away, re-group, come after them later. It was disappointing, but there was no other option.

He stumbled and tripped through the cold and dark, fell once or twice. Branches and stones cut his feet, and he could feel the blood seeping cold through his toes. He pushed on.

At last, he came out on the two-lane highway, spotted the motel on the other side, about a hundred feet to the right. Not bad. He could see his car still in the parking lot, under the soft glow of the motel's security light.

He started toward it, gun ready, trying not to let the wellspring of hope get out of control, trying not to let himself get sloppy this close to escaping.

When he got closer, he saw another car in the gravel lot, a dark BMW sedan.

Two of the killers stood at the trunk—the guy in the yellow parka and Stone.

Damnit.

They watched him, smiling, as he walked slowly toward them. Nathan the Parka Man held a shotgun.

The door to Crowe's shoddy little room opened, spilling out yellow light across the gravel, and there was Larry the cowboy, also with a shotgun.

Stone said, "Hello again, Mr. Crowe," and he actually sounded friendly, not at all threatening. "I'm going to assume you killed Kondrashev?"

Crowe stopped a few feet away, the gun in his hand. It was happening now, and he'd be lucky to take out two of them before they got him. The shotguns were trump cards.

Two more figures came out of his room. Welling first, smiling, and then Murke. Welling had a revolver in his hand. Murke was unarmed.

They all stood there looking at each other for a long moment, fingers tensed on triggers, bodies rigid.

Welling broke the tension with an easy laugh. He said, "You see how it is, Crowe? This could end pretty badly for you, you realize that, yes? But it doesn't have to. Honestly."

Stone said, "Mr. Welling had ideas about you, Crowe. Larry and I have made known our opposition to them, but… opinions are varied."

"To say the least," Welling said. "But we've all come to an agreement. And this is the last time I'll make this offer to you. If you put down your gun right now and listen to the Word, you could very well live through the night. If you don't, well… you've already been sanctified."

Crowe smiled at that. "Sanctified," he said. "Such a pretty word."

Welling said, "Yes, I suppose. But being sanctified isn't pretty at all, I promise you that. The Lord's work isn't always pleasant. So many Christians today, they forget that it isn't all love and peace. That's not what the Good Book is about. God makes His judgments, Crowe, and His wrath is horrible to behold."

At Welling's side and slightly behind, Murke stared at Crowe with his googly eyes. His mouth was wet, face slack.

Crowe said, "Give me Murke and no one else has to die."

"You mean, let you kill him? Just like that?"

"Just like that."

Welling looked at Murke, and Murke started, stared back at him as if unsure what Welling was going to say. Murke took a step back, fear flashing across his narrow face.

Then Welling laughed and clapped him on the shoulder. "Don't worry, Peter," he said. And to Crowe, "I told you before, Crowe, Peter is protected. And let's be honest. You're hardly in a position to offer deals, are you?"

Larry said, "Damnit, we should just kill the sonofabitch. You know he ain't gonna listen to reason. He killed Eckstein already, and Nick too. And he got Percy captured over in Memphis. He ain't gonna listen. We should just kill him."

Stone said, "I agree with Larry, Mr. Welling." Parka Man didn't say anything.

Welling shook his head. "You boys need to have more faith. If you just gave up like that every time you were faced with a disappointment, where would you be now? Of all—"

Larry cut him off, "I'd still be on the road, hitchhiking, killing pretty young girls whenever I felt like it, instead of being stuck here, listening to all kinds of stupid rules and regulations. That's where I'd be now."

Welling looked at him. "You don't mean that, Larry."

Larry grumbled, looked at the gravel.

"Besides," Welling said. "We haven't exhausted all our options yet." He motioned to Stone and Parka Man. "Open the trunk."

Stone fished keys out of his jacket pocket, inserted one into the trunk lock, and popped it open. Inside, someone moaned, and a shadow thrashed weakly. Stone jerked his head at Crowe to come closer, have a look.

Crowe did, making sure his gun was clear and keeping a watchful eye on Stone and Parka Man. As Stone laughed softly to himself, Crowe glanced in the trunk.

Vitower's hands and feet were hog-tied behind him. His good suit was rumpled and bloody, and a big gash ran across his forehead. A ball was stuffed in his mouth, held in place by a dirty brown scarf. He looked up at Crowe, eyes wide with mystified fear. He made a muffled noise that could have been Crowe's name.

Crowe stepped back, away from the trunk.

Welling said, "Nathan," and Parka Man shifted the aim of his shotgun from Crowe to Vitower. He cocked it, and the loud *ka-shunk* sound made Vitower writhe and groan behind the ball in his mouth.

Smiling, Crowe said, "So this is what you have? If I don't hook up with your fucked-up church, you're going to kill Vitower?"

Welling frowned. "I don't really see what's funny about that. Do you think we won't do it?"

"I don't care. Kill him. Knock yourself out. He was next on my list anyway."

Stone glared at Welling, said, "You stupid... didn't I tell you? A complete waste of time."

Welling looked at a loss for words. All eyes were on him

now, waiting to see what he would do, and Crowe got the distinct impression that his days as leader were fast coming to an end. Palpable hatred rolled off Stone and Larry, Nathan the Parka Man looked ready to swing his shotgun barrel in Welling's direction at any provocation now.

The only one still showing signs of loyalty to Welling was Murke. He stood very close to him, like a whipped dog.

Then Welling made his decision, probably based more on self-preservation than anything else.

He said, "Fine. Kill Crowe."

Stone's machete was suddenly in his hand. Nathan the Parka Man's shotgun swung back around in Crowe's direction. And things started happening fast.

Crowe was already moving, diving to the right when the shotgun went off and gravel exploded at his feet. Crowe hit the ground with a painful thud, rolled, aimed blind and got off a shot that ricocheted off the BMW's fender.

Another *ka-shunk*, another round shredding the ground inches from his torso. He rolled again, scrambled to his feet, making for the cover of his car. Welling was firing, and shots bounced into the Saturn, shattering the windows and punching holes in the metal.

Crowe popped up long enough to fire off two or three, didn't keep his head up long enough to see if he'd hit anything. The shotgun went off again and he heard one of the tires pop and hiss. Bullets slammed into the car, whined overhead. Crowe could hear Vitower, still in the BMW's trunk, trying to scream.

Ka-shunk, blam, ka-shunk, blam. And a regular hail of bullets from pistol and revolver. Crowe couldn't get clear to take a shot at them.

From behind him, the loud hoarse boom of a heavy caliber. Crowe heard one of the psychos cry out in pain, and then another boom. The shooting didn't stop, but it slowed down, and Crowe realized they were all going for cover.

He glanced behind him. At the edge of the lot, crouched down in a defensive posture, Detective Eddie Wills fired off another round from his .357, holding it with both hands, his arms steady and his face neutral. He didn't look at Crowe.

Crowe moved around to the front of the Saturn and popped up, this time taking a half-second to target. He couldn't see Welling or Murke, but Stone and Larry had taken up defensive spots behind the BMW. Nathan was sprawled on the gravel, half his face gone.

Larry wasn't as covered as he thought he was, and didn't even have a weapon. Crowe would've preferred a shot at one of the assholes with a gun, but sometimes you have to take the target they give you. He squeezed the trigger and caught Larry in the shoulder. He cried out but didn't go down.

Crowe ducked back down just as another few bullets whined past. Wills had darted toward him, still firing, and was now behind the Saturn with him. He quickly reached in his pocket for ammo, reloaded. He said, "Fella in the suit grabbed the shotgun. Just so you know."

Crowe nodded, popped back up but was forced down by the now-too-familiar *ka-shunk* of the shotgun before he could get a shot off. The round destroyed the hood of the car and a scatter of metal fragments seared into his shoulder.

Wills swung up over the trunk of the Saturn and fired off four rounds in quick succession. He came back down and the shotgun went off again, aimed at his end of the car. Crowe came up, firing, and his second and third shots got Stone in the upper chest just as he was swinging the shotgun around in Crowe's direction.

Stone didn't make a sound, just dropped.

Larry made a weird, strangled noise, stopped shooting. "No!" he said. "Aw, fuck! Goddamnit anyway!"

Wills, crouched there at the tail end of the Saturn, seemed to make a decision. He nodded at Crowe curtly, and then stood up, very slowly, keeping the gun in front of him.

He started to come around the car. "Okay," he said. "Drop your weapon and come out from behind there with your hands over your head."

"Wills," Crowe said. "What the fuck are you—"

A bullet hit Wills in the stomach. Larry howled happily, and fired again, getting Wills in the upper thigh, and then another in the shoulder as Wills fell.

Crowe stood up, saw Larry walking toward their position, still shooting at Wills. Crowe took a second to get a bead on him and then squeezed the trigger twice.

The first one got him in the groin, shredding his cowboy jeans and tearing away a good chunk of him. He dropped his gun, screaming, and the second shot took off the top of his head, throwing blood and brains all over the gravel behind him.

Crowe dropped down again, half-expecting more bullets, but the parking lot was suddenly quiet. No Welling or Murke.

His ears rang, and raw adrenaline still roared through him. He waited five seconds, ten. Nothing.

Wills lay on his back in the gravel. Crowe stood up warily, gun still ready, and made his way over.

Wills' eyes were still open, his chest still moving up and down. Crowe crouched next to him, said, "How the hell did you find me here?"

Wills laughed weakly. Blood bubbled on his lips. "Stupid fuck," he croaked. "You left a… left a goddamn pamphlet. Stupid fuck…"

He pointed weakly at his coat pocket. Crowe reached in, fingers closing on crumpled paper, pulled it out.

The pamphlet about the Society of Christ the Fisher. The one he'd crumpled and tossed away in his motel room, back in Memphis.

Crowe sighed, tossed it over his shoulder.

Wills said, "You… you're under arrest, Crowe." And he laughed again, even weaker. Crowe shook his head, chuckled.

"Ah, well," Wills said. "I reckon that ain't… gonna work out after all."

"No, Wills, I reckon not."

"At least tell me… what the fuck is goin' on here?"

He died before Crowe could answer. Eyes closed, head

rolled over to the left, chest stopped moving. The question still on his lips.

Crowe stood up.

From the trunk of the BMW, Vitower was still wailing and carrying on. Crowe was amazed by that; not a single bullet had penetrated the trunk, apparently.

So there were two of them alive—no, four. Welling and Murke were still around somewhere, and that wouldn't stand.

Fortunately, Crowe had a damn good idea where they'd gone to.

51

There was no shortage of things lying around that could be used to kill people; Crowe took the shotgun, which still had two shells in it, and Wills' .357, along with his last speed loader, and made his way across the road and into the woods, headed in the rough direction of the church.

It was getting colder, but he barely felt it now. He moved fast through the woods, bare feet dead to pain now and crunching dead leaves stiff with frost. Dead bare branches struck his face. Two or three times he tripped, just like before, but this time he never fell, just kept moving.

Just as he was starting to think he'd veered too far off course, he saw the side of the church through the trees. He crouched down, shotgun ready, and crept slowly forward.

Welling and Murke were on the narrow steps leading to the front double doors. Welling was fumbling with a set of keys, trying to get it unlocked. "He'll be coming after us," he was telling Murke. "He's got it bad for you, Peter. We're gonna have to—damnit!"

He'd dropped the keys. They clattered on the concrete steps and he reached down for them. Still doing the faithful pet thing, Murke bent first and scooped them up.

"Here you go, Mr. Welling," he said, and Crowe was surprised at the lightness, the almost adolescent quality, of his voice.

Welling took the keys and again began working at the lock. He said, "There's another gun in the office. I'm going to—"

Crowe came out of the woods, cocked the shotgun and fired.

That tell-tale *ka-shunk* gave them all the heads up they needed. At the sound of it, both men dropped. Welling went straight down, Murke dove off the steps. The blast pock-marked the double doors and shattered the lock that Welling had been trying to open.

The door swung in, and Welling, unhurt, dove inside the church. Murke rolled to his feet like a gymnast, charged at Crowe. He had a Bowie knife in his right hand.

Crowe cocked the shotgun again, started to pull the trigger, but Murke barreled into him and the shot went wild, into the sky. Both of them hit the hard dirt between the trees and the church parking lot.

On top, Murke tried to slash with the knife. He had his left hand around Crowe's throat, pushing him down. Crowe blocked the knife with the barrel of the shotgun, and then slammed the butt into Murke's head. Murke seemed to barely notice it. Crowe hit him with it again, and Murke brought the knife down hard.

Crowe pushed up hard enough to throw his aim off. The knife went into the dirt by Crowe's head. He pounded Murke in the ear with his right fist, pushed the shotgun butt against Murke's throat, trying to gain traction. Murke grunted as the butt grinded against his Adam's apple, and Crowe hit him again with his right, three, four times in the ear.

Murke weakened, finally let go of Crowe's throat to try and get a grip on his hand—Crowe used that second to push up and throw him off.

Now Murke was on his back and Crowe was getting to his feet. The shotgun was empty. He threw it aside, plucked Murke's knife up out of the ground. Murke saw him coming toward him with his own knife, and stark fear showed in his eyes.

The cat came out of the woods then, as if it had been following the whole time.

Its black fur was sleek with blood. The white cross on its head glowed in the darkness, reflecting the moonlight like a pale lantern. It walked right up to Crowe, calm, in no hurry. At his feet it stopped, and the glittering green eyes gazed up at him, and then at Murke.

Murke saw it too. He looked at it, sudden horror twisting his features.

Crowe grinned nastily. "Recognize it, Murke? You recognize the cat you killed, when you were just a little tiny psychopath?"

He shook his head. "No," he said, in his weird, little kid voice. "No, no, no... that can't be."

The cat took a step toward him, meowed. Murke tried to scoot away from it on his back. The cat kept coming, meowing. It rubbed against his shoe, leaving a stain of blood.

Murke kept shaking his head, saying, "No, no, no," but the cat didn't disappear, didn't evaporate in a puff of smoke. It just kept coming toward him, meowing.

Crowe laughed. "Your first victim, Murke. Your very first. Who'd have thought it would be the one to come back for you."

Murke had pulled himself backwards all the way to the church steps, his eyes never leaving the Ghost Cat, his head never stopping its shaking.

The cat hissed at him, spitting blood, and Murke screamed.

Crowe took the three steps toward him, lifted him up by his coat collar, and slashed the knife across his throat. Murke gurgled, spewing blood, and was dead before Crowe even dropped him.

The Ghost Cat was already gone by the time Crowe looked around. Not a sign of it anywhere. It was as if it had never existed. Just like a cat, Crowe supposed, not sticking around to express its gratitude or anything.

But it wasn't in his head; Murke had seen it too. Strangely, Crowe found himself thankful for that.

Welling was still in the church, but Crowe wasn't about to

go in and play games with him. He went over to the side of the building, where he'd left the gas can behind the dead shrubs. He uncapped it and began pouring.

He made his way around the entire church, making sure to slash some along the bottom of the back door and at the two windows on the side. Most of it he poured over Murke's body, sprawled out at the bottom of the steps.

When it was empty, he tossed the can across the parking lot. It bounced two or three times before coming to rest in the gravel.

"Welling," Crowe yelled. "Come out."

From inside, Welling screamed back, "Come in and get me, you motherfucker!"

Not exactly language befitting a man of faith. Crowe shrugged. Truthfully, he was happy Welling wasn't listening. At the moment, he wanted nothing more than for Welling to burn.

He reached in his pocket for the matches he'd nicked from the motel outside Murfreesboro. It took two or three tries, but he managed to get one lit, touched it to the whole book of them. He tossed the burning book at Murke's body.

Murke went up like a bonfire, and heat blossomed out with the flames, so sudden Crowe had to take a step back, certain he was about to catch fire himself.

Within seconds, the fire had snaked around the entire church, encircling it completely, flames licking and crackling and roaring. Through the open door, Crowe could see that they hadn't reached the inside yet, but it would only be a matter of minutes.

He stood near the bottom of the steps, as close as he could without being burned himself, and pulled out the .357. He waited.

To his surprise, Welling didn't come running right out. The fucker was going to see it through.

The fire ate away at the church from the outside in, black smoke billowing into the night sky and the sound of the flames almost deafening. They crawled up the sides of the church, higher and higher, until the steeple on top caught fire as well. The place looked like a birthday cake that had gone horribly amiss.

Crowe could see flames on the inside now. Part of the church collapsed, timbers creaking and moaning. The windows shattered. The front doors burst into flame.

There was a loud cracking sound from the steeple, and Crowe looked up just in time to see it begin to fall sideways. It crashed down, taking out part of the roof, and monstrous flames followed it to the gravel below.

Welling finally came out, screaming. He was on fire. It had caught his hair, and he ran out the front doors, batting at his head, screeching, "Help me! Help me!"

When he was halfway down the stairs Crowe raised the .357 and shot him in the chest twice.

It wasn't a mercy killing. He'd have shot him anyway.

He dropped next to Murke. The flames consumed him.

52

Crowe stood there for a long time, watching the fire destroy the church, watching the flames blacken the two corpses. The heat felt good.

No fire engine came. No citizens showed up to see what was going on. No cops with flashing lights. Nothing. It was as if everyone expected it and no one cared.

After a while, Crowe sighed, put the gun in his pocket, and headed back through the woods to the motel.

Vitower was still in the trunk of the BMW, but he'd stopped struggling. When he saw Crowe, his eyes bulged out, but he didn't move.

Crowe used Murke's knife to cut the scarf off him. He pulled the ball out of Vitower's mouth. Vitower coughed, spat, tried to suck breath.

"Easy," Crowe said. "Breath slow or you'll throw up."

He gasped, tried to get his breathing under control. Crowe gave him a minute. Finally, he said, "Crowe. Jesus fucking Christ. Thank God. Thank God for you… Jesus." He coughed some more. Then, "Get me out of these knots. Help me. Thank

God, Crowe, you saved my life. I don't know… I don't know how to thank you."

"You're welcome," Crowe said, shot him in the head, and slammed the trunk closed.

53

A black wreath hung on the front door. Crowe touched it. Plastic.

He knocked and waited, knocked again, but no one answered. Inside, someone was sobbing, very quietly. Crowe tried the knob and found the door was unlocked, so he went in.

Dallas was on the sofa, her legs pulled up under her, an open bottle on the table and a half-full glass. Her dress was black and her face white and puffy, mascara smeared. She clutched a wadded-up ball of tissue in her pale hand and didn't look up as Crowe shut the door behind him.

He'd taken two days to get back to Memphis, stopping frequently to get out of the car and stretch or think. The first night he'd pulled off in a rest stop and slept, the second night he'd actually gotten a room. He hadn't been in any hurry to get back. The things he had to do here weren't pressing. The cold spell had broken in the meantime, and it felt almost like spring.

But in the apartment, it was still winter. Crowe stood in the middle of the living room, looking at her, and finally her blood-shot eyes set on him. He said, "What's going on?"

Her mouth twisted hard, as if fighting with the sounds that wanted to come out of them. She said, "He's dead. They killed him."

"What?"

"They killed him. They killed him. Right in his… right in his bed."

Fresh tears streamed down her already grief-ravaged face and she looked away.

A bedroom door opened and there was Chester. He wore a rumpled black suit and his face was drawn and blank. Very softly, he said, "Crowe."

Crowe nodded at him.

Chester motioned to follow him back into the bedroom. Crowe glanced at Dallas. She wasn't paying any attention anymore. It was as if he'd already left the room. Crowe followed Chester. In the hall, he glanced through the open door into the other bedroom, the boy's, and saw police tape and the mattress propped up against the wall and covered in plastic. It was black with blood.

Chester closed the door behind them, and sat heavily on the edge of his bed. Crowe stayed near the door and waited him out. He wasn't crying, but he had been. He looked as if he was fresh-out of tears for the moment.

Crowe said, "The boy."

Chester swallowed hard, and when he spoke his voice was raspy and weak. "They killed him. That… that church group Dallas joined. They came in the night and… and we never even heard them. Maybe it was just one guy, I don't know. But we never even heard. We found him in the morning. In the morning."

He looked up at Crowe. "He died all alone, Crowe. He was all alone. He must've been… he must've been so scared…"

"Chester—"

"Jesus, just a boy, all alone. Jesus. Oh God. They… they cut his throat, Crowe."

Crowe became aware of his hands, clenching and unclenching like crazy. He tried to stop them, but couldn't. He felt the weight of the gun in his pocket, the one he'd intended to use on Chester.

Chester said, "We found him in the morning and he was so still. He was so still, Crowe. Like a… like a doll. Oh God. My boy. My son…"

And the tears started, tears he probably thought had dried up for good. He hid his face in his hands and sobbed and Crowe waited.

After a moment, Crowe said, "Chester."

Chester looked up, startled, as if he'd forgotten Crowe was there. And something changed in his face. Something snapped and he stood up very suddenly and hissed, "He was *my* son. You understand, Crowe? *Mine*. I… I raised him and I loved him. He was mine. You understand?"

Crowe nodded.

He said, "The Heretics killed him. I didn't… I didn't even know anything about them, Crowe. I didn't know, until Dallas told me everything. I didn't know, I didn't know. And there's nothing I can do, you understand? They… they have people everywhere. They killed my son and there's nothing I can do about it."

Crowe wondered if Chester knew why they'd done it, why they'd killed the boy in his bed. He wondered if he knew it was Dallas's punishment, not his. *Suffer the children*, Welling had said.

He sat back down, and all the will in him, all the strength, seemed to evaporate right before Crowe's eyes. His face went dull and he sat there and gazed blindly at the wall.

Crowe left him. In the living room, Dallas was his lifeless twin, staring dumbly at a spot on the carpet, the glass in her hand. She didn't look up at him when he passed through the room.

54

In the car, Crowe opened the bottle of pain pills and threw three of them down his throat. He wasn't in any particular pain, but he needed to be numb. He started the engine and drove away.

On his way out of Memphis, he got stopped at the light right before the freeway entrance at Danny Thomas. To the left, the overpass loomed, cars and trucks making it whine and thrum. A dog came lopping out of the shadows under the overpass, stopped and looked at him.

It was a greyhound, but it was hard to tell unless you looked closely. Its fur was matted with blood and bile. Part of its head was gone, skull sticking out whitely, and its hanging tongue was black with age.

Crowe said through his window glass, "I see you, boy."

The tail was little more than a bloody, segmented bit of bone, but it wagged anyway. The dog's mouth moved, a bark of acknowledgment, but of course there was no sound.

Crowe watched, and the dog cocked its head at him before turning around and trotting away, back into the shadows. For a second Crowe thought he saw the boy there, in the shadows waiting, his round white face glowing and cocked at an angle, just like the dog.

But no. There was nothing.

HEATH LOWRANCE was born in Huntsville, Alabama, spent a significant chunk of his childhood in rural Tennessee, his adulthood in more places than he can remember, including Memphis, Tennessee, and currently lives in Flint, Michigan. He's worked as a movie theater manager, a cartoon animal at a kid's pizza place, a private detective, a security guard, and a tour guide at Sun Studio in Memphis. He's the author of the novels THE BASTARD HAND and CITY OF HERETICS, as well as the weird western collection HAWTHORNE, and a trio of self-published short story collections.

ALSO AVAILABLE FROM

SHOTGUN HONEY BOOKS

Buy ***The Bastard Hand*** Today
https://arlo.pub/tbh

Want more Heath Lowrance?

Dig Ten Graves: Stories v1

Read the exclusive short story collections!

I Was Born a Lost Cause: Stories V2

Made in the USA
Middletown, DE
18 November 2021